KIDNAP

A fast-paced, addictive, unputdownable crime mystery with a massive twist

JANE ADAMS

Merrow & Clarke Book 2

Joffe Books, London
www.joffebooks.com

First published in Great Britain in 2022

This book is a work of fiction. Names, characters, businesses, organizations, places and events are either the product of the author's imagination or are used fictitiously. Any resemblance to actual persons, living or dead, events or locales is entirely coincidental.
The spelling used is British English except where fidelity to the author's rendering of accent or dialect supersedes this.

Cover art by Nebojsa Zorić

ISBN: 978-1-80405-082-8

PROLOGUE

Three months previously

Sammy Marvin always did his first and only round at 10.30 p.m., just after the evening shift had left and before the building was locked down securely for the night. He would generally be back in the little office from about eleven, relying on the CCTV and alarm system to protect the building for the remainder of the night. It was not an onerous task. He had a panic button should anything untoward occur, and as long as he monitored the cameras and checked his observations into the book once every hour he was free to get on with his studies. The job had been advertised as being suitable for a postgrad student, and Sammy had been surprised at the explicitness of this, but at interview it turned out that the previous four night-security guys had also been postgrads.

"It's about having somebody there, a presence," Ricky Evans, the man who was now his boss, told him. "Having someone on site and having a decent security system in the warehouse brings our insurance costs right down. We've found in the past that it's ideal for someone who wants to study but needs a job to pay their way through their courses."

It seemed an odd kind of set-up, but Sammy had settled in and found it suited him just fine. He signed the evening shift out at ten o'clock, then checked the paperwork, unpacked his books and snacks, and set off to walk the perimeter at around ten thirty. He was back in the office after locking the main gates and external doors by eleven, and all he had to do then was keep an eye on things till the day shift came in just before six.

"There'll be occasional deliveries coming in late, but they'll be using the rear gates and they've got their own keys, so you don't need to worry about that," he'd been told. "The driver will phone in and let you know when they're about fifteen minutes away."

This he had found happened about once a week. It was usually one of two drivers — cheerful, older men accompanied by a driver's mate to help with unloading. They often chatted on the phone for a few minutes, asking him how his studies were going and teasing him about his lack of a girlfriend. They came in through the rear gates, typically stayed for about half an hour and were gone again. He would watch them idly on the camera in the rear loading bay. They would unload, usually wave at the security cameras when they left, and that would be that. Occasionally it had occurred to him to go down and say hello, offer them tea . . . but there was something about these individuals, friendly as they might appear, that had caused Sammy to hesitate. Something that made him glad there were locked doors between him and them.

For six months this had been the routine — quiet, calm, suiting his lifestyle perfectly. He was home by 6.30 a.m., slept till midday and had the afternoon and early evening to himself. He was expected to be at his post fifteen minutes before the evening shift clocked out, and the daytime security guy always arrived at least ten or fifteen minutes before the end of his own shift at 6 a.m. He had not actually seen the man that interviewed him more than three or four times in all that time, though he checked in with Sammy on a weekly basis

— a conversation that lasted only a few minutes. Otherwise, he was left to get on with things.

All in all it seemed to be the perfect job.

Until the night it wasn't.

He'd gone to the main gates as usual and was about to swing them closed when a car had driven in. Initially he'd been simply puzzled and was preparing to tell them that the place was closed, that the warehouse had shut down for the night and would not reopen till morning. And then a second car drove in after the first and three men got out. Three men armed with guns.

"What . . . ?" The question died on Sammy's lips. He was motioned at gunpoint into the back seat of the second car, driven the short distance to the warehouse and escorted into the reception area at the front of the warehouse.

"Call your boss." One of the armed men handed him a phone.

Hands shaking, Sammy took it and stared at the screen, suddenly forgetting what to do. Forgetting even how to make a call.

"Phone your boss," the man said again.

"Mr Evans? Of course, Mr Evans . . . I mean . . ." Sammy stared hard at the phone trying to remember how. He had taken one look at the gun the man held and his brain seemed to have emptied.

Sighing, the man took the mobile back. "Dumb shit," he said. He swiped the screen and held it to his ear. Reassured that it was dialling, he held it out to Sammy. "Tell him he has to come down to the warehouse. Think you can manage that?"

Sammy nodded frantically, put the phone to his ear and held his breath. When Evans answered, Sammy's words came out in a mad rush. "You've got to get down here, Mr Evans . . . to the warehouse. There's something—"

The armed man took the handset back. Sammy could hear Evans saying his name. "Sammy, is that you, Sammy? What the hell's the matter with you?"

The man hung up and gestured Sammy to go and sit in one of the plastic chairs behind the reception desk, facing the front doors.

"Hands where I can see them."

Sammy placed his hands, palms down, on the desk. "What now?" Somehow he forced the words out.

"Now we wait."

It was half an hour before Evans arrived. Sammy sat in silence. The three men stood stock still, the gun never wavering. Sammy needed the loo, his bladder suddenly full and painful. His stomach churned. He wanted to be sick. He sat so still and tense that his shoulders and back screamed in agony. His hands, pressed and extended on the faux wood of the front desk, prickled with pins and needles.

Then Evans was there, marching into reception and demanding to know what the hell was going on.

He was trying, Sammy realized, to sound confident, to sound like he was in control, but there was no mistaking the shake in his voice. And he'd not come alone — but the men he'd brought with him now stood uncertainly just inside the door, until another of the gunmen motioned them aside.

Sammy had forgotten about the second car. He remembered it now as the doors slammed. Three more men came inside, and Evans took a step back. Sammy watched the colour drain from his face.

"Kyle Sykes," Evans said bitterly. "I should have fucking guessed."

"Not pleased to see me, Ricky?"

"What are you doing here, Sykes? Last I heard, you'd gone to ground. The Perrins had moved in on what was yours and the police were on your tail."

"Well, maybe you heard wrong," Sykes said.

Sammy stared at him. He'd heard of Kyle Sykes, of course. He was all over the news at the tail end of the previous year when he had tried to kill a police officer. The pictures had creeped him out — those dead eyes and that mean little mouth — but that was nothing compared to seeing him here in the flesh, tall and thin but powerful-looking for all that. And those eyes . . .

"And as to what I'm doing here, well, you might call it a hostile takeover."

Sammy looked from Sykes to Evans, wondering what the hell was going on. What had he landed himself in? Sykes glanced at Sammy and gave a little nod as though agreeing to something Sammy didn't understand, then there was a loud noise — but Sammy was in no position to hear that. Sammy tumbled from the cheap plastic chair on to the concrete floor, his blood and brains now dripping off the reception wall.

* * *

Two months later

"It's come to my attention," Kyle Sykes told Ricky Evans, "that you've been holding out on me."

"Holding out? Over what? You've had the lot, Kyle. There's nothing left."

"My accountant tells me different."

"Your . . . what?"

"Accountant, Ricky. Do you not employ accountants? Missing a trick, there, Ricky. No wonder your business has gone down the tube."

My business, Evans thought, *was just fine until you turned up.* He had, however, the sense to say nothing.

Sykes slapped a sheaf of papers down on the table. Ricky stared at it. "It's very simple, Ricky. This is what's called a balance sheet. You see, columns of numbers on both sides, money in, money out — anything left over is considered profit. We had a good look at your bank statements and your business investments and all the little nooks and crannies you've used to hide your assets in, not to mention all the cash transactions and the like, all the stuff you wouldn't want the tax man to see." Sykes smiled, shark teeth bared, eyes dead and cold. "And my accountant tells me the balance sheet doesn't — balance, that is."

Ricky's chest tightened, but he fought to sound calm. "I don't know what you're talking about."

"No? Well, like I say, you obviously need a decent accountant. *I've* got one, trained in forensic accounting." He paused as though tasting the words and finding them to his liking. "*Forensic accounting* — that's all that matters, don't you think, Ricky? And my very able financial adviser tells me that you're holding out."

Sykes slapped the papers. Evans flinched, unable to help himself. Just being around Sykes frayed his nerves and turned his stomach. He felt constantly sick, unable to sleep, scared to answer his own bloody phone.

"So my question is," Sykes continued, "what are you not telling me?"

* * *

Now

It had been easy — almost absurdly so. Despite the size of the house and the sophistication of the alarm system, it had been as simple as carrying a ladder through the long garden, propping it against the back wall and climbing up to the bedroom window. It doesn't matter, he thought, how good your alarm system is if it's only activated for the ground floor of the house. It doesn't matter how good your security lights are if they are so sensitive the local cats set them off — you know this and stop noticing when they come on. It doesn't matter how many locks you have on your windows if you leave a small upper one cracked open to ventilate the nursery at the back.

It was, he thought, the kind of thing everyone did and no one thought about — though it helped to know that the mother was something of a health freak, believing in fresh air and ventilation on all but the coldest of nights.

He slid a gloved finger in through the slightly open window and hooked it around the latch, then swung the window wide enough that he could get an arm through the gap and opened the larger window below. He paused, listening. There were alarms on the windows, but he'd been told they were rarely armed when the homeowners were there. Even so he waited, counting to ten and then twenty, but no alarm sounded and nothing happened to suggest that even the child stirred.

He climbed into the room and glanced around. The door to the landing was closed and the only sound was the soft breathing of the little boy in the cot. A baby monitor stood on a shelf close to where the child slept but it appeared to be switched off, no light showing that it was listening to the quiet room. The child was past the stage of regularly waking in the night, a point of pride for his mother. Her son had slept through the night from six months, and now, eight months on, he rarely disturbed them before six or even seven in the morning — a habit she was much envied for.

The small, blue-clad body in the cot stirred and grumbled, and the intruder paused for a moment to see if the child would wake. Then he took a syringe from his pocket and considered it carefully. Just a tiny dose of sedative, fast acting but not enough to do any kind of harm. Another grumble as the needle pierced the skin. He held his breath, momentarily anxious, but the child soon settled into a deeper sleep, and he scooped him up, together with a blanket, placed the printed note on the mattress and departed the way he had come. He strapped the child, still sleeping, into the car, then strode back through the garden to carefully fold up the lightweight ladder.

Once the ladder was stowed safely in the boot, he took out his phone. "All sweet at this end," he said. "Not a peep out of any of them."

CHAPTER 1

How far must you fall before you finally come to a stop? Not a landing — she had long since given up hope of landing on her feet — just a proper pause would do.

Right now, though, she felt trapped. Like she was in a deep well with no clue as to her next move — climb back into the light or fall some more? She seemed to have been suspended somewhere in the dark with not even a ledge on which to rest her feet. This was an image that infiltrated her dreams and dogged her waking hours, although, upon waking, the well became a tunnel filled with treacle through which she was trying to run.

And that was part of the problem, wasn't it? She had spent hours in the gym, pounding the treadmill, but it got her nowhere. It was not the same as running outside. She missed her morning run along the canal. The evening race across the park, chasing the streetlights as they stuttered into life. Simple pleasures now denied to her after three years undercover in one of the most powerful crime families. Close to the boss, involved with one of his most trusted lieutenants. Friends, genuine friends, with the boss's daughter.

Then exposure. Six months beneath a spotlight so bright she could no longer see in front of her or even behind. She'd been dazzled, frozen, but still falling.

And the worst part? There was so much of it she missed. She thought of her camera stashed away in its bag, untouched for weeks. What had once been her profession, her cover story, her legend, her passion, she no longer had the heart for.

She missed the friends she had made. Carole, Sam, even Billy in a strange kind of way, but that she knew was because she missed belonging. Before that three-year episode in her life, Petra had belonged in the police force, before that she had belonged in the army, before that . . . Well, she never really liked to think about before that. Now, it seemed, she belonged nowhere — her fall had been precipitous and she hadn't landed yet.

Not that she regretted a good job well done. The arrests, the thugs taken off the streets, the girl whose life she helped to save. Seventeen-year-old Lauren, who would not be alive today if Petra hadn't intervened. But that was the thing, wasn't it? No one else in Petra's now narrowed world knew that Lauren was still alive, and for the girl's sake it had to stay that way.

But who was around to save Petra?

She had initially been suspended, of course. That was inevitable, given what had happened, and there had been a few weeks of close protection, while the arrests were made and the tangle of events was sorted out. Then she had been allowed to return to work, pending further investigation. The CPs declared it would be difficult to prove a direct link between her time undercover and the death of Billy Hunter. No one was really buying the suicide theory, but proving a negative was also damn near impossible.

And the fact was she had lived with the man, slept in his bed, been too close to her target . . . Now Billy Hunter's relatives, funded almost certainly by Gus Perrin, were determined not only to have their day in court but to bring a civil case for damages.

But she had been allowed to go back to work. No live cases, of course. Desk duties. Cold cases. Background. Day after day of analysis, collating, chasing down random details. Visits to legal with the Police Federation rep sitting beside her. Not to reinstate her in some capacity, the lawyers advised, would be a declaration of guilt in Billy Hunter's death and an admission that her activities undercover had overstepped the line. So now she was back in the job — a job she'd been away from for so long she could barely remember the day-to-day rules and expectations.

Harder still was going 'home' and not knowing what she'd find or if she could stay. Moving on every few days even though she knew it was fooling no one. *They* knew where she was, and the only thing keeping her from real harm was that her colleagues would know exactly who had caused it. Not that this would stop them for ever — Petra knew that. And she was no longer convinced it was just the Perrins who were causing her grief. She had come to believe that Kyle Sykes and what was left of his organization had joined the party. After all, he knew she was the one his daughter turned to when she ran away from him.

Her bosses acknowledged that this may be the case. They told her to be careful, to report any harassment, any suspicious behaviour, and day after day she did just that. She logged the incidents. They filed them. Nothing changed.

Perhaps when the rest of the Sykes organization was tracked down and locked up there would be some measure of security. Perhaps Gus Perrin would decide she was more trouble than his time and money was worth. But she had slowly got used to the idea that she would probably always be looking over her shoulder. That she would continue to fall.

And then there was the preparation for the court case. Unknown territory, really. Male undercover officers had been hauled through the courts before, charged with having inappropriate relationships. But this — accusations against a female undercover officer — was a new one on most of them. Everyone knew that Billy didn't commit suicide because he discovered that Petra, who had shared his life and his bed, was an undercover officer. Everyone knew that his boss had had him killed because he'd been taken in by Petra's cover story. But everyone knowing did not mean anything could be proved. Billy's family was being supported by Perrin money. Or was it Sykes money? Was there any difference now that the Sykes operations had been acquired by the Perrins? Whatever. They were all holding the line that Petra was the cause of Billy's anguish. That her actions led to his suicide. Petra tried not to think about how high-profile this court case was going to be.

So, day after day, she used the pokey little gym at police headquarters. It was safer than running in the street. Sometimes at the weekend she drove into the country — fifty, a hundred miles away — and then she'd run and she'd allow herself to remember who and what she was before all of this happened. Or some version of it, anyway.

Sometimes she called Lauren. Lauren who was supposed to be dead. Lauren with whom she was supposed to have broken all contact. Who *would* have been dead if it hadn't been for Petra. Sometimes knowing this was all that was keeping her sane.

* * *

Lauren was still Lauren, though everything else had changed. When she had first come to stay with Molly Chambers she had still not been sure who she should be, what new name she should take.

Molly, tough, experienced old bird that she was, sat her down with a cup of tea and a plate of ginger nut biscuits.

"The biggest problem people have," Molly told her, "is that they forget their new identity, especially at first. They forget who they're meant to be. If someone calls your name, you need to turn round and answer them, straightaway. Go with something you can remember. Something you can own."

Lauren had all sorts of unanswered questions in her head, but Molly seemed so sure of herself, so at ease, and that helped her to decide. "I want to be Lauren," she had said. "Can I still be Lauren?" It was the name her mother had chosen for her.

Molly had smiled, her face a maze of creases and lines. "Lauren it is, then. Now we have to give this Lauren a believable and memorable history." And slowly over the following weeks and months Lauren had grown into her new identity.

It was only Petra's phone calls that tied her to the past. These were the one thing that Molly disapproved of.

"She's the adult here," Molly had told her. "She should not be clinging to you for reassurance. Besides that, it's dangerous, Lauren. What if someone gets hold of the phone? You must break that link."

But somehow that had been very hard to do.

"I've been looking over your mother's file," Petra had told her during their latest uneasy conversation.

"My mother?" It had taken a moment for Lauren to realize that Petra meant her mother's murder. "Oh, why?"

"Part of the background. Cold cases . . . You know."

It was Petra that didn't seem to know, Lauren had thought. She sighed, leaned back against the polished wood panelling in Molly's hallway and then slid down until she was sitting on the floor. This, she had sensed, was not going to be a short call. "We know who did it."

"Be nice to prove it."

So it would, Lauren had thought. But what actual good would it do now? Everyone knew that Lauren's father had been responsible for her mother's death, and not just because he had ordered it. He had been the one to murder her. But they had not been able to prove it then, and nobody even knew where her father was, only that he'd disappeared somewhere and police all over the country were looking for him. So far without any kind of success. And when they did catch up with him, and Lauren had to believe it was *when* and not *if*, they could charge him with a whole lot of stuff they *could* prove, including trying to kill a police officer. Surely that mattered more in the scheme of things. She had been a little surprised at this thought and she knew that Petra was slightly shocked at her response. Of course she wanted him charged with her mother's murder. She wanted him charged with a whole lot of things, but had acknowledged to herself that she'd settle. Settle for what could be proved. Settle for anything that might lock him away.

"So," she had asked, "how are you? Do you have a court date yet?"

Hesitation. "No, not yet."

"It might still get chucked out," Lauren had said hopefully. Soothingly. "Petra, I . . ."

"Okay, look, I'd best go. You take care of yourself, now."

Lauren had stared at the now disconnected phone and then deleted the number. Petra would use a different SIM next time she called — she did at least take that precaution.

Soft footfalls and the tap of a cane. Molly Chambers came in from the garden carrying a wooden trug of flowers and freshly picked vegetables. "Oh," she said, one look at Lauren's face telling her. "So she called again."

"I was going to tell her this time. That she had to stop."

"But you couldn't." Molly nodded her grey head. "Come and make tea while I sort this lot out."

Sighing, Lauren got to her feet, glancing at the tall clock that stood in the corner beside the front door. Six o'clock. There had been a time when Lauren had barely been aware that six in the morning was even a thing, but Molly was always up and about early, and Lauren . . . well, sleep was something she still found hard.

"She called you early this morning."

"Before she went to work. I think she'd had a bad night. Oh, Molly, she sounds so lost."

"Yes, my dear. That's because she is. She's a young woman who has lost all certainty in her life. But you can't make it better, my dear. Only she can do that."

"What if she can't?"

Molly parked her stick in the rack beside the front door and gently squeezed Lauren's shoulder, then walked on into the kitchen. She'd had a knee replaced some months before Lauren arrived and she needed the stick when walking on uneven ground. Or so she said. Lauren suspected that she just liked having something to brandish. She had a number of sticks posted around the house — some silver topped or with carved animals adorning the handle. One had a flask concealed in the stem that held a tot of brandy. One contained a long, tapering blade. One even had a mechanism for firing a shotgun cartridge. Molly had shown her how it worked and told her that it had once belonged to some rich bloke who liked to be able to shoot rabbits on his Sunday walks, though Lauren had never seen her use that particular little number.

She followed Molly into the kitchen and filled the kettle, sliced some bread for toast, put some eggs on to boil. The morning routine was familiar and soothing.

"What if she can't? Make it better, I mean," Lauren asked again. She felt Molly's arm snake around her shoulders and turned to bury her face in the soft woollen cardigan — the scent of rose and lavender and early morning garden.

"Others will help her," Molly told her gently. "But that can't be you. Understand that, my dear. That can't be you."

* * *

The police officer that Lauren's father had attempted to murder was at that moment standing alone in the centre of a child's bedroom, peering down at the dismembered body of a stuffed toy.

DI Toby Clarke looked slowly around the room and satisfied himself that this was the only sign of violence. The windows were open. Soft blue curtains decorated with little red boats lifted in the breeze. A white-painted cot stood in one corner of the room, furthest away from the window, and the opposite corner was piled with soft toys and beanbags. Picture books sat on blue bookshelves beside toddler toys.

Brightly coloured outdoor clothes hung on pegs above a pair of tiny shoes. Two mobiles — one of boats, one of dinosaurs — were suspended from the ceiling. He had been told that a child had been kidnapped, but there was none of the activity he expected to find. A senior officer he knew by reputation but had never dealt with before stood in the doorway, watching him. A single CSI brushed the windowsill, looking for prints that Clarke suspected they would not find. Other than that, there was no police presence. The cars outside were unmarked — there wasn't even a scientific support van — and Clarke had been told to park in an adjoining road and come in through the rear garden. The very large rear garden.

He had seen the parents, briefly, talking to a smartly dressed woman he did not recognize but assumed to be a plainclothes detective. The father looked angry — he seemed unable to keep still, the restless rage pouring off him. The mother, in contrast, looked like the walking dead.

He turned back to the man in the doorway, the man who was apparently the SIO on this case, the man who had contacted divisional headquarters and asked for him specifically. Superintendent Deans, about whom Clarke knew very little. Superintendents, in Clarke's experience, sat behind desks and directed operations. They did not take charge on the ground. And kidnappings usually mobilized dozens of officers and an army of technical support, especially when the person abducted was a child — a child of just fourteen months.

"All right, so what's going on?" Clarke asked.

Deans smiled. He looked tired, Clarke thought. And old. Should he not have retired by now? He beckoned Clarke to follow and went back down the stairs. The parents were both crying now — the man in angry, enraged tears, the mother in soft, deep sobs. The female officer he hadn't recognized was no longer there, instead she was waiting in the small room that Deans now led him into. It was clearly some kind of home office, not large, but well equipped with several computers, a printer, a small television in one corner and a two-seater sofa.

The officer was sitting on the sofa, papers spread out on the coffee table in front of her. Deans waved Clarke into the other seat and took the office chair. The woman turned to face him, her outstretched hand tipped with bright-red nails. "DI Sheila Mace," she said. "It's good to meet you, DI Clarke."

"Now," Deans said, "as to what is going on. Some time between midnight and 2 a.m., a person or persons unknown entered this house through the window of the room you've just been in. They took the child from its cot, wrapped it in a blanket and took it back out through the window. We're presuming they had a ladder as there are indentations in the grass below the window, but they must have brought it and taken it away again. The child, Joshua Aaron Banks, is fourteen months old, apparently in good health, and is the only child of Robert and Emily Banks. Robert Banks is CEO of Tyburn Recruitment, a company which specializes in providing high-level computer and technical personnel. The mother got up to go to the toilet around two o'clock, looked in on the nursery and discovered her son was gone. She found a note in the cot."

DI Mace tapped the evidence bags laid on the coffee table. She selected one and handed it to Clarke. Inside was a single sheet of paper:

> *Do not call the police. You will receive details for a bank transfer in due course. Your child will be well cared for and be returned unharmed provided you do exactly as you are told. Call the police and we will kill him. If you are in any doubt as to the seriousness of this, then call this number.*

"The ransom note was emailed just after one thirty," Deans continued. "The number is for Ms Patricia Copeland. About eighteen months ago her nephew and his wife received a similar message when their daughter was taken. They got her back, fortunately, and as promised she had been well taken care of and was unharmed. The ransom on that occasion was a cool million and was paid by a series of bank transfers from offshore accounts that Ms Copeland had access to. The whole transaction took almost three weeks. Apparently the family were given instructions about how much to transfer and where to. The first amount was under ten thousand, so it didn't trigger any warnings relating to our current money-laundering legislation, and we presume this was just a test. Ms Copeland was similarly given a number to call for confirmation that the kidnappers were serious. She was reluctant to give us that contact, but in any case the family concerned have moved permanently to the UAE and are proving difficult to reach."

"We do, however, believe that there are around a dozen families involved," DI Mace told him. "Kidnap for profit is not particularly unusual. In fact, in some places in South America and the Middle East it's commonplace. But those incidents usually involve adults. This is a very unusual set-up for the UK."

"There was something similar down on the south coast a few years ago," Clarke remembered.

"There was," Deans admitted, "but the victims were all young adults or older teens and the gang was successfully rounded up and is now doing time."

"Which doesn't preclude their involvement," Clarke argued.

"And that is a possibility we will be examining. But as yet there is nothing to suggest these latest kidnappings are in any way related."

"So what makes you think there are a dozen families involved?"

"The family Ms Copeland contacted had also been told to phone a certain number. It seems some of the families had talked to one another. These are rich and influential people and are not used to feeling powerless. We are still awaiting details, but it seemed that someone, probably Ms Copeland, hired an investigator, who backtracked and identified perhaps ten or eleven other families."

"An investigator?"

"An ex-intelligence office by the name of Anthony Dronfield."

"The name rings a bell."

"Probably because he turned up dead about a year ago. Fell from the top of a multi-storey car park. Verdict of suicide . . . The family never accepted it."

"You believe he was murdered."

Deans nodded. "It seems most likely."

"So, there's been no police involvement, until this point." Clarke confirmed. "So what changed this time? And given that the family have involved the police, why don't we have a full team on this?"

"What changed was that on this occasion the father is a man who really does play golf with the chief constable." Deans chuckled humorously. "How often you hear people say that. Friends in high places and all that. So the chief constable got a phone call just after two this morning and set things in motion. It was decided to keep the lowest of all low profiles for the time being. It seems he's not the only high-placed friend that Mr Banks has. But anyway, here we are, and here you are."

"About that. Why am I here?"

"You mean why choose you? Because at the moment, DI Clarke, your talents are being underutilized and your time underused. I'm told you're on the mend, but not yet ready for full duties. I also know that you're thorough, careful and have an unusual skill set, shall we say."

Clarke shifted uncomfortably. The bullet wounds on his arm and side still ached and felt tight but, yes, he was on the mend. And, yes, he was bored with light duties. As far as his skill set was concerned, he wasn't sure he wanted to know what Deans thought that constituted. "So what do we have, and where do we begin?" he asked. "And is this it, the three of us and the CSI?"

"I borrowed the CSI, just for an hour or two. Once they've checked the room and determined a likely route out of the garden, they'll be on their way. We have access to whatever other resources we need, but we will be, as I've said, keeping the lowest of low profiles. I suspect that Mr Robert Banks contacted his friend the chief constable on impulse and that had he taken a little more time to consider his actions we'd still be in ignorance."

"I'm not sure that Mrs Banks is ever going to forgive him," DI Mace added. "I can brief you on what we have so far, but then we need suggestions for someone to take my place. Someone who is already, shall we say, digging around in cold-case files, where a little digging in other directions will not be noticed." She looked pointedly in his direction.

"You're not sticking around?"

"I'll be clearing paths and opening doors elsewhere. You can reach out as and when you need other resources," she told him. "Superintendent Deans will, of course, be in overall control, but as he said: discretion. A little subterfuge. I understand that DS Merrow is also currently underutilized," she added, just in case he hadn't already figured it out.

"I take it you have no objections to working with DS Merrow?" Deans asked.

Clarke figured that even if he had, he wasn't being given much of an option.

Did he object? On balance, probably not. But the truth was, despite the drama of their initial meeting, he knew very little about DS Petra Merrow. She had been undercover, and she had been instrumental in getting Lauren Sykes out of danger, but the last time he had actually had contact with her had been at the inquest after Lauren Sykes's car had been found at the foot of a cliff, a suicide note left on a bench on the clifftop and the body presumably washed out to sea. They had also met briefly at the funeral of one of the men Lauren's father had killed. But did he know her? No, not really — neither personally nor professionally.

He also had quite profound doubts that Lauren Sykes had in fact been in the car when it had plunged over the cliff and on to the rocks below. But that was another story.

"You want me to make contact with her?" he asked Deans.

"I'll take care of that. Obviously, you'll need a place to work, so I've arranged for you to have an office in the old schoolhouse on Headington Street. That way you're close to DS Merrow's current post but far enough away from your own divisional HQ that people won't be around to ask awkward questions. You're still on light duties, so you'll just be trading one desk for another as far as anyone else is concerned."

Headington Street, Clarke thought. A dusty old building full of files and spare furniture. He knew there were a couple of offices there used for occasional meetings and that no one could quite decide what to do with the unsuitable and somewhat rundown red-brick building that had once been a Victorian board school. There were, he remembered, two doors — one marked 'Girls' and the other 'Boys' — and a plaque about the board that had set it up. Once the school had closed it had become a library, and then a library with an office for a special constable, and then for a PCSO when community policing had become the latest Big Thing.

"Isn't there a PCSO based there?"

"There is, and a community desk, and one of the classrooms is still used for public meetings. But that shouldn't impinge on you. There are two separate entrances, and you'll be using the one round the back." Deans fished in his pocket and pulled out keys. "It'll probably be a couple of hours before anything is ready for you, so in the meantime, get yourself some breakfast, deal with anything else you need to sort out and get over there by, say, about nine o'clock."

Deans got to his feet and Clarke decided that he was probably being dismissed.

"I'll check in with you mid-afternoon," Deans told him. "In the meantime my contact, for emergencies, will be in the information pack that we'll be sending over to you."

Information pack, Clarke thought. Like he was preparing to attend a conference. "And so far all the kids have been returned unharmed," he emphasized.

"Not only unharmed, but well taken care of."

"You said the last set of transactions took three weeks to complete. The child was away from its family all that time?"

"It did and she was, yes. But I'm told at that age they recover quickly. Unlike the poor parents, I imagine."

He was clearly feeling impatient now, his duty having been done. Clarke sensed he was frustrated with the situation. Maybe he too wanted the full team, not this half-arsed tokenism. Someone from above clearly believed the child was in danger, that the death threat was genuine. That the police involvement should be invisible.

"Are we setting up a wiretap here?"

"What's the use of that? All contact so far has been made via email, from a one-time-use account which disappears within minutes of the email being sent. That side of things is being dealt with elsewhere — the contact will also be in the pack, but I don't imagine it's going to be something you're too concerned with."

"And how many of the families can I . . .?" But Deans was already out of the door.

DI Mace smiled at him sympathetically. "It'll be—"

"In the information pack," Clarke finished for her.

CHAPTER 2

Lauren sat at her desk in the sunny bay window of her bedroom, her bare feet stroking the thick rug beneath her chair. Molly's house was unusual in that it had bay windows both back and front. The rooms at the front of the house were smaller — a study and a somewhat larger dining room. The kitchen was next to the dining room, and then there were two larger rooms at the back, one with a bay window and one with French doors. Upstairs there were three bedrooms. Molly's room had an en suite, and so the other bathroom was pretty much Lauren's territory. It had a deep bath and a selection of bath oils and bubble baths that had been there when Lauren had arrived — Molly's way of making her feel especially welcome.

Lauren's room faced on to the very private back garden, and the big bay window had a window seat beneath its heavy velvet curtains. Lauren had moved the small desk into the space so that she could sit in the sun while she got on with her revision. She had almost finished her exams. She hadn't been able to go back to her school, not that she'd really wanted to, but Molly had insisted that she should have some discipline in her life and had found a place a few miles away that would accept Lauren as an external candidate. Together they had researched the syllabus, and all the textbooks she needed had been provided. Only two more exams to go and she'd be free for the summer, and then . . . Then she wasn't sure. She still had another year of school, and they were looking at options for that, but home study looked like the only way forward at present. Would university eventually be an option? Did she even want to go?

Lauren got up and stretched. Molly had gone out. It was Thursday morning and she and a couple more equally elderly ladies went into town and had lunch together most weeks. Once or twice Lauren had gone along with her. She had expected to be bored, but Molly's friends were as lively as she was and as outspoken, and Lauren had had a surprisingly good time. Neither of them asked who she was. Molly had simply introduced her as Lauren Masterson, a young friend who was staying with her for a while, and that had been that. She got the impression that Molly's friends were used to there being things they did not ask questions about.

Lauren wasn't sure where the name Masterson had come from. It was, she supposed, as good as any. When she had gone to the college to register as an external candidate she'd had to show ID, and it felt strange to be equipped with a passport, a slightly scuffed driving licence, even a library card in the name of Lauren Elizabeth Masterson.

"Should I change the way I look?" she had asked Molly. "My face has been all over the news."

"And unless you have plastic surgery your face will remain the same," Molly said. "Whatever changes you make you must be comfortable with. Have you always worn your hair long?"

"I suppose so. My dad had this thing about women having long hair."

"And would you be comfortable if it was cut?"

She'd thought about it. "I'm not sure."

"Then leave it long but wear it differently. A style that's different but still you, so you don't look and feel awkward about it." She had pointed at a drawer in the massive sideboard that stood in the dining room. "If you look in there, I believe you'll find some hair clips and the like. Take them, play. I prefer my hair short these days so it's easy to take care of. You're welcome to use anything that takes your fancy."

Lauren had expected hair slides and plastic clamps or something of the sort. Instead the pink cardboard box had been packed with combs, silver and enamel slides, and a complete card of hairpins that from the look of the packaging must have dated from the 1960s. Lauren's hair was naturally wavy and somewhat unruly. She had normally straightened it, keeping it neat and smooth and sleek because that was what women did, or so her father always told her. Now she embraced the waves, pinning her hair back from her face or piling it into a loose bun, fastening it with Molly's vintage slides and clips. And she did look different, Lauren had to acknowledge that. Different but still herself.

She changed her make-up too and had not worn foundation in months. A light tint of eye shadow, a little mascara and, if she felt like it, a quick slick of lipstick and that was it. She no longer looked anything like Lauren Sykes, dressed like Lauren Sykes or felt like Lauren Sykes. She was Lauren Elizabeth Masterson, seventeen years old, confident, orphaned, child of a distant cousin of Molly Chambers, and most of the time it was actually quite difficult for Lauren to imagine she had ever been anything else. She was still not certain who or what Molly was. She had apparently been married to some kind of diplomat, and her house was full of souvenirs from their travels. She had loved her husband and had a wonderful life — those were perhaps the only facts that Lauren could be certain of. In the many photographs dotted around the house or that had been placed reverently in the assorted albums, she looked happy. There were images of Molly in elaborate evening dress, surrounded by others in their finery. Molly with faces she vaguely recognized from old news reports. Molly in her garden in her oldest clothes with mud on her face. Molly and her husband with various people she referred to as family — though she admitted none of them were actual relatives. But facts about Lauren's new guardian's life had been harder to pin down. Molly, who had apparently been born in Kenya, had lived a peripatetic existence, and though she was more than willing to talk about her travels and the people she had met, Lauren still had no real handle on what she was or why she had agreed to take Lauren into her home.

She was just very glad that she had.

It was only the knowledge that her father was still out there that caused her to pause, that caused her to fear. Did he believe that she was dead? Her tracks had been covered well, but would Kyle Sykes really believe that she had taken her own life by driving over a cliff? And where was he? Sometimes that question kept her awake at night — frequently it invaded her dreams. People had died to keep her safe. People like Harry, who was like a grandfather to her. Harry, whose gun she still had, in a box under her bed along with what was left of the money she had taken from her father's house. Lauren kneeled down, pulled the box out from under the bed and looked inside. Sometimes she just needed the reassurance that the weapon was still there. Under Molly's careful instruction, she cleaned and oiled it once a week, and a couple of times each month they would drive out to a big and often muddy field owned by one of Molly's friends and hone her skills. Molly was a crack shot. Lauren was definitely improving.

Otherwise, Lauren was doing her best to live a full and normal life. She owed it to Harry, and to the other people who had helped her, to make every moment count and to make sure that her father never found out that she was still in this world.

* * *

DI Toby Clarke called in to work to pick up various personal items he'd left in his desk, and discovered that his colleagues already knew he was changing location. He enjoyed jokes about being put into storage, along with the broken tables and school chairs, and then he went off to find himself some breakfast, discovering that he was surprisingly hungry. While he ate, he jotted down notes on what little he knew so far. The name of Tyburn Recruitment had seemed familiar, and a double check of his own records reminded him that this was one of the companies previously associated with Kyle Sykes. A little further refreshing of his memory confirmed that one of Sykes's most recent suspected victims, Kristy Young, had been an IT guy working for the agency. Sykes had been looking for information about his runaway daughter and the man, Harry Prentice, who had helped her get away. Kristy was known to have been close with Harry.

Sykes — one-time crime lord, now a man on the run and one with whom Clarke had a personal grievance in the shape of painful scars.

Was there a direct connection here? It seemed like a stretch, but there were rumours that Sykes was not such a spent force as the police and the public liked to think, rumours to which Clarke was inclined to give credence. The likes of Sykes always had contingency plans. The Perrin family, once rivals but now the only game in town, might believe they had destroyed him. No, Clarke thought, Gus Perrin and his extended family probably had no illusions about that. Gus was far too skilled a player to count his opposition out. Down he might be, but the ref was still poised at the count of nine in Clarke's book — and, he guessed, in Gus Perrin's too.

He put thoughts of Sykes aside and concentrated on his bacon and eggs, then over toast and marmalade allowed his attention to wander once again. The little café he'd chosen to have his breakfast in was in the heart of Perrin territory. It was next door to a pub, the Three Cranes, in which Gus Perrin had a stake. Both pub and café were in spitting distance of police divisional HQ and as a result did a roaring trade, heavily supported by Clarke's colleagues and by members of the public who believed this made both locations safer, and a few who were just police groupies. Both businesses were, on the face of it at least, totally legitimate, being part of the Perrins' legally owned and legally run expanded business portfolio. Gus must be happy as a pig in muck, Clarke thought, knowing what demographic made up the bulk of his clientele. As it happened, both the Three Cranes and the café had been run under the auspices of Kyle Sykes until late the previous year when Sykes had overplayed his hand, and the Perrins quietly, and with all relevant paperwork in place, filled the gap his absence had opened up. Gus Perrin had undoubtedly slid just as easily into Sykes's not-so-legitimate businesses, but that was harder to prove.

There were other players on the board now, mopping up the dregs Perrin had either missed or, more likely, saw as unprofitable. Clarke had no doubt they had done so with the full knowledge and permission of the big man, and that Perrin would get his cut without expending any effort or manpower.

His mind drifted back to the little nursery with the blue curtains decorated with red boats and his heart sank. The breakfast he had devoured was now suddenly heavy in his stomach. Many and varied were the ways the Perrins and Kyle Sykes had made their fortune, including people trafficking and prostitution, but he'd never heard of either of them targeting young kids. Sykes, in fact, had been known to turn vigilante when it came to known paedophiles, and Perrin had been responsible for scaring a child murderer, newly released on license, so badly the man had suffered a heart attack.

Not that any of that had officially happened, of course, based on the evidence Sykes and Perrin had left behind — which was none.

Clarke glanced at his watch — it was now eight thirty — and drained his mug of tea. It was about a ten-minute walk to his new office. Hopefully they'd set most of it up for him by now, and presumably Petra Merrow would be on her way over. He was still not sure how he felt about that. He liked Petra, but he knew she had been badly affected by her time undercover, by the subsequent threats made to her, and the incipient court case. If he'd been Petra Merrow he'd have been miles away by now, holed up on some little island in the Outer Hebrides or something. He had no doubt that a change of identity could be arranged for her, but she had seemed unwilling to go and the powers that be unwilling to pressurize her into going. It was somebody's idea of fair play that Petra be dragged through the courts over the apparent suicide of Billy Hunter, the man she'd been involved with in the Perrin organization.

Truth be told, Clarke ruminated, what made him uncomfortable was that he wasn't too sure how involved she had been. He was prepared to accept that she had lived with Billy Hunter, slept in the man's bed and appeared on his arm at social events because that was the only way to get close to the heart of the organization. But even Petra would admit that there were people within that organization she'd come to view as friends, such as Perrin's daughter Carole, a talented artist and a woman desperate to strike out on her own. She was someone Petra had been genuinely fond of. Having met Carole, Clarke could understand how that might be. Carole was not only gifted — she was a genuinely pleasant woman.

Leaving the café, Clarke stood uncertainly outside the door, then abruptly made up his mind. He had long since learned to trust his instincts, and they were now screaming at him to guard his back. So, instead of turning left to collect his car and drive to his new office, he returned to the police HQ he had just left and knocked on his boss's door.

Superintendent Craig looked up. "Toby? I thought you'd left."

"Can I have a word?"

Craig took one look at his face and beckoned him inside. "What's on your mind?"

Clarke hesitated, then took a seat. Was he really putting the child at risk in confiding? Did he fully trust his boss? He thought back to the Sykes enquiry. Craig had backed him then, as had Clarke's previous super at another division. And anyway, he figured he was committed now. "A funny thing happened to me this morning," he began, "and I don't mean funny 'ha ha'."

* * *

The technical crew was still setting up when he arrived at the old board school in Headington Street, so he found an empty classroom and a chair, laid his notebook and pen on the windowsill and called Robert Banks, father of the kidnapped child.

Robert Banks sounded first hopeful and then angry when it was obvious that there was no news to be had.

"I don't want you calling here. I don't want any links with the police."

"With respect, sir, you did call us in."

"No. No I did not. I called a friend and he . . ."

And he just happened to be chief constable, Clarke thought. He changed the subject. "Mr Banks, can I ask you about your business, Tyburn Recruitment?"

"What about it? It's not my company, I'm just the CEO."

"And as such, how much contact do you have with those it recruits? I understand the business focuses on technical experts."

"I'm on the board, I'm CEO, so how much do you think? I have other people deal with recruitment."

Clarke ignored the tone. "So you've never come across a man called Kristy Young? I understand he was recruited by Tyburn about eighteen months ago. He was an IT expert."

Banks was immediately suspicious. "You think he had something to do with this?"

"No, he's dead, I'm just following up a possible lead."

There was a momentary silence on the other end of the phone. *For all his bluster, he's genuinely frightened*, Clarke thought. "Is it possible for me to meet up with you? On neutral ground somewhere? Mr Banks, it's possible you know more than you—"

"Out of the question. I can't possibly leave my wife."

Clarke heard him take a deep, controlling breath. "I should never have made that call. Never. Understand this, DI Clarke, I regret that decision more than any I've made in my life."

"Mr Banks," Clarke cut in, "has someone been in touch? Have any new threats been made?"

"No. There's been nothing."

Clarke could hear the regret in the man's voice and knew he'd almost have welcomed a threat. It would have been contact, of sorts. He was a man used to being in control — this limbo was killing him.

"So if we could meet . . ." Clarke tried again.

"I told you no." The tone was sharp, the words ground out. "You don't exist, DI Clarke. I made a stupid mistake. I want nothing more to do with you or any of your kind. Don't call me again."

Something else has *happened*, Clarke thought. *He was scared before, now he's absolutely terrified.* But he knew better than to push. Keeping his voice even he said, "Thank you, Mr Banks, I'll be in touch as soon as I know anything."

Before he'd finished the sentence, Banks had hung up.

Clarke sat back in his chair, staring out of the window. The sense of wrongness he had experienced when he'd stood in the missing child's nursery, a sense of wrongness that had nothing immediately to do with the kidnap, now seemed to fall on to his shoulders like a leaden cape.

How much had he not been told?

He would have given a great deal to speak with the mother. Clarke remembered the quick glimpse he'd had of her as he'd passed the large and imposing living room, thickly carpeted and plushily furnished. The father had been angry. The mother had been utterly devastated, completely bereft. Whatever Clarke was not being told, this poor woman was also in ignorance.

He held on to that thought. A child was missing. His poor mother was in mourning, probably already half believing that her little one was dead, whatever anyone else might tell her. That was all that really mattered, and everything else he would just have to work around. And he was in no doubt now that he *was* going to have to work around . . . the father, his own colleagues . . . and who else? Superintendent Craig had promised to do some careful digging. Clarke hoped to hell it really was careful. Like Banks, he was regretting his impulse to confide — what if it was the wrong move? What if . . .?

He pushed the thought aside. The child *had* to be returned safe. He had put it to Craig that he felt as though he and Petra Merrow were being set up to take the fall if things went tits up. Craig had not agreed, but he'd not rushed to present the opposite opinion either. In his position, Clarke suspected that Craig would have felt the same.

On impulse — that seemed to be happening a lot today — he called the office of the chief constable. After all, he'd been Banks's first port of call. He was asked his name and his business. "DI Clarke, I want to speak to him about some information I believe he received this morning."

There was a pause, a murmur of conversation in the background, the sound of a closing door and then, "I'm afraid he's in a meeting and will be busy for the rest of the day."

The tone was cool — the message clear. Clarke wondered if his superintendent would have more luck.

Glancing down the corridor towards what was to be the office, he noted that tech support had finished setting up. The old schoolhouse reminded him of his own schooldays, redolent of the scent of floor polish and disinfectant and old plimsolls, overlaid with the faint odour of overcooked cabbage. He wondered vaguely how long it had been since anyone had actually cooked cabbage in the school kitchens. It was an odour, he thought, that permeated brick and plaster, no matter how much time passed. The walls of the classroom he was waiting in were painted a pale green, and the cupboard doors were covered in children's artwork and painted messages exhorting you to believe in yourself. It must, he supposed, be used by one of the community groups that met in the building.

The old schoolyard was now tarmacked and used for parking. In the end he'd left his own car back at divisional headquarters, preferring to walk off his breakfast, and currently parked in front of the building were a small blue van and a little hatchback, which he guessed belonged to the technical crew. A third car now pulled in through the narrow gateway and parked up at the other end of the row. Petra Merrow got out. She stood uncertainly for a moment, laptop bag and backpack in hand, looking around anxiously, her expression suspicious. She'd cut her hair very short, Clarke noticed, and had lost even more weight. Always slim, she now looked as gangly as a teenager having a growth spurt.

He watched as she worked out where the entrance was. The end where she'd parked was marked 'Girls' and led into what was now a small kitchen serving a community area. The boys' entrance was around the back of the building. The rooms that would now serve as their offices were sectioned off by an original wall and a locked door. Apparently the big hall on the other side of the locked door was used by playgroups three or four times a week, and Clarke had glimpsed boxes of toys and soft play mats through the windows.

He arrived at the office at the same time as Petra. The tech crew were packing away, about to leave. Two computers had been set up, and there were filing boxes, a whiteboard, a couple of telephones and a long table against the back wall, but that, Clarke noted, was about it. He watched as Petra Merrow stood in the doorway, absorbing the scene. She glanced over at him with a puzzled expression in her eyes, but she didn't speak until the tech crew had gone. "So either they don't want us to succeed, or they don't want anyone to know if we do. Are we supposed to be invisible now?"

Clarke nodded. "Apparently they'll be sending over some kind of information pack," he said. "Other than that it's just you and me, unless we ask for something specific."

She frowned, clearly dissatisfied. "I'll take that desk." She pointed to the one facing the door.

He shrugged, "Sure." He dumped his own bag on the desk set at a right angle to hers, moved the filing boxes on to the long table, then checked the locks on the door. Two new ones had been added, and he now noticed a secure cabinet set beneath the long table. So, someone was taking time to think about security. But it still all felt . . . wrong.

The sound of a motorbike broke through his thoughts. He caught sight of Petra, recognizing her sudden tension. She was pulled so taut she might snap at any moment. Footsteps in the hall, a tap on the already open door. A motorbike courier. No doubt this would be their famed information pack.

He signed the proffered tablet and closed the door on the retreating courier. "We need a kettle, mugs, tea and coffee," he said, turning his back on Petra and giving her a moment to recover. "There's a supermarket round the corner. We can pop in later."

"Sure." She took a deep breath and managed a rather tense laugh. "They never remember the important stuff, do they?"

"Oh, never."

"So—" she took another deep breath, this one calmer — "what do we have so far and what the fuck are we doing here? Just what's going on, Toby?"

"Right now," he told her, "your guess is as good as mine."

CHAPTER 3

"*Where do you hide a tree? In a forest.*"

"What's that supposed to mean?" Sykes demanded.

Ricky Evans felt the small satisfaction he had enjoyed evaporate. "Okay," he said in a more respectful tone, "where do you hide a child? With a lot of other kids. You put the kid where people expect kids to be. So, there's this little charity, places young kids — babies, toddlers, that sort of age — with short-term foster carers. It's usually just until their adopted parents are able to get the paperwork done, but they also take emergencies from social services. We've got a contact in the organization — long and short of it is, they sometimes help place our kids for a short time. All the paperwork's in order. The kids are placed with genuine foster carers, they get looked after, returned to their parents in good shape and . . ."

"Why the hell should I care about that?"

"Because, Kyle, this is a business venture. Think of it as repeat business. You need customer satisfaction. We're dealing with rich parents here. We're demanding over the odds for the safe return of their precious little bundle. We demand silence from them, but as part of our business profile, if you like, we give them the number of a previous . . . client. They phone that number, get told, 'Yes, we paid up, did as we were told, got the kid back in good shape.' So, they decide they'll do the same."

He had explained all this before, but Sykes still didn't get it.

"Look," he said, searching for a comparison Sykes might actually understand, "if you want some building work done on your house, you ask the builder to tell you what work he's done before. You talk to some satisfied customers. You don't give him the job until you've got some guarantee it's been done on time and to spec. For a business to have longevity you've got to have consistency — *you* know that. It's okay if you just want a one-off. Chances are, the parents'll pay up anyway, and if it's a one-off then who cares what happens to the kid? But if you want repeat business, like I said, you have to reassure them you'll keep your end of the deal, otherwise sooner or later they're going to take a chance and go to the police."

"Not. Good. Enough," Sykes said. "I want the kid brought to me. I want it where I can see it. I don't hand over control of any of my assets to other people and neither do my employees. And you—" he stabbed a bony finger in Ricky's direction — "are there to do as you're fucking well told."

Ricky sighed and nodded. "I'll get it sorted now."

Sykes's eyes narrowed, but his attention seemed to have strayed. He waved a dismissive hand in Evans's direction. "Whatever. Just get it done."

Evans allowed his shoulders to relax as Sykes marched out of his office and got into his car, disappearing behind the tinted rear windows. Ginny came in from the front office and claimed the seat Sykes had occupied. "He's touched," she said. "Totally off his head. He was mad before, but at least he knew how to manage a decent business. Now he's shot it."

"Oh, I agree, but what can we do about it?"

"Take the initiative. Let the Perrins know what's going down. Let them deal with it."

Ricky Evans sighed. Ginny had been with him for years and, truth be told, probably knew more about his businesses than he did. She'd made this same suggestion three or four times in the past few weeks and he was now inclined to agree it might be the best or only plan.

When Sykes had first appeared, Evans had been scared witless. Then as the weeks passed and he had displayed no further inclination towards immediate violence, Ricky Evans had settled into a state of more manageable terror. He had lost weight, been unable to sleep, been grateful that he had no immediate family for Sykes to threaten. Sykes seemed wilfully ignorant of Ginny's role in the business or that she might be important to Evans. But then, Sykes did not rate women — it would never have occurred to him that Evans might regard Ginny Afton as an equal partner, and Ginny had the good sense not to challenge that notion by drawing attention to herself.

"It's what the Perrins might do," Evans said. "I've no wish to replace Kyle Sykes with Gus Perrin as a business partner. I just want rid of Kyle Sykes."

"Gus Perrin isn't the only one interested in the whereabouts of Sykes," Ginny reminded him. "A quiet word in the right ear."

Evans shook his head. "No police," he said firmly. "They start digging around and we've lost everything."

"It doesn't have to lead back to us."

"But it would."

She nodded inscrutably then went back through to the outer office. Trouble was, Evans thought, unlike either Sykes or the Perrins, he had no real history of violence. Yes, he was dodgy as all hell, but he'd achieved what he wanted by working smarter, staying below the radar, so he didn't think even the police had any clear intelligence as to the range or scope of his little empire. True, besides the likes of Kyle Sykes he was a minnow, but he was a successful minnow and he utterly resented being swallowed up by a bloody shark.

Evans prided himself on the fact that his was a largely white-collar operation. There were better ways of extracting what he wanted than by shedding blood. Like this little operation with the ransom demands. He kept it clean, ran it, as he had told Sykes, like a regular business, with rules and regulations and what he liked to think of as a basic honesty. He was afraid that was all about to change.

He wondered what Sykes had done with Sammy Marvin's body. That had been a shock, all right. Blood and brains all over reception, and Sykes had left it to Evans to clean up.

Sammy had been a good kid. He'd hated lying to the parents when they'd got in touch, asking where their son might be because he'd not been home or to uni or seen his friends. Not been in touch with anyone.

"We had to let him go," Evans had told them. "He was a nice lad but he kept falling asleep on the job."

No, he'd not liked doing that. But needs must. And he'd have to think seriously about tipping Perrin off. Sykes would know, of course, so whatever Ricky decided to do, he had to get it right.

CHAPTER 4

It had taken the morning to get organized and up to speed. At first Clarke had floundered — this wasn't the first enquiry he had headed up, far from it, but he was used to having a team around him to share jobs and lighten the load. He was not used to being out on a limb with the only support coming from a young DS who, after her time undercover, was unused to working within the usual parameters and jumped like a nervous cat at every unexpected noise. In his honest opinion she shouldn't have been allowed within a mile of active duty until she'd been given time to recover and the support for that to happen.

She was seeing a counsellor, she told him, but wasn't sure it was doing any good. Other than that she would not be drawn.

"So," he said, "our information pack turns out to be half a dozen phone numbers and the names of three previous victims."

She laughed. It was a weak sound, but better than nothing. "You really think Sykes might be behind this?"

She seemed better, he noticed, when she was forced to focus on the work, so he determined to keep her occupied. "It wouldn't surprise me. Okay, so maybe I'm only thinking that way because of the link with Tyburn Recruitment, but it's a place to start."

"So, I'll take that side of things," she said. "I'm already working the files, looking at Sykes's background. I can get access without it arousing any interest. I don't know what you think, but my feeling is we should trust as few people as possible."

He nodded. Sykes, they knew, had previously had informants within the police. Investigations were ongoing, but the suspicion was that there were more than had been identified.

"I'll chase down the families, see what else we can turn up. Trouble is, we've no background. We don't even know when and how the kids were taken or how they were returned. There's no forensics and there's no names, apart from these three. Deans said he believed there were around a dozen families involved, but he's not seen fit to tell us who they are."

"You think he knows? According to what you've told me, all he knows came from the investigation that PI was involved in. What was his name . . .? Anthony Dronfield. He took a dive from a multi-storey car park, we know that much, so what happened to his records? Which of the families employed him?"

Clarke shrugged. "Most likely this Patricia Copeland that Superintendent Deans mentioned. I'll see what I can chase down. You get as much as you can on Dronfield. If he was a registered PI, there'll be something on him somewhere. There'll also be newspaper reports and there'll have been an investigation into his death, even if it was ruled suicide. We work with what we've got and we build a picture." He paused, and she guessed what he was thinking.

"At least the kids have all been given back," she said. "We're working on the assumption that will happen this time as well."

"I think we have to," he said. "There's just you and me and a big wide nothing in between."

It scared him though. This time the parents had deviated from the plan. What if the kidnappers had discovered that? What if they knew? What if that was what Robert Banks wasn't telling them, that the kidnappers had been in touch and told him that they knew what he had done. Joshua Aaron Banks was just fourteen months old. If anything went wrong, what would happen to that little kid then?

"I'd like to be able to talk to the mother," Petra said, echoing Clarke's earlier thoughts. "I don't suppose—"

"As things stand, not a hope in hell. If this had been a normal investigation, we could get a family liaison officer in there, break the barriers down."

"But it's not, is it? Nothing about this is normal. The dad called the police in and then he shuts us out."

Clarke shook his head. "The dad *didn't* call us in. He phoned a friend. That friend happened to be a chief constable. But it goes higher than that, I'm sure of it. This whole operation is closed up so tight you'd think MI5 was running it."

She laughed, and Clarke was relieved that it was real laughter this time. "For all we know, maybe it is. What was it they used to say in *Mission: Impossible*? 'The agency disavows your existence,' or something. So, get it right and some other bugger takes the credit. Get it wrong and the two of us — well, we're expendable, aren't we? No one knows what the hell to do with me. If they suspend me, they look like they were wrong to send a woman in undercover. Put me back on active duty and they're second-guessing the outcome of the internal investigation and the court case, and the press and Gus Perrin would just love that. Hiding me away on a no-hope, off-the-books operation like this — well, there's no risk, is there? And as for you, you're the DI that exposed corruption within the force, so you had a hand in bringing it into disrepute. You know how these things usually go: the quiet report, the chance for the guilty party to retire on full pension. But no, you have to make waves."

Clarke raised an eyebrow but didn't interrupt. He could understand her anger. She really had been hung out to dry. But the bitterness caught him off guard, as did the sneaking feeling that she was right. Another thought occurred to him, a deeply uncomfortable one. He voiced it anyway.

"I'm wondering, does anyone apart from Superintendent Deans and the chief constable actually know we're even undertaking an investigation?"

"What about the woman, this DI Sheila Mace, and the CSI? You said there was a CSI there."

"One CSI. A woman I never spoke to that Deans said he'd borrowed for a couple of hours. And as for DI Mace, I looked her up."

"Of course you did."

"And she's currently on secondment. In Edinburgh."

"So? It's only a few hours on the train. Or to drive. It's possible."

"It is, but it's still—"

"Bloody weird," Petra finished.

CHAPTER 5

Petra arrived back at the room that she had called home for the last three days. It was a rundown B & B — not that she ever had the breakfast — in a backstreet just a short distance from the main police station, though the proximity didn't give her any better sense of confidence. There was no one at the front desk when she came in — a bell on the counter instructed prospective guests to ring for attention, and the reception was not manned as often she would have liked. The place was noisy too. It was used by the local council's emergency housing team and as a cheap place to doss down by so-called commercial travellers, though what they were selling was anybody's guess.

So she was not so much surprised as horribly disappointed to find the door to her room ajar. Cautiously, she pushed the door open. The room had been turned over, bedding and what little clothing she had left behind strewn across the floor, one pillow left ostentatiously in the centre of the bed, and on that pillow a photograph. She didn't need to look to know that it was a photograph of Billy Hunter. She should report it . . . again . . . Petra thought. But what was the bloody point? Instead she gathered up what remained of her possessions and walked out, leaving the mess behind.

At least, she thought, no one had pissed on the sheets this time. Or worse. And the only thing of value, her camera, was stowed safely elsewhere.

Walking back down the street she glanced around, wondering if she was being watched. She had come to the conclusion that the observation was not 24/7, that it was sporadic but frequent enough for them to keep tabs on her, and infrequent enough for her not to be able to anticipate a pattern or summon her colleagues. They didn't need to monitor her all the time. It was bad enough, worse perhaps, to know that they did it at all. It kept her on edge. It impacted on her concentration. Who was she kidding? It impacted on every aspect of her life.

She drove to a chain hotel, booked in for the night and decided she might feel better if she was booked in for two. She felt safer in places like this — the front desk manned all the time and CCTV in lifts and corridors — but she could not afford to live permanently in even the more modest of the chain hotels. What savings she had were dwindling. What reserves she had in terms of self-confidence or respect were down to almost nothing. She could not afford to go on as she was, not financially, emotionally or in terms of her general health.

She had been offered a place in a safe house and an extended suspension from duty, but after a near-death experience, when the safe house she and Lauren had occupied had been attacked, she no longer trusted . . . anybody.

She could, she knew, have asked for the same people who were now protecting Lauren to help her, but that would have meant giving up everything. She would lose everything she was now or ever had been and she would have to start from nothing. As time went on, Petra was not sure she had much left to lose. She was increasingly certain that one day she would make that call, despite the strings that would be attached and the final loss of everything she might feel she had achieved.

Dumping her stuff in the hotel room, locking the door behind her, she took a deep breath. She checked the room over and looked out of the window. She had made sure she knew where the exits were.

The only thing that made her relatively safe, Petra thought, was that the Perrins and Billy Hunter's family did not actually want her dead. They wanted her to suffer — they wanted their revenge to be long and cold. They wanted to make her life a misery, drag her name through the mud and then through the courts and ensure that in the end she *did* lose everything, including her dwindling sense of self-worth. And Petra was under no illusions — if the police force and the powers that be needed a scapegoat, she was most certainly it. She didn't like to think what Sykes might want or why he might be holding back. He must have bigger fish to fry just now. Maybe he was waiting for a day when he had nothing much on to deal with the minor annoyance that was Petra Merrow.

Just for a moment she was tempted to phone Lauren. She took the cheap, pay-as-you-go mobile from where it was hidden in the lining of her coat pocket and stared at it. There was only one number in the contacts list and Petra changed the SIM card regularly. She hesitated and then put the phone back into its hiding place, knowing that she wasn't being fair. This was not Lauren's problem. It was just that Lauren was the only person Petra knew who had any notion of what she was going through right now.

* * *

Clarke approached his own home with caution, but this was more from the memory of the day Sykes had been waiting for him than it was from real fear that something bad would be there. It was caution born of remembered pain, rather than expectation of a repeat of the experience. Since the day when Sykes had almost killed him, security in the building had been beefed up. There were now separate key codes on the front door, on each landing and on each flat, and CCTV cameras in all of the public areas. He knew that his immediate neighbours blamed him for the increase in service charges, but on the whole he didn't think anyone was too upset.

He let himself in through his front door and automatically checked each room before returning to double lock the door and shoot the bolts top and bottom. He would not describe himself as a paranoid man, but he would acknowledge that he was more acutely aware of his own personal safety than he ever had been. He supposed that getting shot would do that to a person.

He had stopped off on the way home to buy takeaway, and he now forked noodles and chicken on to a plate and got himself a beer from the fridge, then settled in front of the television for a while, trying to take his mind off the day.

Fat chance of that. He chased the conundrum that had begun at five o'clock that morning round and round in circles. He understood that the family did not want official police involvement, but even so, none of this made proper sense. And then his mind turned to Petra, and how much she had changed since he had last seen her. She had lost confidence, shrunk into herself, diminished both physically and in her sense of self, and that saddened him. She could, he knew, be a force to be reckoned with, an excellent investigator and definitely not lacking in courage. Living three years undercover, when any slip-up could quite literally have cost her her life, must have taken its toll, but it was events since that had undone her, Clarke thought. Not just the threat of the court case and all the media accusations, but more acutely than that, the knowledge that her colleagues blamed her for the death of the man who had been her handler for those three years, who had been tortured to death without giving her away. DCI Frankland was supposed to have been retired, but he had continued to monitor Petra in her undercover role, reluctant to pass this off to someone else, knowing just how difficult her job had been and how essential a familiar point of contact was. Frankland was a well loved and respected officer, and his violent and painful death had shocked everyone who had known him. Clarke knew that

Petra blamed herself, and many of her colleagues blamed her too. Unfair as that was, he felt that Petra understood it. There is no logic, Clarke thought, to grief and despair. We look for answers and we look for someone to blame, and as the man believed to have killed Frankland was on the run with Kyle Sykes, there wasn't even a day in court to satisfy the very human need for revenge. Or justice, if that was what you wanted to call it.

* * *

Kyle Sykes was at that moment with the unfortunate Ricky Evans.

"It has come to my notice . . ." Sykes said, and Evans's heart sank. What now? ". . . that you are holding out on me. Again."

Evans sighed. "Kyle, you've stripped me bare. There's nothing more to tell."

Sykes pulled out a chair and sat down on the opposite side of Evans's desk. He leaned forward. Behind him Paul Benson, Sykes's favourite muscle, hovered in the doorway. Evans knew that he had once worked for the Perrin family, but it seemed things had changed and he was now Kyle Sykes's man.

"It seems you have an inside man," Sykes said.

"An inside man where?"

"Where do you think?" He sat back, smiling. Behind him Benson was snorting and oinking. "Your little piggy," Sykes's smile widened.

Evans felt his stomach churning, but he did all he could to keep his expression neutral. "Like *you* don't," he said. "The police have their snouts, we have ours. That's the way it is. I suppose that's the way it's always been. People don't stop needing a bit of extra cash just because they put on a uniform."

"Well isn't that the truth?" Sykes said. "But yours, if my information is true, is already better paid than most. So what's his problem then — gambling? Ex-wives? What does he need the money for?"

"Constables aren't paid that well, and that's as high as I get. Community policing. They keep their ears to the ground, tell me when raids are planned, tell me what new initiatives are out there before we get to hear about it publicly. If you think I've got access to anything higher up than that you're sadly mistaken."

Sykes's eyes narrowed. Evans was certain now he was just shooting in the dark. He had no firm information for the very simple reason that Evans's high-ranking informant was not a 'he' at all but was very, very definitely a woman.

Evans jerked back as Sykes hammered on the desk, coming out of his seat now to lean over it, his face so close to Evans's that he could feel the man's breath. Sykes sprayed him with spittle as spoke again, barely keeping his anger in check.

"Names," he said. "You'll give me names. I don't give a shit if they just clean the toilets. You don't hold out me. I own you, body and soul."

Evans breathed again as Sykes pushed back from the desk, then left the office as suddenly as he had appeared. Paul Benson followed. Ricky Evans wiped his face. "Fuck's sake."

Ginny Afton came through from the outer office. She took one look at her boss and poured them both a stiff drink. "How much more of this are you going to put up with?" she asked. "I'll come in one day and find you with a bullet in your head or your throat cut, and that's if you're lucky. You know what he likes to do to people." She set the glass down in front of him. "Talk to Gus Perrin, or let me do it. He and I go back a long way, you know that. He'll listened to me, and Sykes is less likely to take any notice of what I'm doing. You go within five miles of Perrin and he'll know about it. Me, he thinks I'm just the bloody secretary."

"I can't, not yet. Let's get the kid back first, let this deal go through."

"He doesn't know where the kid is. The kid is safe enough."

He nodded, but there was clearly more on his mind, and Ginny, sensitive to his moods, sat down. "What are you not telling me?"

"When Sykes first learned about all this, about the kids and the payments and that side of the business, he came up with a . . . proposition, he called it. Like I had any chance of refusing it—"

"And you told me nothing about this? Fuck's sake Ricky. Didn't you—"

"Trust you? Of course I trust you. But you'd have done something, or said something. I didn't trust you not to land us both in it, just because you'd have tried to help."

She sipped her drink and glared at him. He could feel the anger coming off her in waves.

"Like I said, he had a proposition. A suggestion for the next kid, the next one to take. The family weren't as rich as some of those who we've dealt with, but the father could lay his hands on money easily enough, even if that meant he had to take it out of the company. He has access to the company accounts."

Her eyes narrowed. "You mean Robert Banks, the CEO of Tyburn Recruitment. I thought it was an odd choice, Ricky. So it was *his* idea." She frowned. "Didn't Sykes once have an interest in the company?"

"A sixty-per-cent stake, yes. It seems Robert Banks found this out, complained to the board, said he didn't think Sykes was a fit partner. He made trouble."

"And so Sykes has taken his kid in revenge."

"Sykes wants money. The revenge is just added sauce."

He watched as Ginny's brain ticked through the possibilities. "You think he's really a threat to the kid? You think he'll—"

"I think he's capable of anything."

"Then you've got to get rid. You've got to go to Gus Perrin now. Look, Ricky, this has been a good little earner, but everything has its day. We agreed the kids would always be sent back safe and sound. You can't risk—"

"And if I move against him, before he's got the money, we're dead. Understand that. He needs finance, ongoing finance, and he sees this as a way to get it. He won't hurt the kid. He needs the kid. He needs what the kid is worth. He needs the money."

"You believe that, you know nothing about Kyle Sykes," Ginny said.

"And you'll do nothing to get in the way," Ricky told her, and he saw the fear in her eyes because she knew that he was serious.

* * *

Clara Etheredge examined the paperwork presented by the woman with blond hair, and it all looked to be in order. It wasn't usual for a member of the team to turn up unexpectedly. Even emergency placements usually afforded a little more notice, and it was so unsettling for the child. He'd cried for his mother that first night but had seemed much more settled today, playing with Zara, Clara's four-year-old, and Bo the cat, and she'd been hopeful that the little boy, whatever trauma he'd been through that had brought him into the system, would realize he was now in a safe and untroubled place. But now the blonde woman was back and said she was going to take the child away.

"So, what's happened? I thought I'd got him for at least the next couple of weeks while the adoption paperwork was sorted. You said there was just a small, last-minute glitch." She knew her tone was a little accusatory, but she really didn't like to see already traumatized kids further distressed.

"I know and I'm sorry. I know this isn't ideal. Look, if you want to call my supervisor, her number's on top of the form, there." She pointed.

Clara glanced at it, absently registering the woman's immaculately painted, bright-red nails. She recognized the name and number, having dealt with the supervisor on a number of occasions. She made up her mind.

"Okay, look, I'll get John to pack his things for him, but if you don't mind I'd like a word with Mrs Jonas. This really isn't on, you know. I'm used to kids arriving unexpectedly in the middle of the night, and that's fine. I'm not so happy about the lack of notice when it comes to taking them away again. Josh is beginning to settle here. It's just not right to uproot him again."

"I know, I do know, and I agree. But unforeseen circumstances . . . you know how it is."

That was the thing, Clara thought. She didn't. Once kids were in the system very little was actually unforeseen, at least at her end of things. She sighed again. "Okay, look, if you want to wait in the living room, I'll just call Mrs Jonas. I want her to know I'm objecting, at least." She relented slightly, seeing the woman's troubled look. "It's not about you, it's just . . . well, it's not right, is it?"

She directed the social worker through into the small living room where Josh and Zara were both playing and went back down the hall and into the kitchen to collect her mobile phone. Her husband John was cooking and glanced over as she came in.

"Trouble?"

"Not sure. Something's off. I don't believe in kids being shunted pillar to post like this. It's not right."

John looked puzzled but didn't interrupt as she picked up the phone and scrolled through the numbers. Then a sound from the front of the house had Clara running into the hall, her husband following close behind. A quick glance into the living room told her that Josh and the woman were both gone. She flung open the front door just as the social worker's car sped away.

"Josh!"

John came out of the living room with their daughter in his arms. His face was white with shock. "Josh is gone."

"That lady took him," squeaked Zara. "We were in the middle of a game."

John patted his daughter's head. "I'll call the police."

Clara nodded, not able to speak. She was never certain afterwards how she managed to pick up her phone and speak to the switchboard and then to the senior supervisor, Mrs Jonas, but she must have done and she must have made a kind of sense because by the time the police arrived, Amanda Jonas was also there and then their little house became a crime scene.

"Clara," Mrs Jonas said gently, "we need to go upstairs and pack some things for you all. You'll have to leave for a while so the police can do their job, and you need to think about this really carefully. The woman who took Joshua Perry, did she touch anything? If she left fingerprints, the police might have her on record."

"But she had all the right documents." Clara was bewildered, her brain desperately clinging to what little certainty she had. "She had a clipboard and all the right documents. She said I should call you if . . . Oh my God, she took him away. She wasn't real, was she? But she brought him here on Friday morning. An emergency placement, she said. She said —"

"Clara, was that the paperwork?" John was pointing at something on the hall table. The clipboard, the forms the woman had presented to her.

She nodded. Through the open front door she could see the scientific support van that had just arrived, the CSI suiting up. "Fingerprints," she said. "She wasn't wearing gloves. There'll be fingerprints so you'll know who she is."

Mrs Jonas put an arm around her shoulders. "And she never went anywhere else? Just the hall and the living room? So we can go upstairs and collect clothes and anything you'll need for the next few days."

Clara stared at her. Mrs Jonas was speaking as much to the young constable standing awkwardly in her hallway as she was to Clara.

"Yes," he said. "That should be fine. But if you can go out the back way?"

Minutes later they were leaving, with Clara sitting in the rear seat of the supervisor's car, Zara in a child seat beside her, John in the front passenger seat and the cat in a carrier on John's lap. They were going to her sister's, Clara remembered vaguely. To stay with Connie for a few days. Someone had taken the little boy she had been meant to protect and care for. They had snatched him from Clara's own front room. How, just how could she live with that?

CHAPTER 6

Patricia Copeland had not been keen on arranging an appointment with DI Clarke that Saturday morning. He had finally managed to contact her late the previous evening, and it had taken a good half hour of his best persuasive arguments to get her to agree. In the end he was pretty sure it had been the certainty that he would bother her again rather than anything he had actually said that had swung it for him. He set out on the two-hour drive on the Saturday morning still not certain he would get through the front door when he arrived.

Clarke was horribly conscious of passing time. It was two days since he had stood in that beautifully kitted-out and desperately sad little nursery. There could be no talk of golden hours on this occasion, just, to his mind, one wasted opportunity after another.

Would he have behaved differently, he wondered, had it been his child? He rather thought he would.

Once on the A1 and heading for a village five miles from Leeds, he allowed his thoughts to drift. His parents had separated when he had been just a little kid of four, but he had been lucky, never in any doubt that he was loved by both. His parents, he thought wryly, had managed their separation far better than they had managed their marriage, and birthdays had been doubly exciting with the occasion celebrated with both families. Christmases happened twice too, his parents taking it in turns to have him on Christmas Day, usually at the home of one or other set of grandparents, and then repeating the exercise on Boxing Day. His childhood might have been unconventional and in some ways very difficult, but there had never been any doubt that he'd been loved.

The kidnapping brought to mind one particular incident in Clarke's life. He'd been, he reckoned, about five or six and had gone after school to play with a friend. The friend's garden backed on to what had been a field and was now a building site, and the diggers and piles of bricks and timber had been too much for the pair of them to resist. They'd squeezed through a gap in the hedge and gone to explore this much bigger playground.

It could only have been a few minutes before their absence was noted. The poor mother was frantic and had called Clarke's mother, and of course, she had called for backup. Twenty minutes later, four cars had screamed into the close — Clarke's father and a dozen of his cronies, prepared to tear the place apart until he was found. Meanwhile, Clarke and his friend, in a state of blissful ignorance, had been wandering this wonderful, cratered landscape, climbing up on the diggers and tractors until they were spotted by one of the workmen and escorted into one of the site Portakabins. As is the nature of kids who know they are in trouble, they played dumb.

Soon the local constabulary had joined the search, in strained lockstep with Clarke's dad and his tooled-up associates.

Of course, Clarke thought, one look over the garden hedge and he'd figured out where they must be. He'd also once been six years old and enamoured of anything with tracks or giant wheels.

"An hour, maybe," Clarke remembered, speaking to the memory of his long-dead father. To the mother now happily remarried and living abroad. "We were missing for an hour and grounded for at least a month."

He remembered his parents shouting at him, hugging him, his dad crying tears of relief and not caring who saw them. This big, tough man that most people figured had no regard for anyone or anything. This was his boy and he would move mountains to make sure he was safe.

Though, of course, Clarke had not appreciated that at the time. He'd just been concerned with all the play dates missed and the lack of chess club and taekwondo after school and the unfairness of it all.

So what was so different in this case? In those other cases they knew about — or sort of knew about, information in the so-called information pack being on the slim side of scanty — the parents had toed the line and kept their silence, trusting to strangers that their child would be returned.

He supposed, on one level, they'd had no choice. Where could they even begin to search? Who could they call on for help, apart from their bank manager or whatever it was that rich people had? Clarke's dad had taken one look at the building site and remembered his own childhood curiosity. No one, after all, had taken his son. No one was demanding anything or threatening them or . . . but what if they had? He had no doubt that his dad would have torn them limb from limb. But that would suppose he knew who they were and that he could get hold of them — though remembering the people his dad had run with, it would not have taken long for them to have found out.

That was, Clarke figured, the difference here. The families had no choice — there was no one, nothing to grab hold of, just the hope that a bargain would be kept.

* * *

Petra Merrow was back in her cramped little space sifting material as she had been most days in the past months. Today, though, she felt as though she had a new purpose

— something specific she could look for and that might, just might, produce a concrete result. She began with a general search for Tyburn Recruitment, refreshing her memory. The company had existed for more than a decade but had only risen to prominence in the past six years, when it became a limited company and shifted emphasis to internet security, data protection and recovery, employing specialists in those areas and using them to create 'tailored packages'. Robert Banks had been CEO for five of those years — headhunted from some corporation that Petra had never heard of but which she gathered was a big deal in the tech marketplace. She made a note of the name, BellisCo, in case it should be relevant later.

She skimmed the details of Banks's education and career and then googled the man himself. She'd already established that he had no record — the only thing she'd found on him was that he had once attended a speed awareness course, which presumably meant he had been caught driving above the limit on at least one occasion.

He was on the board of several local charities, all to do with young people and education. She studied the photographs taken at various posh-looking dos, but recognized no one from either the Sykes or Perrin camp. He'd made some keynote speeches at local Financial Stability Board and Chamber of Commerce events and run the London Marathon in aid of one of his charity interests.

There were pictures of his wedding and an announcement of the birth of his son and a few articles, co-authored and appearing in business journals and banking newsletters.

Then something made her heart beat just a little bit faster. It was a letter of complaint written to a national newspaper. It might completely have passed her by, being several pages into the search and uncovered only when she played around with cross-referencing various key words and phrases. The one that scored was 'shell companies'. Banks had been writing publicly about his concern that criminal activities might be concealed 'like Russian dolls nested within legitimate concerns' and that the boards of those companies may or may not choose to know that this was taking place.

So why put this in a letter? And a letter to a mainstream newspaper at that?

She read more closely and began to understand. Banks named one such shell company, said that he had presented his worries to Tyburn's board and had been flatly told that it was none of his concern. Shellard Tech, a limited company dealing in the development of tailored solutions — that phrase again — in the banking sector was in fact owned by a known criminal. In the shape of one Kyle Sykes.

It took a bit more digging and a lot more cross-referencing but at last she found more. Sykes, via Shellard Tech, had bought a controlling interest in Tyburn Recruitment around the time that Banks had been appointed to the board. It seemed that Banks had not known about Sykes and his less legitimate dealings at the time. Shellard was simply a parent company and Tyburn one of several in its portfolio. Then suddenly, about eighteen months earlier, Banks had woken up to the fact that Karl Sykes might not be a simple businessman after all. Not only that, but Banks was prepared to make some noise about it. A little more digging had revealed an article, co-written by Banks and published in the online version of a business magazine, asking how easy it might be for criminals to infiltrate legitimate business.

"Child's play," Petra muttered and noted that the article had reached the same conclusion. She took a note of the name and contact details of the co-author and searched further to see how this had played out.

It seemed that Banks had kept the pressure on, asking difficult questions and eliciting a public statement from Shellard that, yes, Mr Sykes was a major investor but that, as a limited company, the accounts were on public record and available for scrutiny. At one point it looked as though Banks would resign, but then, last November, life had turned sour for Sykes and he was now a man on the run.

"So, you decided Banks would be your target," Petra said thoughtfully. This man had crossed Sykes, even though it had looked, at the time, as though he would be the one to come out ahead. Until it hadn't. Until Lauren had put paid to many of her father's ambitions, drawing the focus of his rage on herself and anyone foolish enough to help her escape. And because Petra, then embedded with the Perrins, had reluctantly been dragged into the mess, she had now invoked the ire of both the Perrins and what remained of Sykes's organization.

She paused, hands raised above the keyboard, and glanced over her shoulder — her anxiety, never absent, suddenly spiking as the enormity of it all overwhelmed her.

She took a deep breath, let it out slowly. Tapped her fingers one by one on the wooden surface of the desk. Right, then left, then right again, focusing only on the movement of her hands, the feel of the wood grain beneath the pads of her fingers.

They don't want me dead, she told herself. At least not yet. Had that been the case, she'd be gone by now — from a bullet in the back of the head or a blow from the ubiquitous blunt instrument. And that's if she were lucky . . . She was under no illusions that at any moment this might change, but for now she was alive and, she supposed, that was something.

She turned back to the computer and began to search again.

* * *

The signs for Leeds reminded Clarke of the rainy day the previous November when he had driven to the city to collect Lauren Sykes from where Petra had stashed her, in one of the chain hotels close to the station. He recalled his first sight of her — small, waiflike, but possessed of such determination and, he soon realized, courage. Several times recently he had wanted to ask Petra if Lauren was really dead.

He looked for his exit and twenty minutes later was pulling up outside a modest, stone-built cottage, centred in a small, fenced garden, at the end of a long lane. He checked the address — this, somehow, was not the sort of place he had envisaged as home for Ms Patricia Copeland. He had imagined some posh place, like the Banks house. Modern and plush.

The door opened and a woman stood on the threshold. She had bobbed grey hair, was slim and tall and wore straight-legged jeans, an expensive-looking dark pink sweater – and an expression that told him she was seeing him under sufferance. He must be in the right place, then, Clarke thought, remembering his somewhat fraught conversation with Ms Copeland the day before.

She watched as he emerged from the car, made no response to his greeting but instead turned and went back into the cottage. At least she'd left the door open. Clarke followed her in.

For a moment he thought there was going to be some kind of stand-off in the small sitting room — the woman standing, arms folded, on the hearthrug, he just inside the cottage door, wondering whether or not he should close it or beat a hasty retreat. And then she sighed.

"Oh, for God's sake, sit down. I'll make us some tea. We may as well be civilized while we get this over with."

Clarke closed the door, took a seat and watched her flounce through into the kitchen and fill the kettle.

From his position beside the empty grate, he took the opportunity to look around. Kindling and dried logs had been stacked in an alcove below shelves of paperbacks. A small sofa faced the fire and chairs were set on either side. It was, he thought, more of a winter place than a summer one. He could imagine a blazing log fire, curtains closed against what would be very dark nights, so far from light pollution. But this time of year, even on a bright day, the cottage felt oddly bleak. Or perhaps that was just the woman's mood impinging on his sense of the place.

Stairs rose up from the end of the room. In the space beneath was an old-fashioned bureau-style desk, a modern filing cabinet — looking oddly out of place — and a high-backed dining chair that he presumed was used whenever she sat at the bureau.

She didn't live here, it occurred to him. This was a bolthole, a safe and neutral place for her to meet this unwelcome visitor.

Patricia Copeland came through with a tea tray. "Grab that little folding table, will you?" she said, jerking her chin towards the alcove on the other side of the fireplace, behind the chair Clarke occupied. He jumped to do her bidding and she set the tray down between them, taking the other fireside chair.

"So," she said, occupying herself with mugs and teapot, "they've taken another child."

"They have, yes."

"That brings the total to either thirteen or fifteen, including this one," she said.

Her hands were shaking slightly as she passed him his mug. She was wound almost as tight as Petra, Clarke thought. "Thirteen or fifteen?"

"Not all the families will talk. I know for certain about twelve. I suspect two more, but the parents won't give me the time of day." She shrugged. "I can understand why they don't want to talk, not even with all the precautions we take."

Clarke was startled. "The families are in contact?"

"Three of us. We have established something approaching friendship, I suppose. Each of us has made some kind of contact with other families. Sometimes just briefly, sometimes for longer. I suppose we've become a support group for one another — that and a source of what little information there is. Sometimes all that can be offered is reassurance. The children have always been returned, have always been cared for. But the families, on the whole, avoid all contact with the authorities. They're scared that if they break the rules their kids *won't* come back alive and cared for. They'll come back dead or not at all." She folded her hands around the bright-red mug she held and stared into the empty grate as though wishing that a fire burned there, and to Clarke the cottage felt suddenly chill.

"*Have* some of them come back dead. Or not come back at all?"

She hesitated. "Hard to say. No one really wants to talk. Not even to those who've been through the same thing." She shifted uneasily in her seat and then went on. "You have to understand, most of the families have nothing in common apart from the fact that they were targeted, presumably by the same gang, and their children . . . their very young children were taken away and a ransom was demanded."

"Nothing in common apart from wealth," Clarke pointed out.

"I'd have thought that was a given," she said coldly. "There's not much point kidnapping a toddler from a council estate, is there?"

"No, I suppose not." He kept his voice steady but she had managed to make him feel both slightly stupid and . . . somehow soiled and unclean. Her tone was disdainful, as though those other children, the ones not worth taking, were in some way of less value.

"Look," she said, as though suddenly making up her mind. "I have records of everything I know, everything I've managed to find out, everything the investigator I hired, Dronfield, managed to find out before he met with his accident."

"It wasn't an accident."

"Well, suicide then," her expression told him that the word tasted bad. That 'accident' was more acceptable.

"Likely not suicide either."

She met his eyes with some reluctance and nodded. "I hired him on the recommendation of a friend. Someone he used to work with. At the ministry, I suppose, or something like that. We never discussed his CV. You don't, you know, with people at a certain level. He seemed to be getting nowhere."

Clarke was reminded that pressure was being brought to bear on this case from very high up. Or so Deans had told him. "So either Dronfield was getting closer than you or he realized or someone thought he was."

For a moment Clarke thought she was going to lose that fragile grip she had, that all-too-thin veneer of control. Then she lifted her mug and took a casual sip of tea.

"You're scared," he said. "Has something happened? Something more, I mean?"

"I've been frightened for a long time," she said, but Clarke got the impression she was almost proud of that. She was terrified, but she went on anyway, continued with her task, whatever she considered that to be.

"How long has this been going on? Do you have a sense of that?"

"Almost four years, we think. As I said before, it can be hard to discover the details because—"

"No one wants to talk."

"As I told you, these families have nothing much in common. They were all resident in the UK when it happened, but not all are British nationals. Not all are obviously wealthy — they tend to be more discreet. Some are old money, some are entrepreneurs or whatever. Their children are taken from them and they are told not to report it to the police. They are given a number to call, a contact with a family who has already endured what they are going through. They are told, do what these people say. We got our child back. Safe and unharmed. So they comply. What would you do, Inspector?"

It was the question he had asked himself on the drive here. "I don't know," he admitted.

"Quite. None of us knows until we're in that situation. I find it best not to judge when you've no idea . . . no idea what it feels like."

There was a moment's silence and then, glancing around the small sitting room, he asked, "Is this your place?"

"It was once a holiday let. One of several I owned around here. I sold the others, kept this on. It's my sanctuary, I suppose."

"I'd like contact details for the families you're in touch with."

"Not going to happen."

"I could arrest you for obstruction."

"Then do so. I have a very expensive lawyer on speed dial."

"I have some of the names already. Maybe they'll lead me to others."

"If you have, then you can work with what you've got, like the rest of us have had to."

She confused him. On the one hand she seemed eager to help. On the other she seemed determined to obstruct. He wasn't sure how to break through the barriers she'd erected. "What happened, when the child was returned to your family? How was it done?"

"Amelia was dropped off at a local park. My nephew and his wife were given a time and a location. They arrived to find their daughter playing in a sandpit as though she'd not a care in the world. She was dressed in the clothes she'd been wearing when she was taken."

"It's a miracle she hadn't wandered off."

"It was one of those fenced-off areas. Fenced off to keep the dogs out, I suppose. With swings and rocking horses on big springs and a sandpit." She wrinkled her nose as though the idea of a public sandpit was distasteful.

"And she was . . ." he wasn't sure how to put this.

"She was fine. Healthy, well fed, happy to see her parents but totally unfazed by it all. I had a doctor examine her and he found a mild sedative in her bloodstream. Just enough to keep her calm. She kept asking for someone called Jenny and for a boy called Pete. It seems . . . it seems as though she was kept with other children. She came back with a liking for porridge and . . . and she was no longer frightened of the water. Her mother had taken her to the swimming pool so many times and she'd just screamed blue murder. After . . . after that she couldn't get enough of it. Tiny little tot that she was, Inspector, she could almost swim. Can you imagine how her parents felt about all that?"

"Terrified, but better than her being harmed."

"Oh, don't you get all sanctimonious with me. Of course it was, but can you imagine how complicated and conflicted their emotions must have been?"

Clarke supposed he could. He remembered his own parents' reactions when they had found him that day — after only a short time, admittedly. The pure, unadulterated gratitude of his father's tears.

"So you think she was kept among other children. Did any others go missing at the same time?"

She shook her head.

"And do any of the other parents report anything similar?"

"One other that I know about. Their little boy kept asking for his big brother. He doesn't have a brother. The others were by and large too young to verbalize their experiences."

Clarke thought about this. In the previous investigation he had remembered all the abductees had been older. It was their evidence, pieced together, that had finally broken the case. That and the murder of one of their number. It was unlikely that this was the same gang — that one had been thoroughly smashed, but many of the details were public knowledge, reported in the press and on television. Anyone getting it into their heads to take a similar route would have an easy lesson in how to proceed and what mistakes not to make.

Patricia Copeland got to her feet, set her mug on the tray and crossed to the filing cabinet he had noticed earlier. She began to empty the drawers, then stopped. "Look, just take the whole damn thing, will you? I'm sick of the sight of it."

He tried to hide his surprise. "Sure." He eyed it suspiciously. "Can the drawers be taken out?"

She cast an exasperated look in his general direction. "See for yourself. Look, I need to be on my way so . . ." He watched as she crossed the room, collected the tea tray and took it back into the kitchen. He heard her running water to wash the mugs and wondered if she was also imagining washing him and all the grief that had dominated her life down the plughole as well.

He had taken the drawers out to the car and was returning for the cabinet itself when he saw her again. She stood in the kitchen doorway and watched as he wheeled the cabinet out from under the stairs. "It broke my family," she said. "Not just when it happened, but after. My nephew and his wife, they divorced a year later. They couldn't seem to deal with the guilt or the grief or the fact that Amelia still asked if she could play with this Pete child for weeks after she came home. Then when they found out I was trying . . . trying to get to the bottom of it all, they broke all contact. They said it would only bring trouble, and so it has, I suppose. Dronfield dead, other families still suffering."

"And you?"

"I lost money, of course I did. Taking that much cash out of the equation is not going to happen without ramifications. I was — by most calculations, I still am — a rich woman, but it took time to plug the gap and it took a lot of lies. I blamed my 'losses' on bad investments, and in business bad investment equals bad decision-making, which equals bad leadership. And you might say that the buck stops with me. So in the end I downsized and regrouped and, well, I took a different direction. That, Inspector, I could deal with. I had experience and acumen and I'd had setbacks before. I treated it, on the business side, just like any other setback. But as I say, it broke our family. I discovered far too late that I didn't have the experience or the resources for that."

"You did what you thought was best. You didn't want other families to suffer."

She laughed, the sound crow-like and harsh. "I fix things, Inspector. All my working life I've gone in and I've fixed things. I turned failing companies around, looked for new ways of working, convinced myself that there was nothing in life or work that could not be managed by the correct application of carrot and stick. I was naive."

He looked curiously at her, trying to read her expression. The notion that she was trying to tell him something but did not have the words hardened into certainty. Why, he thought, hand all of her research over now. "Has someone threatened you? Threatened your family? Recently, I mean?"

"I know what you mean. Inspector, when I walk out of here today it will be for the last time. I'm going away for a good long while. I have good people I can trust to run my business day to day, and these days I can just as easily manage anything else from California or Berlin as I can from anywhere in the UK. And no, I'm not going to tell you where I'll be. My family have already gone, hopefully far enough away."

"What happened, Ms Copeland?"

He could feel her reluctance to say more. As though by speaking about the threat it would bring it closer. Allow it entry into this little room.

She ducked back into the kitchen and returned with a padded envelope held between her hands. "It was about a month ago," she said. "In the post one morning. Photographs. Then one of the families called me to say they'd received something similar. A week ago there were more and yesterday I woke up to find this on my doorstep. Here, in my safe place."

She held the envelope out and Clarke took it from her.

"No. Don't look inside. Just take it. The photographs are in there too. Just go, please. Everything I know is in those files, but I'm done with it now. There are some things I just can't fix, so I'm doing something I've never done before and I'm running away from it all."

He nodded. "We could—"

"Don't. Just go." She paused for a moment. "If you'd not called me I'd have burned the whole damn lot, you know that?"

"I'm glad you didn't."

That laugh again, jagged and desperate. "When you called, my first instinct was to tell you to fuck off."

"As I remember it, you did." He smiled and saw it returned, but saw also that she was close to tears.

"Then I thought, right, this is an opportunity. To be rid. To hand it all over to someone else."

"Thank you. I'm grateful."

She straightened, squared her shoulders and smoothed her hair, and in that moment all weakness disappeared and he glimpsed again that public persona. It was his cue to go.

A few minutes later he was driving away with the drawers from the small filing cabinet laid across the flattened back seats of his car. He drew the car up on the verge before joining the main road and, pulling on a pair of latex gloves, took the padded envelope from the passenger seat. Inside were a half-dozen photographs of children. Three of a little girl playing on swings in what looked like a park. The second showed a little boy, somewhat younger, splashing in an outdoor swimming pool.

There was a second padded envelope, which he guessed must have been left on her doorstep. It contained a sleepsuit, toddler sized and pale blue. And stained with blood.

* * *

Ricky Evans watched as Kyle Sykes picked the child up, held him at arm's length and inspected him as though he were some kind of exotic toy. The child burst into tears and Sykes, losing interest, dropped him back on to the chair.

"We got him back for you." Ricky's voice was cold but far from calm.

"And so you did. You see life runs far more smoothly when you do as you're told." He turned to Paul Benson. "Put it in the car."

To Ricky's alarm, Ginny stepped forward and said hesitantly, "Maybe he could stay with me, Mr Sykes. He's just a little mite, he'll need some looking after. You won't want to be bothered with all that."

Ricky held his breath as Sykes turned to stare at Ginny.

"Put her in the car too," Sykes said, and Ricky's heart sank.

"No, I need her here. She does all the admin and . . . This place doesn't run without Ginny." His words failed him as Sykes's scrutiny turned back to him. Coming under his gaze, Ricky thought, was like being stripped to the bone.

"Then maybe you'd like to come along with her?" Sykes said, and Ricky, to his shame, found himself shaking his head. Ginny didn't even turn to look at him as she began to follow Paul Benson to the car.

Sykes halted abruptly. "On second thoughts, maybe you'd better keep her. I wouldn't want my business plans interrupted because you can't manage a bit of admin."

He gave Ginny a shove towards Ricky. She stumbled back and Ricky caught her before she fell. They watched as Sykes and Paul Benson drove away.

"Ginny, you daft cow!"

She shrugged him off, eyes blazing. "He's just a little kid. You know what he's fucking well capable of!"

"And you think you could protect the kid, just by being there?"

"I think I could have tried."

"If Sykes decided you were getting in his way you'd have ended up like Sammy Marvin — or worse," he told her sharply. He saw the tears in her eyes and reached out towards her, laying a hand on her arm. Again, she shrugged him off. Ricky watched helplessly as she walked away, got into her own car and drove off.

"What an absolute fucking mess," Ricky said bitterly.

CHAPTER 7

They had arranged to reconvene at the office in the old school, and by mid-afternoon Clarke pulled into the car park and noted that Petra was already there. She must have seen him through the window because the kettle was on. She gestured towards two long, white paper bags bearing the name of a local shop. "I found a good little cob shop round the corner," she said. "I bought a couple of baguettes. I thought you might be hungry as well. I'm starving."

She looked better, he thought, as she handed him his coffee. More alert, more like her old self. He sank down gratefully into one of the low armchairs she must have filched from somewhere else in the building and reached for one of the baguettes, not too fussed about what was in it. It was food and he'd not eaten since early morning. It was now almost four.

"So," she said, taking the other chair and the second baguette. "Who goes first?"

"You," Clarke said. "I suspect your day might have been more straightforward and I can't really tell you about mine until we unload the car. And we might need a bigger secure cabinet."

She gave him a speculative look and he could see she was itching with curiosity. She pointed to what must once have been a stock cupboard. "I found the key to that. It's a good size and has shelves. I brought some boxes with me and there's another lockable filing cabinet inside too. I have the key."

He felt oddly relieved at that. Through the window he could see his car and knew he'd feel a whole lot better when the contents were inside.

"I'm hoping Superintendent Deans will call," he said. "I phoned him on the way back. He wasn't there but I left a message. We need forensic support."

"Oh?"

Clarke sighed. He took a bite of his baguette, ham and cheese salad, decent bread. Fine. He could see this little sandwich shop getting a good deal of custom over the next . . . well, however long.

"Maybe you'd better go first after all," she said.

Half an hour later she was up to date with what he had learned that day. She took his keys and left him to finish eating while she fetched the papers from the car, neither of them really comfortable until they were locked away.

Together they eyed the stack of documents laid out on the table. "Are these in any kind of order?" Petra asked.

"Hard to say. Most of the folders are dated. She seems to be an organized woman, so I'm guessing there is logic in here somewhere."

"Okay, so how about we get things into date order and work through chronologically, then we can examine it thematically and any other which way when we've got a timeline." She nodded towards the back of the room and the old stock cupboard. "There are shelves in there so we can lay things out as we go. And then . . ." She hesitated for a moment. "As well as locking it we can maybe arrange the table or a cabinet or something in front of it so it looks as though nobody's ever gone in there?"

Clarke cast her a speculative glance. "A little paranoid?"

"Neither of us feels comfortable about this," she countered. "We both know this is not how things should be done. I'm not paranoid, I'm just . . . uncomfortable."

Clarke nodded. The truth was, so was he. "Give me a sec." He had spotted something earlier that he thought might be useful. He dodged out of the room and moments later reappeared with an old noticeboard, designed to be hung on a wall. A further scrabble around the mothballed building produced a hammer and nails and together they hung the noticeboard so that it covered the door but could be removed easily. "Now set the table in front, put those two small filing cabinets underneath and the door vanishes. Let's make it a rule that we take out one stack of paperwork at a time and replace it as soon as we're familiar with the contents. I'll take our notes back with me and lock them in my safe at home."

She nodded, and for a moment they just stood looking at one another. Clarke felt the sudden clench of fear in his chest. Maybe it was just paranoia, but whatever it was, it was catching. "And I think maybe we stay quiet about the results of my visit to Patricia Copeland this morning," he said quietly. He wasn't sure who they could trust. Everything about this was wrong, everything about this felt dangerous, and it had not escaped him that this highly sensitive case, one which should have been set up with specialist teams and experienced investigators, had been placed in the hands of two people who were already pretty much expendable so far as the higher-ups were concerned. He because he was not yet perceived as fit enough to be on active duty and Petra because of all the baggage she carried from her time undercover.

"So far the kids have been returned safe, every time," he reminded her, but he knew he was trying to reassure himself as much as Petra.

"So far," she said, turning away from him to sort through the folders. A moment later Clarke had joined her and they worked in silence, swiftly and anxiously, almost irrationally desperate to get this evidence stowed away before there was a chance of anyone else seeing it.

After about an hour, most of the folders had been sorted and stowed away. The motorcycle courier they recognized from the previous day came to pick up the bloodied sleep suit, stowed in its evidence bag, then concealed in a large manila envelope.

"We don't know that it belongs to the little boy," Petra had said hesitantly. "We don't know that it's human blood."

"No, we don't," Clarke said flatly. They turned back to their tasks and for a while did not speak.

At five o'clock Petra said, "We seem to have broken the back of the work. If I leave you to finish up, I can phone the journalist who collaborated with Banks on the business article. I might just catch her before she leaves for the day. And then I'd like to get hold of the guy who wrote the article on Dronfield's death. Tomorrow is Saturday — if I don't manage to catch them today, likelihood is it'll be Monday."

Tony glanced at his watch. "I think you'll be lucky anyway."

Both desks were still covered with paperwork, so Petra took a notebook and her mobile and sat just outside the door to make her calls using the deep windowsill as a makeshift desk. He heard the murmur of conversation, then a pause, and then another conversation begin. He turned his attention back to the folders laid out on the desks. They had arranged them in date order and found that this also correlated with families whose children had been taken. There was something like a three- or four-month gap between each kidnapping — in some cases the amount of material ran to three or four manila folders, crammed full with press cuttings of background information on the families, what was known about the kidnappings, how much had been paid for the safe return of the precious children and how each child had been returned. In other cases there were perhaps only two or three single sheets of A4 paper with scribbled notes, mostly speculative. He guessed that even the redoubtable Patricia Copeland had failed to get these families to cooperate with her.

He heard Petra ring off and then dial another number. It seemed to be quite a while before she got a pick-up on this call and he sensed she was about to give up when he heard her say, "Oh, hello, is that Jonathan Roan? I'm so glad to have caught you. No, thank you for picking up, I won't keep you long."

Clarke gathered from the initial conversation the man had been about to leave his office for the weekend. Soon he could hear Petra's voice but not the words, and glancing through the door he saw that she was pacing up and down the short corridor. Although her words were soothing, he could see that she was slightly annoyed. He gathered the journo was beginning to regret answering the phone.

A few minutes later she re-entered the room. He had started stacking the folders on the shelves in the stock cupboard and she began to help.

"Any joy?"

"I finally got put through to a work colleague of Maisie Rooney, that's the journalist for the business magazine who wrote that article with Banks. She's apparently away and might not be back for a couple of weeks. They wouldn't give me her mobile number and, frankly, there was nothing I could say that would put pressure on them to do so."

She sounded pissed off about that, Clarke thought.

"I had to give them some spiel about checking background of an old case, but that sounds just *sooo* dodgy. Anyway, as her colleague pointed out, most of Maisie Rooney's work is in the public domain so I can just look it up myself."

Clarke laughed. "Well I suppose she has a point. And the second call? What did Jonathan Roan have to say for himself? You ever met that guy, by the way?"

"Can't say that I have. What's he like?"

"Young, keen, wants to make a name for himself. Likes digging the dirt, fancies himself to be—" he set down the folders he was holding and made air quotes — "an investigative journalist."

"He any good?"

"Hard to say. He's run a couple of so-called exposés on local drug culture, and about three years ago did the thing on dodgy council officials — I forget the details, backhanders for building contracts, I think."

"But from what I can see of the Dronfield article, it was very much 'just the facts ma'am' — the fact that he died falling from the multi-storey, a bit about his background, hints about him being ex-military and possibly ex-intelligence, that sort of thing. He led on to a series of articles about midlife crises and male suicide, which I suppose was useful in its own way, even though it's probably wrong in the Dronfield case."

"Was there anything to suggest he'd been pushed?"

"Coroner's verdict was death by misadventure. You and I both know they often bring that in to avoid embarrassment to the family, even when it's widely believed to be suicide. But my guess, and I think yours too, is that he was helped on his way."

Clarke nodded. It was a distinct possibility. They closed and locked the door to the stock cupboard, positioned the noticeboard and set the table and the filing cabinet in position. It wouldn't pass close scrutiny, Clarke thought, but it would do. He glanced at his watch. "Time to call it a day. Shall I pick you up first thing in the morning? Save on petrol? Or do you want to sleep in on a Saturday?"

"I don't sleep in," she said, then realizing he had meant it as a joke, she added, "I don't really sleep."

"Where are you staying tonight?"

She told him and they agreed that he would collect her at eight in the morning. They had each selected a stack of documents, and he watched as she stuffed hers into her backpack, noticing that her anxiety seemed to have returned with full force. He had heard that she had been constantly on the move for these last months and knew that it must have been taxing, but he had not given it much thought until now. Looking at her he registered the strain that had aged her, the lines around her eyes and the pallor of her cheeks, and he noted again how thin she was. He wondered how he could make it better, a sudden surge of sympathy making him want to at least say or do something.

"See you in the morning," she said, and the moment was gone. Watching her leave, he told himself that there was nothing he could help her with, that he actually barely knew the woman, that she should ask their bosses for help if she needed it. He swore then, knowing he was making excuses for himself and that their bosses had not exactly been useful to either of them since the Kyle Sykes case had blown up in their faces. He almost called after her but realized he had no idea what to say and even less what to do. She should leave, he thought. Go far away and start again. But start again as what? And how could she really go anywhere with the court case hanging over her and the weight of public opinion weighing so heavily on her shoulders?

* * *

A couple of miles away, Jonathan Roan sat glaring at the phone and trying to make a decision. The phone call from DS Merrow had been a surprise. He had been following her story, of course, and already had a series of exclusives with other parties organized for when reporting restrictions had been fully lifted and the court case put away. He was surprised that she was still a serving officer — though his sources told him she was assigned to 'tidying up the filing' in the archives. So what was she doing poking around into Dronfield's death? Jon had always suspected there was more to that story than first appeared, but despite his best efforts had failed to come up with anything concrete.

Giving in to the inevitable, he picked up the phone and dialled a number he knew far too well. Just pressing that sequence of buttons on his phone was enough to set off the incipient ulcer Jon was certain was his destined lot.

"Hello, yes, it's Jonathan Roan. I just—"

The person on the other end laid the phone down heavily on something hard. Jon winced. He heard the murmur of voices and a moment later the phone was retrieved. "Good evening, Mr Roan."

Jon caught his breath. Even with a phone line between them, the man still creeped him out. No, tell it how it was, the man scared the bejesus out of him, as his gran would have said. He knew better than to preamble.

"I've just had a phone call from DS Merrow. She was asking about an article I wrote about a private investigator, Anthony Dronfield. Fell to his death from the multi-storey on Melbourn Road about eighteen months ago."

"I recall the incident. What did she want to know?"

"About any background material I'd collected, if I'd spoken to any of his associates, that sort of thing." He took a deep breath. "Nothing very specific. Just fishing, as far as I could tell."

"So, what do you think she was after?"

"I don't know," Jon Roan admitted. "I'd not even thought about the man since I wrote the report."

"So what would this man have been investigating?"

"Apart from a couple of divorce cases and a lawsuit over a business partnership, I don't know of anything."

"Not the sort of thing that would interest DS Merrow," the voice said coldly.

"No," Jonathan agreed unhappily, knowing what was to come. Gus Perrin liked to get his money's worth, and Jon would be the first to admit he'd not provided much for his retainer.

"So you'd better find out," Gus Perrin said.

CHAPTER 8

Petra sat on the bed in the hotel room and dialled the one number in the phone's contacts book. A moment later she heard Lauren's reluctant hello.

"How are you?"

"I'm fine. You?"

Petra did not bother to answer. They both knew the truth of the matter, what was there to say?

"Kyle Sykes. To your knowledge was he ever involved in kidnapping?" She had long since stopped referring to Sykes as Lauren's father. The girl had told her this was no longer the case, reminded her that Lauren Sykes was officially dead.

She could sense Lauren thinking.

At last the girl said, "I suppose if you count snatching someone off the street and then killing them, then you and I both know that happened on more than one occasion. Someone would threaten him and he would deal with it."

"No, I mean something more organized. Kidnap for profit." She took a deep breath knowing that she was piling more agony on to this young girl each time she asked about her past. "Specifically children." She heard Lauren's quick intake of breath.

"No," Lauren said quietly. "I know nothing about that. What makes you think . . ."

"Probably no connection," Petra said, though she knew how hollow that assertion must sound. "As you know, I'm looking through cold cases. Something came up, so I needed to ask."

She hung up soon after because there was nothing left to say. She had been aware of Lauren slowly withdrawing from these conversations as time went on and she knew that she had no right to keep what could be a very dangerous connection going. She had justified it to herself, because Lauren knew about her father's business dealings, both legal and illegal. She was an intelligence asset — albeit an intelligence asset that everybody else believed dead and gone. There was a limit to her usefulness, in the sense that Petra could not reveal her source. She understood that Lauren wished these conversations to end, that she should be getting on with her life and consolidating a new identity and that Petra was pulling her back into her past. She knew that if Lauren was to have any chance, not just of surviving but of thriving, then Petra should let her go, but she found it so hard to do.

Impatient with herself, she dropped the phone on to the bed and told herself she'd better order room service, especially if she planned to spend the evening going through the files she brought with her. Lauren owed her nothing, she told herself sternly. Yes, Petra had stepped up when Lauren had needed her, but the girl had more than repaid anything Petra had done and it really was time to be letting go. She was just surprised at how much that knowledge hurt.

* * *

"What did she want?" Molly Chambers asked.

Lauren told her.

"Kidnap for profit," Molly said thoughtfully. "It's not an uncommon action in many parts of the world. More unusual here, I would have thought. And you don't remember hearing about anything like that?"

Lauren shook her head. "But then I think he was capable of anything. I wouldn't rule it out." She looked thoughtfully at the mobile phone she still held in her hand, then set it down on the table. "Molly, I am grateful, I know what she did for me, but every time she phones I get scared. I feel safe here, or as safe as I can feel anywhere, but what if . . ."

"The next time she calls let me speak to her," Molly told her firmly. "As I said before, you are not the adult here and you cannot solve her problems for her. She has to do that for herself."

"That feels so harsh."

"Because it is. She can reach out and ask for help elsewhere. The police force has a good counselling service, and in extremis she could ask for help from those who helped you and brought you to me."

"I don't understand why she doesn't do that."

"I suppose because it would seem like giving in. And if she left her life behind, as you've done, I'm not sure she'd know what to do with the new life that was given to her. Not everybody can make that adjustment."

Lauren absorbed this. "I feel selfish," she said. "But Molly, every time she calls me I feel like she's asking me for help and I have to give it. I don't mean information, I mean . . ."

Molly took her hand. "I know what you mean. But my dear, you cannot give her the kind of help she needs. It would be like sticking a plaster on a broken heart. Until Petra Merrow works out what she wants, no one can give her what she actually needs."

Lauren leaned into the older woman's embrace. She had come to love Molly almost as much as she had loved Harry, a man she'd known all her life as a surrogate grandfather. That love was what had got Harry killed — she tried not to think about that. She was terrified that she was bringing danger to Molly, though she was pretty certain that it would not have been the first time someone in Lauren's position had done that. She had gleaned that Molly Chambers had a colourful past.

Molly hugged her tightly and dropped a gentle kiss on Lauren's hair. "I can put out feelers," she said. "See what my contacts can turn up. That's if you want me to."

Lauren hesitated. "I don't want anyone else put at risk," she said. "If someone else starts asking questions and they get hurt, I'd . . . Molly, I feel like I'm responsible for enough people hurt and dead."

"No one will be put at risk, I promise you that. And the weight of responsibility for what's happened in your life really isn't yours, my dear. Kyle Sykes took those people's lives, not you."

"But he killed them because I ran away."

"He killed them because that's what he does. He's a killer, a psychopath, a man who deserves to be put down," Molly said harshly. "The world has never benefited from having men, or women, like that living in it."

Lauren raised her head and looked at the older woman. Molly had a gentle, lined face. Her thick white hair curled softly, brushed to a shine. Blue-grey eyes, crinkled by smile lines. And yet . . . and yet, there was steel behind that gentleness. Fierce, protective determination that in different circumstances, Lauren felt, would give anyone pause.

"Always know your enemies," Molly said gently. "Know where they are and what they might be doing. That way you can either avoid them or, at worst, be prepared for the fight."

* * *

Superintendent Deans sat opposite DI Mace and stirred his coffee, despite the fact that he did not take sugar. His hands were shaking and the spoon rattled against the rim of the cup. He was aware that she had noticed. She held her own cup delicately between long fingers, her blood-red nails in stark contrast with the white of the china. He cleared his throat nervously. "What will you do now?"

"That depends on what happens next. Hold your nerve and you'll be fine. You kept it together when you were briefing DI Clarke, so I don't see what the problem is now."

"That was before I knew *he* was involved."

"It alters nothing. You play your part and it will all be fine."

"You're a cold-hearted bitch, you know that?"

"I never denied it. Look, sudden attacks of conscience are an emotion we can ill afford. Just play your part, keep your mouth shut and we'll all get what we want."

"And the child?"

She sipped her own coffee, peering at him over the rim of the cup. Then she set it down. "I've no doubt that they'll get their kid back in due course," she told him. She gathered her bag and her coat, and he watched as she left, the café door clanging behind her.

CHAPTER 9

As Clarke collected Petra the next morning, the radio was broadcasting an item on the eight o'clock the news about a child taken from a foster parent's house by a bogus social worker. There were few details, just some speculation that the child might have been taken on behalf of a disaffected parent.

Petra turned up the radio to listen. "You think . . .?"

"Let's hope not. Like they say, maybe a child custody issue gone south." But he felt deeply uneasy. He comforted himself with the thought that this case at least had a full investigation supporting it and not just two outliers like himself and Petra. "We can't go on like this," he said abruptly. "We've got to call in some help."

She nodded. "Yeah. It's just stupid."

By half eight they were settled in the office, collating the information they had gathered from their reading the evening before. Clarke checked for further information on the abduction they had heard about on the radio. No name or description had yet been released. Press speculation suggested the child was a two-year-old male. The police computer told them the name of the officer in charge and that the child's name was Joshua Perry. Beyond a description of the incident and a series of actions, taken and proposed, there was little information.

"Joshua," he said. "His name is Joshua."

"Coincidences happen," Petra told him, but he could see the added anxiety in her eyes. Having each taken a case file, the first and second in the sequence of snatched children, and familiarized themselves with the contents, they now took the opportunity to exchange information.

"The first kidnapping was just over three years ago," Clarke began. "The child was Karina Shore and she was ten weeks old. As far as we know she was the youngest one ever taken. The father, Ian, was a multimillionaire, inherited wealth and a whole portfolio of business interests, and the mother was a catwalk model before she took early retirement at twenty-five to get married."

Petra looked at him, noticing something in his tone. "What happened?"

"The family was killed in a road accident about six months after the kidnapping. Patricia Copeland seems to think that our private detective, the late Mr Dronfield, was looking into the events surrounding the crash. There are notes in the folder to that effect. It seems she gave him carte blanche to go where he liked and proceed as he saw fit. There are a lot of his notes in this folder too."

"Really? Mine had mostly background stuff. Anyway, carry on."

"The accident happened at something of a black spot on the A5. The report says that Mr Shore probably lost control on a patch of ice when trying to overtake a lorry on a stretch of dual carriageway. He clipped the front of the lorry and the car spun out of control and rolled several times before coming to rest about a hundred yards down the road."

"Which all sounds very feasible," she commented. She spotted photographs of the accident scene and spread them out on the table. "The car's a hell of a mess. What was it?"

"Top-of-the-range Mercedes, fully loaded with airbags, traction control, the works. The airbags had deployed and there was some indication that the driver had exceeded the speed limit when trying to overtake the HGV — in really poor driving conditions, no less. So as far as the accident investigators were concerned it wasn't suspicious."

"So why was Dronfield investigating?"

"Well, according to his notes here—" Clarke extracted a sheet of paper from the folder — "a friend reported that the family had been harassed — silent calls, photographs sent to them that had been taken when they were out and about, death threats sent to the home, that sort of thing. No evidence was found, which fitted with the friend's statement that Mr Shore had burned it all. On the face of it he just dismissed the whole thing."

"On the face of it?"

"Turns out he had someone looking into it. His business was big enough that it had security to do background checks on prospective employees, and they were told to look for disaffected ex-workers. They didn't get very far before the accident happened."

"And back when the kidnapping happened, how was the child taken?"

"The mother parked at front of the house and left the child in the car as she took some shopping inside. She was gone no more than two minutes, but when she returned the child was missing and there was a note in the car seat telling her to wait to be contacted."

"God, she'd never forgive herself," Petra said.

"Seems the husband never forgave her either. The fact that they were all in the car the day the accident happened was an anomaly. They were going to a wedding, daughter of a business acquaintance, some really big affair. Shore wanted to put on a united front in public and was threatening financial consequences if she didn't play along."

"Nice."

"Actually, they were to be divorced and the mother had already moved out of the house. The father was suing for sole custody."

Petra wasn't sure there was a good response to this. "And how was the child brought back? After how much time?"

"We don't know how much the ransom was. Dronfield and Patricia Copeland fitted the pieces together and figured out that the child had been missing for about two weeks. Dronfield interviewed staff that had worked at the house, who finally admitted that, while the mother had been distressed when the child had gone missing, it seemed to have been covered up — the father told them he'd taken her and not informed the mother. As the marriage appeared to have been shaky even then, they believed him. Or decided it was politic to do so. And none of them broke their silence at the time. We can't even be sure of the facts I've just relayed to you. As you'll see from Dronfield's notes, a lot of it's circumstantial and inferred, but it's all we've got to go on."

"How certain can we be that this was an accident?"

"There was no suggestion at the time, but then the accident investigation didn't know what had happened previously, or they might have been more suspicious, I suppose. The child was returned, but maybe something went wrong. Maybe the family let something slip and the kidnappers took action. Maybe it was a tragic accident. We just don't know for certain."

She nodded and took up the narrative. "The second case was about six months after the first, a little boy of eighteen months called Robert Cohen- Brown. Facts about the kidnapping are very thin on the ground for this one. It seems the parents wouldn't speak to Ms Copeland and Dronfield doesn't seem to have been involved, at least there are no notes from him. Most of what I have is press cuttings and some speculation. I've had a glance at the third and fourth cases, and it much the same. Lots of background information on the business, the parents, the timescale that the child was missing in each case. According to Copeland's notes she worked that out only because in each subsequent kidnapping the parents were told to call the number of a previous victim, and small details emerged. It suggests a lot about her persuasive capacities that anybody's told her anything, to be frank. I mean, in their situation, would you?"

He shook his head. "Probably not. Why take the risk? And they wouldn't tell the likes of us. Patricia Copeland was part of their circle, or at least part of their business and social milieu. Not like us common plods."

"True. I get the impression you like her." She watched as he considered what she'd said.

"I think I *could* like her."

"Could?"

"I didn't meet her at her best. Yesterday she was just another scared witness, wanting nothing more than to be rid of me. The more I see of what she achieved, the more I admire her capacity for investigation. But I'm also pissed off by the idea that she knew all of this and did nothing. She could have tipped us off anonymously, sent what she had to any police force in the country, and someone would have taken notice."

"You think?" She eyed him closely, realizing now that what she had taken for liking was in fact more complex.

"I do. Anyway, Petra, she's a woman with power and influence. She knows people in the same way that Robert Banks knows people. His son was kidnapped, so what did he do? Called the chief constable. My bet is, even if there'd been no threat to the contrary, he'd never have soiled his finger dialling nine, nine, nine. That's for the plebs."

She laughed at him. He sounded so outraged. "Classist," she said.

"Damn right. But no, I think if we'd met socially, I would have liked Patricia Copeland. But when I met her yesterday she was in full flight mode. Everything she thought she could control has been taken from her, and her life is in free fall. She thinks she's still got the resources to run away and put distance between herself and her family and all of the trouble she's now inadvertently brought down on their heads. So she's doing what she's always done and thrown money at the problem. A first-class ticket and a succession of five-star hotels, no doubt."

"It's still frightening, even if she is doing it in style," Petra told him a little sharply.

He looked momentarily startled. "I know it is. I just feel that a woman in her position, with her resources and privilege and education, might have acted more wisely."

"People don't," Petra said. "Most of the time they react on instinct. It's hard to be wise when you're shit scared."

"Which I agree, she is now. But—"

"Look, she's not the one behind all this," Petra reminded him. "If you're going to attempt to profile anyone, maybe it should be the kidnappers."

He laughed at that. "Easy. We're looking for complete assholes."

She helped him move their barricade away from the door and replaced the files they had read, withdrawing two more stacks. Clarke began to move the furniture back.

"No need," she told him. "Not until we pack up for the day. We just lock the outer door. Anyone wants to see us, they can ring the bell."

He looked momentarily abashed. Then nodded. "Right, so we split the rest, work our way through quickly. Anything else?"

"I want another look at Dronfield," she said. "I'd like a better picture of the man, especially if he's made notes on the cases, then I'll pick up my share."

They spent the morning working in near silence, broken only by the tap of a keyboard or the scratch of a pen and the making of coffee. By the time they broke for lunch, Petra felt they had both made headway.

"Dronfield," she said. "Military background, possibly special forces. There are little hints on his web profile. And other little hints that he had connections in the intelligence community. Lots of testimonials on his site — which may or may not mean anything — and he was a member of all the usual professional associations."

"So . . ."

"So absolutely bloody nothing. The testimonials are glowing but none actually tell me what he did. There's a list of the areas he covers — everything from missing persons to looking for lost heirs. Lost dogs too, for all I know. But when you start to dig down, there's nothing. It's almost like a cover story, you know?"

Glancing at him she got the feeling that he was thinking that she was probably the expert on cover stories, but he didn't say it and she didn't challenge. "I suppose Ms Copeland didn't say how she got in touch with Dronfield?"

She watched as he flicked through his notes and then shook his head. "At the time I just assumed she'd googled PIs or maybe looked in the phone book. Does anyone look in the phone book anymore? Anyway, thinking about it, maybe it was personal recommendation. Sorry, can't tell you any more than that."

She nodded. "There's an emphasis on discretion."

"I suppose there would have to be."

"Sure, but, you know, more than you'd expect. Maybe this was a cover. Maybe Dronfield did find evidence for divorce cases and the odd lost dog, but maybe he did more than that, on the quiet."

"Discreetly." He grinned at her and she found herself smiling back.

"One thing for sure, though. He was meeting someone the night he died. Someone he trusted. And you've got to ask, a man with his background, what kind of person would take him so much by surprise they could shove him off the top of a multi-storey car park?"

She watched as he considered that, but then Clarke reminded her, "We don't know for sure it wasn't suicide. We don't know there was anyone else involved."

"True. But the odds are . . ." She picked up the next folder. More human misery, she thought. More parents scared for their child. And what about the little boy that was missing now? The others had all been returned. But that didn't mean anything.

Clarke seemed to read her thoughts. "All we can do is follow the evidence. We need to know the background. Everything there is to know. If there are answers, then they'll be in the files."

"And if they're not?" Her despair was sudden and absolute. She fought it, placing her hands flat on the table to stop them from shaking.

"For now this is all we've got," Clarke said quietly. "So we get on with the job in hand. That's all we can ever do."

* * *

By the time they broke for the evening they had an all-too-clear impression of a dozen families who had gone through hell and a dozen children who had survived against the odds, but they were no further on than they had been on that first morning.

Remembering the south-coast operation from a few years before, Clarke had accessed the details and even spoken to the SIO, a DI Sebastian McGregor. But there had been differences in the MO and the gang responsible were all serving hefty prison sentences.

McGregor had been curious as to Clarke's interest, and Petra got the impression Clarke was uncomfortable fobbing the man off with his vague 'checking background' excuse. He had also pointed out that the details were well known, the media having scratched away at the case until the very bones were picked clean. It would not take a great leap of imagination to replicate and improve on what had been done before.

Twice in the day they had attempted to get hold of Superintendent Deans, but he seemed to be unavailable. DI Mace was similarly absent. "I don't like this at all," Clarke said as he failed for the third time to contact the only two officers who officially knew about the case.

"So, what do we do about it?"

He looked uncomfortable. She guessed, "You already did something, didn't you?"

She listened as he confessed to bringing Superintendent Craig into their confidence.

"And you were going to tell me this when?"

"I just did."

For a moment or two she regarded him with annoyance verging on anger, but she had to admit she was glad that someone else was in the loop. She'd had a lifetime's worth of being out on a limb and without a safety line. "So we call him. Now?"

He glanced at his watch. It was almost seven. "I'll try him at home."

But that too was scuppered. The phone rang out. "No one there."

"Try later."

He nodded. Looking at him she guessed that he had never felt so alone or so isolated. For Petra that was a familiar feeling, but DI Toby Clarke had spent his career as part of a team, knowing he had colleagues he could depend on and who would share both workload and responsibility, with senior officers who would when necessary make the difficult decisions. For a moment or two she was angry with this apparent weakness. She had operated alone and without any real support for three long years, with only her own knowledge, experience and nerve to back her up. Then she stopped being angry. That was then and this was now, and there was more at stake than a bit of professional pride.

CHAPTER 10

The following morning all plans were thrown into disarray. The body of a child had been found. Clarke heard the news on the morning news as he was driving to headquarters. It had been found together with a more decomposed body of a young male. The waste ground by the canal on which they had been dumped was familiar to Clarke. Earmarked for redevelopment that never took place, warehouses and old factories long demolished — though odd walls and basements remained — it was a place where people walked their dogs in daylight and addicts hung around after dark.

It had also been a favourite spot of Kyle Sykes for getting rid of what he saw as unwanted waste. Clarke turned the car around and headed for the crime scene.

Petra must have heard the same bulletin — her car pulled up behind his just as he got out. They stood together watching the familiar scene beyond the cordon of police officers and forensic support, in their pale blue bunny suits, moving purposefully or consulting in small, tense knots.

"I should stay here," Petra said. "You might get through the cordon — what reason have I got for being here?"

He started to argue but she silenced him with a look. "Go. Find out if . . . if it's our kid."

Our kid, he thought. He nodded. She was right, in a way. Every waking hour in the past few days had been spent on trying to find some kind of lead. The weight in the pit of his stomach and the tightness in his chest told him that they had failed.

He could see the crime scene manager, Paul Collins, talking to DC Denise Allwood and their immediate superior DCI Tucker, who had replaced DCI Henderson a few months before. He wondered if Tucker was to be SIO on this case but then decided probably not — Tucker was far less hands-on than Henderson had been and would delegate. He'd probably only shown up for the photo opportunity, Clarke thought bitterly, and then rebuked himself for the thought. Tucker might have a more stand-back attitude than Henderson but he was also a first-rate investigator and a much better people manager than Henderson had ever been. He was here because he cared, not because the gathering press would expect him to be. Glancing back towards where he'd left his car, Clarke noted that Petra had got back inside her own, probably wanting to keep a low profile.

Recognized by the constable on patrol, he was allowed to duck under the tape and was directed towards the common pathway laid out earlier by the CSIs. Tucker spotted him and looked puzzled. Denise Allwood just looked intrigued, but then she always looked intrigued.

"What are you doing here?" Tucker asked.

"I heard on the morning news. I need a word."

Denise Allwood's interest was piqued further. Tucker took in the look on Clarke's face and nodded. He dismissed Allwood and followed Clarke back along the pathway on to the road. "So?"

"The child, has he been identified yet? I think I know who he is."

Tucker frowned, his demeanour changing from one of mere curiosity to something close to suspicion. "Go on."

Clarke took a deep breath. This was not going to be easy or pleasant. He wished fervently that when he had gone to speak to Superintendent Craig he had asked that Tucker be brought into the meeting. His boss would not like the idea that he had been kept out of something as crucial as this, no matter what the excuses. "The child, it's a little boy? If I'm right then his name is Joshua Aaron Banks."

Tucker's frown deepened. "And what information do you have that we don't?"

"Sir, this is going to take a bit of time, and I think we need to speak to Superintendent Craig as well. But could I see the body?"

It was, Clarke thought, to Tucker's credit that he stood back and gestured towards the crime scene without asking further questions. He was surprised that Tucker did not follow him back. Collins, the crime scene manager, accompanied him to where a small body lay on a pile of rubble. Clarke had seen pictures of the child — there was one in the folder back at their makeshift office — and even though this little body was marble pale, there was no doubt. The world seemed to shift sideways, and he realized a moment or two later that Paul Collins had taken hold of his arm to steady him.

"It's always more of a shock when it's a child," he said quietly. "The baby's only been there for a short while. The ground beneath is wet, but the child is not."

"Time of death?" Clarke managed, but his voice sounded strangled and strange.

"I wouldn't like to speculate. It's harder to get a handle on these things with infants, but perhaps twenty-four, forty-eight hours, something like that. The other individual has been dead a lot longer, certainly."

He had been so preoccupied with this tiny human being that he had almost not registered the second, but Collins's words suddenly made him very much aware of the smell of decomposition. The second body lay just a few feet from the first and was in a far worse state. "Any idea?"

"As yet, no. Best guess is he was dumped here recently rather than left here at the time of death. This area, as you know, is frequented by dog walkers and kids getting up to no good, so someone would have seen it or smelt it. In fact, it was a dog that found them both this morning. The owner, an elderly man, called it in."

"Is he still here?"

"No, your boss had him shipped off to the local hospital. You can imagine the shock he was suffering. Tucker wanted to get him checked out." Now Collins was looking at him speculatively. "You know something about this, don't you?"

"I think it links with a cold case I've been looking into," Clarke managed. He sensed that Collins suspected there was more to it, but knew he would ask no more questions. He walked back to where he had left Tucker. His boss had moved. Petra's driver's door was open and Tucker was squatted down talking to her. *Shit,* Clarke thought. *Well, he's got to know sooner or later.* And he would also have to know that he had confided in Superintendent Craig. Was Petra telling him? He had been grateful for her lack of reaction the evening before, when he had told her what he'd done. She might not be too happy about it — though he had felt she might actually be relieved — but he had been afraid she would assume he had not told her immediately because of a lack of trust.

Was it? Clarke wondered. Did he trust her? Since she had returned from her undercover role he knew that she had been viewed with a degree of suspicion by her colleagues. They couldn't help themselves — could someone who had been in as deep and for as long as she had really be trusted anymore? Whose side was she really on? And she had been engaged in a long-term relationship with one of Gus Perrin's closest associates and a friend of Gus Perrin's daughter. So what, the argument went, did that say about Petra Merrow? Perhaps he had been touched by the same concerns, even though his experience with her told him they were unfounded.

As Clarke approached the car, DCI Tucker straightened up, his face grim, and Clarke guessed that Petra would have felt compelled to at least begin to explain what they had been doing and why. Petra's face was pale. Clarke nodded — it *was* their kid. He saw the blood draining even from her lips.

"The pair of you had better come back to the station," Tucker said. "I think you have some explaining to do." He turned on his heel and walked towards his own car, and Clarke bent down to peer into Petra's.

"Are you okay to drive?"

She nodded.

"What have you told him?"

"About you being called out in the middle of the night, about Superintendent Deans and DI Mace, and that they've arranged everything." She hesitated. "I didn't tell him about the files from Patricia Copeland. I know we have to, but . . ."

He nodded. She closed the door and he got into his own car, and in convoy they drove out through the press pack at the end of the road, knowing that it was only a very short time before it would be reported that the infamous DS Petra Merrow and the dubious DI Clarke had been at the murder scene. Conclusions would be drawn.

* * *

"It is a general rule," Molly Chambers commented, "that the younger the victim of crime the more column inches that crime will generate. Or internet links, I suppose, would be more accurate these days."

Lauren nodded. There was a certain sardonic humour in Molly's words, but her tone was sombre. They were, as had become their habit, watching early morning television on the small set in the kitchen while eating their breakfast.

"Do you think this was what Petra was asking me about?"

"Hard to say. If the child had been found anywhere else, you wouldn't even consider that possibility. It's only because the poor mite has been found in your home town that you're making the connection. And no, you are not going to contact her to find out, no matter what unwarrantedly guilty thoughts are churning about in your head. You know how foolish that would be."

Lauren scowled, then gave up. Scowling had no effect on Molly, especially when she was right. "I promise I won't. It just crossed my mind, that's all."

"Of course it did." Molly's tone was gentler now. "You're only human."

When Lauren had first come to live with Molly she had used the word 'promise' quite liberally, but it had soon become clear that this was not acceptable to her protector. "Never," Molly had told her, "promise anything unless you intend, come hell or high water, to keep your word."

Lauren remembered that she had laughed. "It's just a word, it's like—"

"It's a precious word," Molly had said. "You can tell me you'll try, you can tell me you'll do your best. You can tell me to go to hell and not interfere in your life, or whatever phraseology young people today use when they are instructing someone in sex and travel."

"Sex and travel?"

"Think about it."

"Ah." Lauren remembered she had laughed. "Rather than just 'fuck off'. I like that."

"Good, but if you give your word, if you make a promise, then it must be given with total honesty and the expectation that you will do whatever it takes to keep that word."

Lauren had only known this elderly lady for a few days at that point and was inclined to think this was a bit over the top. She had shrugged. "Whatever." But in the days and weeks that followed she began to realize that Molly had been deadly serious. That Molly had given her word many times in her life and that promising something meant that it would be done. That sometimes it had meant she'd quite literally risked her life to keep another person safe.

"Did you promise to look after me?" she had asked, after a time, keeping her tone light.

"No," Molly said frankly. "I said I'd do my best to make sure no harm came to you, but as I didn't know what I might be dealing with or even if I'd like you enough to care, I couldn't do that. Not at first."

Lauren had wanted to ask, *Do you like me enough now?* but couldn't summon the nerve. Molly saved her the agony. She'd dropped a light kiss on Lauren's hair and said, "But don't you worry, my dear, I've no doubt I'd give as much as Harry gave to protect you now."

Harry had died for her, Lauren thought. But she believed Molly. And what was more, she had in the past months come to realize that the feeling was mutual.

The television news had moved on to the previous history of the waste ground by the canal. Of the three bodies dumped there the previous year. Three men tortured by Lauren's father. In person, she thought, he was not one to delegate a task he enjoyed so very much. "So, what if he's mixed up in this?"

"Well within the realms of possibility," Molly said. "It could be the Perrins, I suppose, but it seems, from what I've been told, more Kyle Sykes's style than theirs. It seems unlikely someone else would move into territory occupied by such an established family, especially as they have taken over so much of Sykes's domain. Though it's possible, of course." Lauren noted the cool, curious gaze turned upon her. "And what do you think?"

Could he have done this? The man was technically her father, however much she wanted to forget that. "It's showy enough," she said. "But I've never known him do anything to a kid. Not even to me when I was little. I mean, to be honest, I didn't have a lot to do with him until I was seven or eight, even though we all lived in the same house. He'd show me off, make a fuss of me in front of guests and then lose interest. Father–daughter time was always best dress, combed hair and best behaviour. To be honest, I think he just found kids boring."

She sat back, rocking the kitchen chair on to two legs, then remembered from previous experience that this was a bad idea and tilted it forward again. Molly was clearing the breakfast table and preparing to wash the pots. The television had moved on to other stories and Lauren turned it off. Could her father have done this?

She put the marmalade back in the cupboard. Took the tablecloth to the back door and shook off the crumbs, examining it carefully to see if it would do another day or needed to be washed. Folded it and put it back in the kitchen drawer. The usual routine they had established was soothing, and she almost resented this reminder of her other life. She waited until Molly had finished running the kitchen taps. "He'd have to have a reason for something like this," she said. "If the parents paid up and he killed the child, then he must be out to punish them for something. Punish them twice, I suppose. He must really want them to suffer. So it must be personal. If the parents didn't pay up, then killing the kid must be to send a message. What if he plans to do this again?"

Molly plunged mugs into hot water. She nodded. "You think he has someone in mind? If we could discover the identity of the child, that might give you a better idea of what's happening here."

"You sound like you want to investigate."

"I sound like I want to know my enemy," Molly corrected her. "From what you've told me and from what I've been told by others, Kyle Sykes is a calculating bastard. Someone who wrings every situation dry of everything that can be of possible benefit to him but stays far enough in the background that he's always got an alibi. Of course, we're making a lot of assumptions here, but you're right. It is — what did you call it? — flashy. Cruelly so. He's shouting out for everyone to take notice — police, parents, media . . . the Perrins, presumably. And he's committing what most people see as the worst of crimes to do that. The killing of a child is heavy with symbolism. Every bastard in history has known that and taken advantage of it."

She dried her hands and looked thoughtfully at Lauren as she put away the breakfast things. "I'll make a phone call," she said. "We need intelligence on this and from someone a lot higher up the food chain than young Petra Merrow."

* * *

Miles away Kyle Sykes watched the same bulletin. He had started the day with a celebratory glass of champagne and, Ricky Evans thought, looked set to finish that and several more before the day was through.

He's totally nuts. He's totally lost it, Evans thought. In his view Sykes had always been a couple of sandwiches short of a picnic, but now he seemed to have forgotten the picnic altogether.

Evans watched the bulletin and watched Sykes watching the bulletin, reminding himself that this was no joke. A kid was dead and he was right up to his neck in the middle of it, and that was a place he never wished or planned to be. Ginny was right, he had to do something, and she was probably right that the only thing he could do was go to Gus Perrin, spill the lot and hope that Big Gus had some solution to the problem that was beyond Ricky's imagination or means to see, because right at this moment he could envisage no way out.

Could he even get to Perrin without Sykes knowing? Ginny had suggested that she make contact on his behalf as she had more chance of doing so unobserved. By and large she was off Sykes's radar. He just saw her as the hired help, a woman who should know her place and stay out of his way. Ginny played the part to perfection, keeping her head down, both literally and figuratively, and rarely even making eye contact with the man. Ricky Evans wished fervently that he could do the same.

"You're not celebrating," Sykes complained.

Celebrating that you killed a little kid, Ricky Evans thought. "You know the police will be round here. They'll identify Sammy's body and that will bring them to me."

"And?"

And, Ricky thought. What did Sykes care?

"You didn't have to kill the kid. He was just a baby. We've always sent the kids back alive and unharmed. I mean, some of them have gone back in better shape than they were when we took them."

Even as he said it, he was aware of how absurd this sounded. He had almost managed to justify himself in the past, telling himself that the kids were fine, the parents could spare the money, no harm done. If there were problems, they could afford to send the kids to counselling, though Ricky himself was no fan of shrinks. In his book, if you did something, or something was done to you, you dealt with it. You moved on. Then Sykes had come back on the scene and Ricky couldn't convince himself of anything much anymore.

"Why do you care?"

"Because it was a kid."

Sykes shrugged. "Everybody's somebody's kid." He poured a second glass of champagne, got up and dumped it on Ricky Evans desk. "Drink."

Ricky Evans did as he was told.

CHAPTER 11

The longest day didn't really cover it, Clarke thought. He and Petra had the first hour with Superintendent Craig and DCI Tucker 'explaining themselves', as Tucker had phrased it, though to Clarke's relief Craig had taken their side. Clarke, he said had been placed in an impossible position and had done the sensible thing and reported the situation to Superintendent Craig. He pointed out that DCI Tucker had not actually been in the building at that point or he would have been included in the briefing. Clarke had no idea whether or not that was true, but it gave everyone an excuse and, as Craig also pointed out, there were far more important things to be getting on with.

"And what about the involvement of the chief constable?" Tucker wanted to know.

"I've tried to speak to him," Clarke explained, "but I can't get past his PA."

"We've had a conversation," Craig said. He didn't sound too happy about it, Clarke thought. He risked a glance at Petra, and from her frown she didn't think so either. "He assures me that he believed Superintendent Deans had everything in hand. That they would keep everything low-key until he'd established the facts and then act accordingly."

Tucker made no comment, but Clarke could tell that Tucker didn't like it. The man glowered, and his dark eyes surveyed Clarke, Petra and the superintendent with deep suspicion. Tucker was quite an intimidating man, Clarke supposed — solidly built and with a way of carrying himself that made him look taller than he actually was. His once-jet-black hair was now an attractive salt-and-pepper grey, and he always managed to look smart, even at the end of the day.

Clarke pulled his thoughts back. Tucker was speaking to him again.

"So, this Patricia Copeland woman, she gave you some information."

"Some background, yes. To be honest, a lot of it is newspaper clippings and the odd bit of speculation. Nothing solid."

He felt rather than saw Petra move restlessly in her chair, but she said nothing to contradict him. And, Clarke reassured himself, a lot of it *was* newspaper clippings and the odd bit of speculation.

"Have forensics come back on the blood-stained sleepsuit?" Clarke asked. He had told them how this had been dumped on Patricia Copeland's doorstep, how this had been the final straw that had brought her to the decision to go as far away as she could.

Tucker ignored the question. "And she gave you no sense of where she was going?"

"I got the feeling she was going to America. She has business dealings there and she mentioned some family connection. But I couldn't demand to know. I could have brought her in, but she still wouldn't have told us, and my sense was that would have put her in further danger. I could hardly arrest the woman, could I? I suppose I could have threatened to charge her with withholding evidence. At that point there was no official investigation apart from whatever it was Petra and I were meant to be doing. I was up there on my own, the local constabulary hadn't been informed I was fishing on their patch, and until I got there I'd no idea she could tell me anything useful. She was just one of the very few leads we'd got." He faltered, the excuses sounding hollow. "I tried to speak to Superintendent Deans again. I could have done with some official guidance, but—"

"But we've not been able to get hold of him or DI Mace since that first morning," Petra said. She looked at Craig. "Sir, have you . . ."

"He's not been home in two days, and a woman we've identified as DI Mace can prove that she's not left Edinburgh in the last week." He sat down at his computer and called out a personnel file. "This is DI Mace," he said.

Clarke looked at the screen. "That's not the woman I met. She had dark hair in a kind of bob, blue eyes, was quite thin and smartly dressed." He recalled her careful make-up and bright-red nails. "This isn't her."

The woman on the screen was blonde, round faced, smiling and though not overweight, definitely not thin, and her clothes might have been described as smart casual but not tailored. It suddenly struck him that the woman he had met at the crime scene had been almost overdressed. Too expensive, somehow.

"So who the hell was she?" Tucker wanted to know. "Didn't you ask for identification?"

"I'd met Superintendent Deans before. I knew him a little," Clarke offered in defence. "If a senior officer introduces me to another officer, I have to assume he knows what he's talking about. What about the CSI?"

"We've not yet identified who that might've been. I don't suppose you have a name?"

Clarke shook his head. "Barely spoke to them. I asked if it was all right to touch certain things, where I should walk, the usual stuff. She directed me like I'd expect the CSI to. She was suited and masked, but she wasn't someone I knew. I recognize the locals even when they're masked up. Have the forensics from the scene been logged?"

Craig shook his head. "Someone was taking you for a fool, possibly Deans too," Craig said.

"And picked on two officers that no one's going to miss," Petra said bitterly. "DI Clarke is still not on full duties, and I'm . . ."

"They picked on two officers known to go above and beyond in pursuit of their duties, even if that means using unorthodox methods." Tucker had taken her completely by surprise, Clarke could see. He'd surprised the hell out of him too. He had expected out-and-out disapproval.

"Yes, you are both available for specific reasons," Tucker said, "but it occurs to me that Deans would have hand-picked you in any case. You both have a wealth of experience that others do not. Clarke's background and yours are both unusual. You both also have a tendency to be loners, acting on your own initiative with discretion and caution. No, Deans chose you not because you wouldn't be missed but because of who you both are. Actually, I find that far more worrying. And where the hell is he?"

"What about the sleepsuit," Petra reminded them. "Sir, have the results come back?"

"The sleepsuit belongs to the child, but the blood wasn't human, it was pig's blood. Most likely it was just for effect. The child was probably still alive at that point. It's possible — likely, even — that they intended to return him once the ransom was paid and that something happened to change their minds."

"Like our involvement becoming known," Clarke said bitterly.

"We don't know that."

"If the sleepsuit was deliberately bloodied to reinforce the threat, then why not send it to the parents? Why send it to Patricia Copeland?"

No one had an answer for that.

"There might be other forensics on it," Petra said.

Tucker nodded. "We can always hope."

A quiet knock on the door interrupted them and a note was passed to Tucker. The second body had been identified. "Sammy Marvin, twenty-one years old, reported missing three months ago by his parents. He had been working night security for Ricky Evans, on the industrial estate off the Colby Road," Tucker said.

"Shall we bring him in?" Clarke asked.

"Not yet. Let's pay him a visit first. I want to see him on his own ground. We leave him to sweat for a bit before we bring him in."

Tucker, who had been perched on Craig's desk, now slid off and beckoned to DI Clarke. "That will be our second stop of the day. The first will be to the parents of little Joshua Banks. I expect you to make the introductions."

Clarke winced, then, with a sympathetic glance in Petra's direction, prepared to follow his boss from the room.

"So what do I do?" Petra asked.

Craig waved his hands. "You carry on doing what you were doing before. Checking the background. But first, you and I will brief the rest of the team."

"What? Surely DI Clarke would be better doing that."

"You know as much as he does. Possibly even more."

Clarke saw Petra shift, uncomfortable at the reminder of her close connection with the Perrins, and her subsequent interference in the life and business of Kyle Sykes.

"Ready?"

She nodded.

Clarke smiled at her. He knew she'd be okay, but could see she was relieved that at least the superintendent would be sharing responsibility for the briefing.

CHAPTER 12

The Banks house looked different in daylight. Set back from the road behind the high hedge, it managed to feel isolated even though it was only a few yards from a fairly major suburban road. The house itself was imposing, with whitewashed plaster between sections of red brick, and sash windows that looked authentic at first glance but which Clarke knew from being up close were just posh-looking UPVC.

A young woman opened the door, someone Clarke had not met before. She introduced herself as Jocelyn Mulligan, Mr Banks's PA, and led them through into the main living room. Clarke recalled the last time he had been to this house and the tableau of Mr and Mrs Banks sitting together in this room, the woman sobbing uncontrollably. He was caught by the odd sense that this scene had been frozen in time, it was so like that which he had witnessed on Thursday morning. Mr Banks was sitting on the deep-red sofa alongside his wife. He had his arm around her, but it was clear that she was pulling away from him, bent in on herself with her arms wrapped around her own body and her head bowed. And she was sobbing. *Still* weeping, Clarke thought to himself. He exchanged a quick glance with Tucker, noticing that his boss seemed just as moved by the sight.

"Mr Banks, I'm sure you remember me. This is DCI Tucker, he's—"

"Get out of my house." Banks's voice was low, but there was no mistaking the fury and the anguish.

"Mr Banks, I—"

He was on his feet now, advancing on them. "I said get out of my house!" His anger was clearly directed towards Clarke. Tucker gestured that Clarke should leave.

"Mr Banks, we've come to talk to you about your son," Clarke heard him say as the PA ushered him back into the hall.

"They saw it on the news," she told him. "They guessed. They guessed it had to be him. Poor little Josh." She was obviously close to tears too, and was only holding it together because, Clarke supposed, someone had to.

"When they had the phone call saying that you were on your way over — well, that just confirmed it for them."

The door to the living room had been closed, but the voices were loud — Banks's the loudest of all, against a background of his wife's sobs and Tucker's more placating tone. The PA looked somewhat embarrassed. "He's got it into his head that it's your fault. I don't know why, do you?" Her tone sounded accusatory now. "Why should he think that?"

"I suppose in this kind of situation people need someone to blame." It was all he could think to say.

She frowned, but nodded. This was too big a problem for her to deal with just now, so for the moment any explanation would do.

They were standing close to the front door now, but Clarke had no intention of going through it. "DCI Tucker will take care of Mr and Mrs Banks, talk them through what's happened and what needs to happen now, but I need to talk to you, you understand that? You're close to the family and therefore considered a witness. You may have seen something without realizing the significance of it."

For a moment he thought she would argue, then she nodded. "You'd best come through to the kitchen, then at least we're out of the way." She turned and led him back down the corridor towards the back of the house and then down some steps into a well-lit room. It would have been a simple basement when the house was built, but now it was a modern, stainless-steel kitchen that would not have looked out of place in a restaurant. Hardly homely, he thought.

She must have registered his surprise. "It was like this when they moved in. To be honest, it doesn't get used all that much — neither of them likes to cook and there's an ordinary stove and microwave in the side room there." She pointed, and Clarke glanced through into what had probably been a scullery but was now a small but perfectly adequate kitchen space. An odd set-up, he thought.

"Why not just convert it into something else?"

"This big kitchen gets used when they have the caterers in."

"And how often does that happen?"

"Big events? About once a month, on average. Mr Banks does a lot of business entertaining, and Mrs Banks doesn't like to cook, like I said, so when they have dinner parties, which is about once a week, or bigger evening dos, which happen at least once a month, they just get someone in to do it." She gave him a sharp look. "My God, that means so many people could know the layout of the house. I mean, not just guests, but the kitchen staff and the waiting staff and . . ."

Clarke nodded. He pulled up a high stool to a bench that could, he supposed, just about be described as a breakfast bar and laid his notebook down, gesturing to her to take a seat. "Look, I know this is difficult, but I'm going to need to know about regular staff, names and addresses, about the catering staff, anybody that makes regular deliveries to the house, any business associates that come here, guest lists from recent events. I'm going to need everything you can tell me about the day-to-day running of Mr Banks's business affairs and the household. About anyone or anything strange you might have registered in the last few months, and particularly in the last week or so."

She looked startled for a moment and then nodded, and he could see that she was glad to be settling into a task that she understood. "I look after his diaries and I have his address book, so we can start with that. Mrs Fincher comes in daily. She's like a cook housekeeper, and there's a nanny, but she's on holiday at the moment. I think her mother was ill or something, so she's been gone about three weeks."

"You have her mother's contact details?"

"Of course."

She went through to the little prep kitchen and opened a drawer, withdrawing a notebook and pen. The notepad was long and thin, the kind people wrote shopping lists on. She came back and sat beside him. "Now tell me. Give me a list of what you need. It might take me a little while to get it all together."

She was all business now, and he realized that she really was glad to have something to do. He ran through his list of required information and then walked back round to the front of the house to wait in the car. A scientific support van drew up just as he reached it, and rather than disturb the Bankses again he escorted the CSI to the kitchen and explained to Jocelyn that they needed to examine the nursery before moving through the house.

"Do you know a Patricia Copeland?" he asked.

"Of course. She's not really a business associate of Mr Banks. Her expertise is securing finance for major infrastructure projects, but she worked with Mr Banks on a community not-for-profit scheme a while ago. A tech thing for unemployed kids from deprived backgrounds. He does a lot of charity stuff."

"Would you happen to have details of that too?"

She looked puzzled, but asked no questions. "Yes, of course, I'll add that to the list."

"It's likely the Bankses will be asked to move out for a few days," he told her gently.

She nodded. "Sounds sensible. I imagine the media will get hold of this fairly quickly."

"I imagine so. And it's also distressing for parents, with the CSI here."

"I can take them up the back stairs," she said. "It occurs to me you might need a map of the house, the layout. I still have the details on file, I think. Mr Banks likes to keep hold of things like that, along with the deeds, will that be helpful?"

"Very helpful."

* * *

It was almost two hours before Petra left the police station and returned to the schoolhouse. She had DC Allwood with her and instructions to bring everything they had back to HQ for processing. Petra had been assigned a small cupboard of an office and envisaged spending the next few days just inputting data into HOLMES and other databases. She resented that but at the same time was grateful to be part of something again, to be an acknowledged part of a team — even if that did mean being shut away in a broom cupboard.

Eyebrows had raised when she and the superintendent entered the briefing room to deliver the morning update. A picture of little Aaron Banks, smiling and alive, had been placed at the centre of the evidence board, just in case anyone could have any doubts as to what all this effort was about. A second board was arranged with images of Sammy Marvin. No picture of the living Sammy had yet been supplied — all they had were images of a man long dead and past easy recognition. Beside these pictures was a photo of a wallet and its contents, and Petra realized this was how they had identified him so quickly. Money and bank cards featured in the picture, though no driving licence or student ID card. *So not theft, then*, Petra thought wryly. But if whoever killed him didn't care that he might be identified, why keep the body? There was no way it could have been on the waste ground all this time — too many dog walkers, as had been proved that morning — so it had to have been stored somewhere. Why and where?

Craig motioned her to the front of the room, and she realized she'd been unconsciously hanging back. All eyes were on her now. Questioning, curious, mildly hostile. But Craig's presence provided her with an authority she usually lacked. She squared her shoulders and came to stand beside him.

"About 1 a.m. on Thursday morning this child, Joshua Aaron Banks, was taken from his bed by person or persons unknown." Craig began. "We know the time he was taken and something about the events that followed on that morning because a couple of hours later DI Clarke received a phone call from Superintendent Deans, who you'll know is based at Millwood, about twenty miles from here. The events that unfolded placed both DI Clarke and DS Merrow in a very difficult position, one which they handled to the best of their capacities. I will now hand over to DS Merrow so that she can explain what happened from that point. DI Clarke is currently with DCI Tucker interviewing the parents and gathering evidence at that end — you'll understand why in just a moment. DS Merrow, if you'd like to take over."

The silence in the briefing room was absolute. All eyes were turned on Petra. In some the hostility had hardened, but most she realized were merely curious and anxious. Petra took a deep breath. She had no proper notes to offer, had had little time to prepare and fervently wished Clarke was here. This was a pivotal moment as far as her career was concerned, but she chided herself for even thinking about that and began.

* * *

A couple of hours later, she had delivered all the information they had to hand, speculated about the other cases, answered what seemed like endless questions and now, accompanied by Denise Allwood, was tasked with bringing everything back from the schoolhouse. She wondered how Clarke was getting along and felt both relief that she wasn't the one dealing with the parents and then a touch of guilt about feeling that.

"My sister's husband went to school here," Denise Allwood told her.

"Yeah? I think it just gets used by community groups now, and we keep offices in the back. I'm not sure what they normally get used for, from the look of it, it's mostly storage."

"At least it's still getting used," Denise said doubtfully. "There are too many good buildings just being left to rack and ruin in this part of town."

Petra led her in through the entrance at the back. She paused before going into the office as an odd feeling assailed her.

"What's wrong?" Denise was quick to catch her mood.

"I'm not sure. You know that feeling you get when . . ."

Denise nodded.

Petra reached forward, put the tips of her fingers on the door handle, pressed down and then pushed the door open. Paperwork had been scattered around the room, desks pushed aside and drawers opened. Petra went immediately to the filing cabinets beneath the table. "I locked these," she said. She produced the key from her pocket. "They're not locked now."

"What's in them?"

"Not a lot. One is completely empty and the other just has a few notes." She stood up. "Help me with the table."

Together they moved the filing cabinets out from beneath, being careful not to touch areas where there were likely to be alien fingerprints, shifted the table aside and then the large noticeboard.

To Petra's relief the cupboard door was still locked. She took the key from her pocket and opened the door and breathed a sigh when all of the folders and storage boxes were revealed exactly where they had left them.

"What is all this stuff?"

"This is what Patricia Copeland gave to Toby. To DI Clarke," she corrected herself.

Denise Allwood grinned at her.

"We were making notes as we went along but we didn't leave them here. We locked all this stuff away, and DI Clarke took the notes back to his flat at night to put in his safe. We thought we were being a bit paranoid, but it seems not."

Denise was on the phone. "We need to get CSI in here. But I think we're okay to take the stuff from the cupboard, that's not been disturbed. We'll see if there's CCTV footage too — there's a camera out front, I think, and there might be something from the shops opposite."

Petra nodded and began to stack the folders ready for removal. She wanted to be able to take them in just one trip, a bundle each — suddenly the idea of leaving this intelligence in the car unattended, even for a moment or two, was too much. She wanted out of here and she wanted the evidence to be safe.

Denise had finished on the phone and came to join her; it seemed she felt a similar urgency. Minutes later they were out at the car, piling the previously carefully sorted evidence into the boot. Petra told herself she could put it back into order at her little office. Now she just wanted to be away.

She locked the main door, and they were both relieved when a marked car arrived and she could hand over to the officers, who would control the scene until the CSI arrived.

"Well, looks like you've rattled *somebody's* cage," Denise commented as they got in the car and drove away.

"Question is, whose?"

"Maybe the journalist you contacted got curious and did some digging of his own, maybe that alerted someone. Or maybe . . . Maybe it was the Perrins wanting to know what you were up to." Like all of her colleagues, Denise was aware that Petra had been persecuted these last few months.

"Most likely," she agreed. "Maybe the Perrins have something to do with this business."

"You think?"

"No, not really. It doesn't have the feel of the Perrins, it's more like Kyle Sykes."

She could almost feel Denise *not* saying, *Well, you'd know more about that than I would.* But the other woman refrained and instead murmured her agreement. "Though it feels unusual even for Sykes. But then—"

"What is normal for Kyle Sykes?" Petra nodded. "But like you say, we must have rattled somebody's cage."

* * *

Clarke had of course encountered Ricky Evans on a number of occasions, but he could not recall ever going out to this warehouse complex on the industrial estate. At this time of day the large gates in the six-foot chain-link fence were open. They parked up just outside the warehouse, and Clarke, on getting out of the car, looked around with interest. The warehouse was on an industrial estate occupied by small businesses, a sizeable self-storage unit and a caravan sales park. Unusually this particular warehouse had been fenced off from the rest and stood slightly apart on the edge of the estate.

"A second entrance at the back—" Clarke pointed — "opens on to that side road and gives access to the rear loading bay."

"And what gets loaded or unloaded?" Tucker asked him.

"Apparently legitimate merchandise, most of the time. Dodgy booze and cigarettes some of the rest. But Mr Evans is very good at having all of his paperwork in place whenever we turn up to examine it."

Tucker raised an eyebrow. "You think he has someone dropping him the word?"

"I think he runs his business carefully most of the time. He takes only as many risks as are profitable but not so many that he treads on other people's toes. However . . ."

Tucker nodded and they made their way into the small reception area. A few minutes later they were in the presence of Evans himself in the back office. Tucker took the proffered seat and Clarke stood by the window, seemingly transfixed by the gravel and scrubby weeds outside.

"What can I do for you?" Evans's tone was affable, but his eyes were wary.

"You have heard about the bodies found on the waste ground this morning. One of them is an ex-employee of yours, a young man by the name of Sammy Marvin."

"Sammy?" Evans looked genuinely shocked. Shocked about something, anyway.

"He worked for you," Tucker reminded him.

"Yes, he did. Then I had to let him go. Kept falling asleep on the job. I mean, I know it's boring, but the lad didn't have to do that much, just keep an eye on the cameras and update the log once an hour. The rest of the time he could get on with his dissertation or whatever it was he was doing."

"That sounds very altruistic of you."

"Not a bit of it. I've employed a lot of postgraduates and even a couple of postdocs over the years. As I say, the job isn't demanding, it just helps out with the insurance if we have a body here." He flushed slightly and backtracked. "I mean, someone in charge. I'd be the first to admit the wages aren't good, it's only minimum wage after all, but it doesn't take much effort. They get to earn some money and have time for studying, and by and large they're a conscientious lot." He paused as though aware that he was waffling unnecessarily. "I was disappointed in young Sammy. He was a nice lad."

"And now he's a dead lad."

"And I know nothing about that. Dropped off the planet, didn't he? I had his mum and dad phone me, see if I knew where he'd got to. He'd not been home and hadn't been in touch, not with them or any of his friends or anyone at the uni. But I couldn't tell them anything. I told them I had to let him go, but that was all."

"And now he turns up dead."

"Nothing to do with me."

"And the funny thing is he must've been dead a while, before his decomposing body was dumped on the waste ground. We reckon he must've died around the time he 'dropped off the planet'."

Clarke watched as a car came in through the gates and pulled up beside theirs. There seemed to be a single occupant, but he didn't get out. The phone rang in the front office, and the woman who had greeted them and had introduced herself as Ginny Afton picked up. She spoke briefly and the car drove away. Clarke leaned against the window trying to get a view of the driver and frowned. He turned his attention back to the conversation between Ricky Evans and DCI Tucker.

"And who do you employ now?" Tucker was asking.

"Didn't fill the position again after Sammy went," Ricky Evans told him. "Decided it wasn't really worth it."

"Even if that put your insurance up?" Tucker queried.

"Or perhaps you employed your security from elsewhere," Clarke said. It was the first time he had spoken since the initial introductions.

"I don't know what you mean," Evans said. He was trying to sound calm but he was evidently rattled. The words came out just a beat too fast.

"I just watched a car drive in, park up, then drive off again," Clarke told him.

Evans eyed him warily. "So what?"

"I recognized the driver." Clarke smiled at him.

Tucker looked interested now. "Enlighten us."

"Well, if I wasn't mistaken the man looked very much like Paul Benson. Used to work for Gus Perrin, switched allegiance to Kyle Sykes a few months back. I have reason to remember the man very well, seeing as he tried to kill me." He was watching Evans closely. The man was twitchy and increasingly unsure of himself, his eyes darting this way and that, his hands fiddling unconsciously with papers on his desk. He was scared, Clarke thought, but not of the two police officers, however inconvenient their presence might be, however unwelcome their questions about Sammy Marvin.

"Coming to see you, was he?" Tucker asked. "I'm assuming you got his registration number, Clarke?"

Clarke nodded and handed his notebook to his boss. He watched Evans as Tucker called this in and put out a watch for the car and for Paul Benson.

Ricky Evans had grown increasingly pale. "You don't know it was him. Maybe it was someone just came down to ask directions. How should I know what he wanted?" He glanced beyond Tucker, and Clarke became aware that Ginny Afton had come through from reception and was standing in the doorway.

"You've got a meeting in half an hour," she said. "Did you want me to call and delay it?"

Evans took a deep breath and then shook his head. "I don't think there's anything I can tell you gentleman," he said. "I'm sorry about young Sammy. We're both sorry," he added, glancing in Ginny's direction. "It was young Sammy's body they found in the waste ground this morning," he told her.

Ginny's gasp of shock was undoubtedly real, Clarke thought. She raised a hand to cover her mouth, and he was certain he could see tears before she blinked them away. For a moment he wondered if she was going to faint. Too shocked, he thought, considering Sammy Marvin had just been a young employee that she probably hadn't met all that often — Ginny worked days and Sammy worked the night shift. He exchanged a glance with Tucker, who nodded. Time to go. The seeds had been sown and further questioning just now would most likely lead to Evans clamming up or lawyering up, and neither would be desirable.

As they drove away, Tucker was on the phone seeing how easily he could get a warrant for the telephone records of Ricky Evans's warehouse operation. Clarke drove along the main thoroughfare through the industrial estate for a few hundred yards and then, spotting a quiet side road, pulled in, turned the car around and positioned it so that they could watch the warehouse. The angle wasn't great, but it would have to do.

"You're certain about it being Paul Benson? You can't have seen him very clearly, not from where you were standing."

"It's not a face I'm going to forget in a hurry," Clarke said with feeling. He was healing well, but the wounds were still sore — as, to be frank, was his pride. "I thought I recognized him as he was driving down from the gate, but I got a better look as he was driving away. And I'm pretty sure he phoned the reception to see who we were." He realized his boss had already deduced that, hence the desire for the phone records, but Tucker nodded anyway.

"So is somebody coming here for the meeting or is he going elsewhere?" Tucker wondered. "Of course, it could be a legitimate meeting as opposed to a *meeting* kind of meeting."

Clarke laughed. Not likely. "There's a car pulling out from behind the building. If it comes this way are we following?"

"We'd be spotted straightaway. Chances are he'd just drive off somewhere else. No, we take a note of the vehicle and the reg, set up observations once we figure out which direction he's going in and then follow the CCTV cameras."

"So we have to hope he turns left. If he turns right at the main road he's out of town in a quarter-mile and we lose CCTV coverage." He started the engine and they watched as the car went by the end of the road. Clarke waited and then pulled out. The car was just in view — one occupant, and it looked like Ricky Evans. Clarke crept forward, glad that there was so little traffic around the industrial estate so there was no one to see his odd behaviour. He hung back so that he could just keep Evans in view but wasn't crowding the man. At the main junction Evans turned left.

"Yes!" Tucker sounded celebratory. He was on the phone again, quoting make, model, reg number. "Now let's see where the bugger goes."

"We'll look pretty stupid if he's just gone to get his laundry done," Clarke observed.

* * *

With two of them in the tiny office space it felt impossibly crowded, but Petra was glad of the company. She'd just started to organize the files when Denise breezed in with two mugs of hot chocolate.

"Sod coffee," she said. "I need a treat."

Petra looked at her curiously.

"Don't tell me you weren't spooked," Denise said. "All the time we were there it felt like someone was watching us." She shuddered elaborately, but Petra got the impression it was only partly put on.

"I feel like they're always watching." The words came out before she could stop them. She bit her lip, suddenly feeling awkward.

To her surprise, Denise just said, "That stinks." Seeing Petra's reaction, she went on. "Look, none of this team has really been undercover, not like you were, anyway. For what it's worth, most of us think you were cut a really bad deal. We're not your enemies, you know."

"I never thought . . ." Petra protested. She looked away. That's exactly what she had thought, what she had felt all these months.

"Here, have your chocolate. Let's start sorting through this stuff, shall we?" Denise smiled at her and held out a mug.

Petra nodded. "Thanks." She sipped the chocolate. It was sweet and rich and dark and exactly what she needed. "It shouldn't take too much sorting out. We did go through it once, so it should just be a case of putting the folders back in order and then I'll talk you through it, shall I?"

She had begun to relax with Clarke — after all, she had got to know him a little bit — but Denise and the rest of the team were largely strangers to her. In her three years undercover she had almost begun to view them as the enemy, and that feeling of opposition and of being the outsider had stayed with her after her return to work, exacerbated by the fact that she had still not returned to full duty. Until now, of course. It looked as though the death of little Joshua Banks had changed a great many things. From being the outsider she was now right at the centre of things whether she wanted it or not. She knew from what Clarke had said that Denise Allwood was a nice woman, genuinely kind and helpful and capable of working on her own initiative. Petra wondered if she was ever going to be able to let her guard down completely.

For the next hour they sorted, collated and made notes. There was to be a briefing at four o'clock, and Denise seemed to take it for granted that the two of them would give it together. Petra found she was grateful for this.

Denise stepped back from the table and surveyed the work they had completed. "My God, these poor families. Can you imagine what they went through?"

"At least they got their kids back." Petra shook her head uncomprehending. "If you look at it coldly they were on to a good thing. The parents paid up, the kids got returned, the next set of parents were told what happened and how to play the game. They could at least be reasonably sure that they'd get their kid back unharmed. Yes, what they went through was unbelievable, sickeningly horrible, but something must have changed. Drastically."

"Why kill this time?" Denise agreed. "Sounds like a horrible way to put it, but you don't kill the goose that laid the golden egg, do you? And what about the other body, Sammy Marvin? What did that poor beggar have to do with anything? He was just working his way through university and he ends up dead."

"He was a nightwatchman," Petra said. "Maybe he watched the wrong thing. Who knows? Why dump the body now?" She sighed. "I think I need another hot chocolate. Okay, let's forget about Sammy Marvin just now and think about the kids and the families. Ms Copeland put all this together. She did background research into each one, and even if she didn't know much about the kidnapping she's managed to put together enough material that we can understand who these families were, why they might have been targeted and if there were any connections between them. Now, I've had a good look through these notes before and some of them are the kind of things that you might find by a good trawl on the internet, but some of this information is really specific. She was able to put it together because of the kinds of circles she moves in socially. After all, her family was targeted too, so I'm thinking—"

"That whoever put the information together to target the families was probably part of the same circles as they were," Denise finished for her. "It's a different perspective — worth trying to chase down. We need to build a kind of family tree, draw it out, make links."

"We need to get a whiteboard or something in here," Petra said doubtfully, looking around the space and wondering how that was going to happen.

Denise shook her head. "No way, but I know what we can do. We can wheel a couple of them into the hall opposite the office door. We just expand your office outwards into the corridor. You can make the chocolate, I'll liberate a couple of whiteboards and we can pin anything else to the wall."

Petra raised an eyebrow, wondering how that was going to go down with the boss, but she decided that Denise probably knew what she was doing. As she headed for the kitchen she began to wonder if perhaps, just perhaps, she might be on the way to making friend. She was shocked at just how much she hoped that might be true.

CHAPTER 13

The afternoon briefing brought a flurry of activity and information. The initial post-mortem findings had been sent over, the two bodies having jumped the queue. Ricky Evans's destination had been tracked on CCTV and there were possible leads beginning to emerge from the information they had on the different families.

"Sammy Marvin was shot," DCI Tucker explained, "probably at quite close range from the amount of damage that was done. Probably with a nine mil, which doesn't narrow things down very much. Decomposition is reckoned to be in keeping with death occurring at around the time he was reported missing. Which begs the question, where was the body kept and why, and why was it then dumped so publicly? There was no attempt to hide either victim. The child, Joshua Banks, seems to have been killed by a single blow to the head." Tucker paused and indicated pictures placed on the board. "The skull was hit hard. Cause of death was blunt-force trauma." A soft murmur of shock drifted about the room, and Clarke, standing beside Tucker, caught Petra's eye. She was still pale, he thought, still strained, but there was a purposeful look to her now. He turned his attention back to DCI Tucker.

"Time of death was probably within hours of the child being taken from the foster family. It would seem there was no intention of waiting to see if the ransom was paid. At the moment it's speculation, but it would seem perhaps that this was not about money." He jerked his head towards someone wishing to ask a question.

"Are we still working with the theory that this latest kidnapping is linked to the previous ones?"

"Yes. But my conclusion is that we should work both possible lines of enquiry. One team continuing with the assumption that this is linked to the previous crimes and a second that this might be a purely independent attack on the parents, probably the father. It might be linked to those previous events, but it might equally be more specifically to do with the husband's business dealings or some personal matter. We can't rule out some kind of grievance against the wife either, and we can't afford to miss anything. A third team will focus on Sammy Marvin — his background, his history, anything that might suggest criminal involvement — but keep your minds open. It may well be that he was just in the wrong place at the wrong time, and at present our best guess is that wrong place was Ricky Evans's warehouse."

Clarke took up the story. "While we were there today, we happened to spot an old . . . I hesitate to call him friend." He pressed two CCTV pictures of the car on to the evidence board and a third highlighting the registration number. A fourth with a picture of Paul Benson. "I'm sure you're all familiar with this individual. Paul Benson, one-time casino manager and enforcer for Gus Perrin. Last seen in the company of Mr Kyle Sykes. If Benson is back, chances are so is Sykes, and we also know that piece of wasteland was one of Sykes's preferred dumping grounds. I don't need to remind you of the three bodies found there just before Christmas last year, or the death of DCI Frankland." He didn't look at Petra, but even across the room he could feel her wince. She was only alive because of Frankland. It was believed that the man who had tortured and killed him had been Paul Benson, at that time still employed by Gus Perrin. By the time Clarke had encountered them in his flat, he had either switched allegiance to Kyle Sykes or at the very least Sykes had become his paymaster. "We have every reason to believe that Benson was responsible for Frankland's torture and murder. He took great pleasure in admitting as much when he was trying to remove me from the realm of the living.

"CCTV footage reveals that Benson is a regular visitor to the warehouse and has been for at least the last month. On a couple of occasions there have been two people in the car, and though we can't get a clear view, it's entirely possible that the second one is Sykes. Now, he's risking a lot coming back here. Not only are *we* looking for him but so are the Perrins, so what does he want that's so important, and is he behind this latest spate of violence?"

DCI Tucker stepped in. "CCTV footage from today indicates that Ricky Evans went for lunch at the Jimmy Dear pub down by the canal. He arrived around noon and left just before two. We've spoken to the waitress who served him, and the bar staff, and the description they gave us of the man he met matches that of Paul Benson. When shown photographs of Benson, the waitress was eighty per-cent sure, the bar staff a little less, but it would seem logical that if Benson couldn't meet him at the warehouse, he would set up a meeting elsewhere. This other man didn't stay for lunch — he was there for about fifteen minutes and then went on his way. Ricky Evans, however, did the full three courses followed by coffee and a small brandy. The staff reckon he's not a regular customer and it's very unlikely he'll be gracing their restaurant again, I would have thought. You'll agree perhaps that the proximity of the pub is interesting, being only a few hundred yards from the waste ground where the bodies were found."

"Are we bringing Evans in?"

"Not yet. He's far more value to us at the moment attracting the flies than he would be in here stinking up the place with his lies and his expensive lawyer. No, we'll leave him hanging out there for a while. He's going to be having a very uncomfortable time of it, and the more uncomfortable he is by the time we get to interview him, the easier it will be."

Clarke frowned. They had argued this through in the car on the way back. Clarke had been all set to bring Evans in to interview immediately. He saw the logic of waiting, but what he didn't think Tucker appreciated was that Kyle Sykes, if he actually was involved — and it seemed more and more likely — had very little patience with associates who might be weak links or in some way endanger his position. They had a tendency to end up in the canal, or beside it.

"So, we have several lines of enquiry opening up. I'll be allocating teams after the briefing and each team will report to DS Allwood and DS Merrow."

Clarke saw Denise's look of surprise and Petra's look of horror. He smiled reassuringly at them both.

"They've already done a lot of the spade work on this, so they already have a handle on the different angles. They're in a better position to see the possible links and to see if you're wandering too far from the mark."

The faint ripple of sound that crossed the room told Clarke that the team was as surprised by the decision as Petra, but Clarke saw the sense in it. Any doubts the rest of the team might have would be put aside, for now at least, and all the focus would be on finding those responsible for these two deaths. The fact that Denise Allwood seemed to be working closely with Petra Merrow would also silence the critics. Allwood had been close to Frankland, their murdered colleague, and initially she had been deeply hostile to Clarke and Petra. If her attitude had softened, that would certainly smooth the way for Petra. It eased Clarke's mind that Denise was not the kind of person to be friendly to your face and then stick the knife in once you trusted her enough to turn your back. DS Allwood was as honest and open as daylight — if you pissed her off, you'd soon know about it.

The meeting broke up shortly after, Tucker calling small groups into his office to assign tasks. Clarke wandered over to where Denise and Petra were standing. He could see down the corridor to the two whiteboards and the noticeboards that they had set up, which were already filling up with information.

"You've been busy."

"We have," Petra nodded. "Want to come and see?"

They were due to distribute their collated information the following morning. Clarke stood in the doorway to the tiny office and surveyed what at first looked to be a confusion of data. He soon realized it was slowly beginning to coalesce into a series of links, some quite literally connected by pieces of string.

"We started trying to write it all out," Denise said, "but there are so many interconnections. People who were married to other people who sit on boards for other companies who have a financial stake in other holdings . . . It's incestuous, that's what it is."

She sounded vaguely outraged and Clarke found himself laughing. It felt nice to find something funny after dealing with the horror of the past few days. It made him feel slightly guilty as well. He could see Petra watching him and guessed that her feelings were much the same.

"It occurred to us," she told him, "that Patricia Copeland was able to put all of this together because she was on the inside. At first glance you look at it and you've got a lot of news clippings, online articles, public domain stuff that a thorough search might turn up. But when you look closer at the information you see she's making connections, she's drilling down in a way that you can only do, we think, if you actually understand the culture and society that these people inhabit."

"You make them sound like aliens."

"In terms of money and privilege," Denise told him tartly, "they may as well be. Anyway, we came to the conclusion that whoever was organizing the kidnappings must be in the same sort of position as Ms Copeland is. An insider. Somebody who understands who to target and why and how."

"We've made a tiny bit of progress," Petra told him. "We managed to get through to one of the numbers Patricia

Copeland had in her files. They've agreed to speak with us, or at least a representative of the family has, together with the family lawyer. We're just waiting to hear where and when."

"That's if they don't get cold feet."

"Then we'll keep calling until they change their minds or threaten legal action," Denise shrugged. "I got the feeling they will cooperate, though. They heard about Joshua Banks. They're scared."

Clarke nodded. "So how is all this set up?" he mused.

"*How* is simple. You just take their kid," Denise said. "That's the lever, it's not how. This—" she glanced at Petra, and Clarke guessed this was part of what they were still trying to work out — "this looks as if it's more complicated than just a kidnap and ransom. After it happened, most times, there was a lot of repositioning of business. I mean not every time, but at least half of the dozen cases we know about. People suddenly selling shares, or giving up their place on the board, or simply leaving the country, and we wondered if that was part of the payment."

"Speculative," he said. "But worth chasing down."

"I don't suppose you have any idea where Patricia Copeland went to? We really could do with her input on this."

"She didn't say. I'm assuming she flew out, so she must have left via one of the major airports, I'd have thought."

"That's just it," Petra said. "There's has been no record of her leaving the country, not by air, by ferry, by Eurotunnel. Of course, a woman with her resources could have flown out from a private aerodrome and someone just made a false declaration. There are many ways a woman in her position could have got out of the country, but as yet there's no evidence she did. Only that she's gone to ground."

"Let's just hope the evidence is wrong, for her sake. She was scared, and the more I see of this business the more I think she had reason to be."

"We could do with another member on the team," Denise said. "There's going to be a mountain of material to handle, especially with the different lines of enquiry."

Clarke nodded. "How about DC Hopkins? She doesn't have a lot of experience yet, but she's familiar with the background from when Lauren Sykes went missing last year."

Denise Allwood nodded. "Sophie, yes. Good choice. Will you clear it with the DCI?"

Clarke nodded.

A phone rang in the main office, and a few moments later they were being summoned back into the incident room.

Tucker once more stood in front of the assembled troops, his face grave. "Another kid's been taken," he said. "A little girl called Gracie Moore. She's sixteen months old and she's the grandchild of Superintendent Deans."

CHAPTER 14

Paul Benson took the back road out to the farm, pulled the car off the road and into a small copse of trees and entered Gus Perrin's extensive domain on foot. Technically this was a public footpath and Gus Perrin was careful to maintain it according to his legal obligations. In summer, hikers and families could cross the field behind the house, enjoying the birds and the hedgerows and the wildflower meadow, most of them in total ignorance of their close proximity to organized crime. A small gate led off this path and up towards the house. An equally small and very discreet notice announcing that this was private property warned off the hikers, and an infrared sensor alerted those inside the house should anyone happen to stray. Benson knew that Gus Perrin would have been alerted and would be waiting for him.

He took a straight route across the lawns and spotted Perrin sitting in his wheelchair in the large conservatory at the back. Perrin saw him at the same moment and raised a glass invitingly. Minutes later, somewhat relieved, Paul was seated opposite him nursing a glass of whiskey.

"How goes it?" Perrin asked. "I hear our man is making waves."

"He's totally off his nut," Benson told him.

"No change there, then."

Benson shook his head. "Oh, everything is changed. The man could at least be relied on to put business first, now it's all about just what he fancies doing, and that changes moment to moment. I tell you, he's lost it. He was dangerous before, now he's just . . ." He shrugged helplessly.

He could feel his boss regarding him closely, considering. He knew Gus Perrin had little patience with shows of weakness, but he also knew that he had been a trusted Perrin employee for a long time and that Gus would at least listen.

"He knows I'm still reporting to you, I'm sure of it."

"Of course he knows. The man might be off his rocker but he's not stupid. Or at least not stupid that way."

"Truth is—" Benson found it hard to say but knew he must — "I don't know what the fuck he's going to do one minute to the next. He killed that kid, Gus. That was never in the script. Ricky Evans had a scheme going, but it was business, it didn't involve murdering little kids. I want out, Gus."

Gus Perrin laughed. "Out of the question, and coming from you, squeamishness seems a little, how shall we say, misplaced. Hypocritical maybe?"

Benson scowled at him. "I never killed kids."

"No, you just tortured a policeman to death, attempted to kill another, and, well, we'll gloss over the rest, shall we?"

Benson was about to retort but he saw Gus's expression change and held back.

"No, but you're right. His behaviour is extravagant, even for Kyle Sykes. So you'd better do what you can to control it, hadn't you?"

"Might be too late for that. He had something else lined up."

"Like what?"

"I don't know. He's not always the confiding type, only when it suits him and only then when it's going to get a reaction."

"Then stop reacting to him."

"Easier said than done."

He could feel his boss regarding him with something close to contempt. But he didn't really care anymore. Kyle Sykes made Gus Perrin look like a harmless old tomcat, wanting nothing more in his retirement than to curl up by a warm fire and sleep his late years away.

"And how is our friend Ricky Evans doing?"

"Shit scared and with good reason, especially with the police turning up today, followed by yours truly."

"A nice touch, I thought. Of course, when he thinks about it, DI Clarke will feel it was a little coincidental. I agree it wasn't subtle, but it did the trick didn't it?"

Benson refrained from replying that it was fine Gus Perrin sitting there and telling him everything was going to plan when it was him that had been at risk, if Clarke had suddenly managed to call in reinforcements and Paul Benson not been able to get away in time. He drained his whiskey glass and set it down. "I'd best be off. If I'm gone too long he starts chewing the carpet."

Gus Perrin nodded, his large, bony head looking too heavy for his shoulders. He was, Benson thought, a shadow of his former self physically, but he'd lost nothing of his power to intimidate. The thing was, Benson had now had months of dealing with Sykes, so Gus was starting to look like a rank amateur when it came to his ability to terrorize, as far as Benson was concerned, anyway. He headed back across the lawns, knowing that Gus Perrin would watch until he was out of sight and then listen for the chime of the alert as he passed through the rear gate and on to the path. This was not through any sense of threat but from sheer force of habit. Perrin was like Sykes in that regard — he liked to know where everyone was and what they were up to, especially since that fiasco with Petra Merrow. The Merrow woman had wormed her way right to the heart of the Perrin organization, befriending the daughter, Carole, and sleeping with Billy Hunter for close to three years. Worse, as far as Paul was concerned, they had all genuinely liked her. And, he knew,

Billy had felt a whole lot more. Well, Billy had paid for that, hadn't he? Paid with a bullet to the head.

Benson could countenance all that. It was business, and everyone in the Perrin organization knew the rules and was playing the game because it suited them. They'd chosen.

He opened the gate and stepped through on to the path.

But seeing Sykes with that little kid, that was something else again. That was something he wouldn't forget in a hurry. It reminded him of the horror stories his grandad had told him about the war, how he reckoned he'd seen some SS officer pick up a kid by the ankles and dash its brains out against a wall. He'd assumed the old boy had been exaggerating, his mind wandering, but now . . .

He got into his car, started the engine and sat for a minute or two fiddling with the radio, suddenly very reluctant to move. He'd done some appalling things, he knew that. He had dealt in death, and death was often painfully slow for those in Benson's charge. On balance, he could live with that, but he didn't like the way things were going now and his sense of self-preservation was too finely tuned to continue along this road at other people's direction.

He drove slowly out from between the trees and to the crossroads, where a right turn would take him back to town, to his ersatz employer, Sykes.

"Fuck that," Paul Benson said.

* * *

Sunday evening, just before eight, Ricky Evans was sitting in an interview room attempting to look unconcerned. Ginny Afton, even less effective in her attempt at nonchalance, had been placed in a second interview room just along the hall. On the floor below, Petra Merrow and Denise Allwood were with a distraught Superintendent Deans trying to piece together what had happened.

Petra had been shocked to have been given this task. It was not at this stage a formal interview or even statement taking — though she and Denise were making copious notes — all of that would come later. For now they just wanted the man to talk.

His daughter, the child's mother, was at home, heavily sedated. The husband had insisted on accompanying his father-in-law to the police station, dimly realizing that the older man knew more about the loss of their child than he was letting on, but was still not able to comprehend exactly what or how. He was now ensconced in some quiet corner nursing a cup of tea and speaking reluctantly to the surprisingly able DC Hopkins.

Clarke sat in the viewing room, quietly monitoring it all.

"So, who was the woman impersonating DI Mace?" Petra asked. "We know that the real DI Mace has been in Edinburgh this past month. She's barely left the city and she's certainly not been here, in Wandsborough, colluding with you."

"Colluding!" Deans exploded. "You think I ever wanted this?"

"No," Petra's tone was even. "I don't suppose you did, but it undoubtedly happened because you had some previous involvement."

"Previous involvement? I was called in because the Banks child was taken and his father called the chief constable. I suppose you'll accuse him of collusion too." His expression was one of pure disdain, Clarke noted, but Petra was in the zone and seemed totally unconcerned. Beside her Denise Allwood sat back in her chair, waiting to be tagged when Petra needed a change of pace. Clarke allowed himself a smile.

"If I find he's involved, then of course I will," she told him. "But what I would like to know is why he then called *you*. And how this phony DI Mace came into the equation."

"I had no idea she wasn't what she seemed to be. She was at the Banks house when I arrived, waiting for me. I assumed she'd been summoned by the chief constable. I assumed he regarded her as a safe pair of hands. How was I to know—"

"I suppose it is hard to keep track of all the officers you've worked with over the years," Petra said.

"What do you mean? What are you accusing me of now?"

Petra glanced at Denise, who produced a photograph from a folder on the desk. She pushed it across to Deans.

"What is this?" Impatiently he thrust the paper aside. It fell to the floor. Denise retrieved it and set it back on the desk.

"For the benefit of the tape," Petra said, "we are showing Superintendent Deans a photograph of him presenting a special commendation to DI Mace. This was less than a month ago."

"How am I supposed to remember?" But the bluster sounded less confident now.

"You had your pictures taken for the local newspaper. You attended a small reception for DI Mace and others who had been honoured on the same day. The press photographer spent a little while taking informal shots of the ceremony and the reception. You spent quite some time speaking to DI Mace. She seems to have made an impression."

Denise passed more of the pictures across the desk. Clarke's smile broadened. He guessed that a simple internet search would have turned this up, but even so it was impressive. And careless on Deans's part. Had he not been prepared for this unknown woman turning up? Had he needed to pull a name out of the air and picked on Mace at random?

"In fact," Petra continued in the same quiet tone, "you signed off on DI Mace's secondment to the Edinburgh force just prior to that. You knew she'd be well out of the way, so presumably decided hers was a safe identity to borrow."

"So who is this mystery woman, posing as DI Mace?" Denise pressed. "Just turn up out of the blue, did she?"

"I don't know who she is," Deans said. He looked broken, Clarke thought, but the two women interviewing him seemed unprepared to cut him any slack.

"So when did you first meet her?"

"Like I said, she was waiting at the house when I arrived."

"Really? How convenient for you." Petra's tone never changed, Clarke noted, but there was no mistaking the contempt she felt for the man. "And were you told that she'd be there? Did your friend the chief constable tell you that when he called you in?"

"Don't use that tone with me, DS Merrow," Deans said coldly. "You're on dangerous enough ground yourself, don't you forget that."

Clarke noted that Denise raised an eyebrow, but Petra seemed barely to register the comment. She may be damaged, he thought, recalling how lost she had looked when he had met up with her a couple of days previously, but she was tough. She had survived three years deep undercover. She had coped — somehow — with the aftermath and the persecution by the Perrins, the loss of face and friends and status. But now she was back, doing what she was good at, and she was recovering strength almost as he watched.

"So this woman was waiting for you. Who did she tell you she was? I can't see her coming up with the name and cover story — that seems more likely to have come from you."

He stared at her for a moment. "I want my solicitor. I've nothing more to say until he arrives."

"Fair enough," Denise told him. She stood and began to gather her papers together. Petra followed suit. Deans's face was a picture of disbelief, Clarke thought. He had clearly expected a fight, not this casual agreement, as though it didn't matter to them one way or another.

"I'll get someone to bring you a cup of tea, shall I?" Petra asked. "And give you some time to think about what might be happening to your grandchild."

She signed off for the benefit of the tape and the two women left. A constable took up position by the door. Clarke left the viewing room and met Denise and Petra at the coffee machine.

"You could maybe have pushed a bit harder," he suggested. "He looked about to give in."

"Maybe," she shook her head. "He needs space to work out what he can tell us and still get out of this alive. I think he hopes to get the child out alive too, but he's so scared I don't think that side of things is quite real to him at the moment."

Clarke looked at Denise, but she seemed in general agreement. "I'll take the lead when we go back in?" she asked.

Petra nodded. "His solicitor will be here soon, so we'll give everyone time for a break so we can make a fresh start when he's had time to consult with his legal eagle." She sighed and, Clarke thought, looked suddenly deflated. "Meantime, we don't know what's happening to that little girl. How's the father holding up?"

"He's not. Sophie Hopkins is with him. He's scared as hell and trying to make sense of it all. The kid was in the garden, literally feet from the back door. The mum had just stepped inside to grab something when she heard the gate and the dog barked. A man ran in, grabbed the kid, and fled. The dog tried to attack the guy's leg and got kicked for its trouble. The mum raced after him and into the road in time to see a car driving away. The husband heard her shouting and came running out and—" he shrugged — "here we are."

"So were the police or Deans called first this time?"

"The father dialled the nines. The mother called her dad. It seems he told her not to do anything until he got there. She couldn't understand what he was on about, and the husband took the phone from her to see what his father-in-law was saying to cause so much upset. He's got it into his head that Deans knows something — which, of course, he does — but he's still trying to make sense of the senseless."

A constable came to tell them that Deans's solicitor had arrived.

"I need the loo," Petra said, "then we'll discuss strategy before we go back in?"

Denise nodded. "We should listen to what the father had to say, I think. See if anything useful came up."

"Good idea."

"So, you're getting on okay?" Clarke asked cautiously, as Petra walked away.

"You mean, do I still blame her for DCI Frankland's death?"

"Something like that."

"Right. Well, you see, we had a talk and it seems both of us saw the man as a mentor and friend. So we're both gunning for the bastard who tortured him to death. Petra knows she owes him her life. I know there was nothing she could have done to have stopped what happened. So I guess we're both on the same side." She hesitated for a moment. "I think there are all sorts of moral questions to be asked about her relationships with Billy Hunter and Perrin's daughter, but she did what she was assigned to do. And I know I'd never have had the courage for it, not even with Frankland's backup. I'd have told him to stuff it."

Clarke grinned at her and nodded. "Me too."

* * *

Knowing that they would not be called back into the interview room for a little while, Petra took a moment to go outside for some air. She had her other mobile in her pocket, the one with just Lauren's number programmed into it. She would not normally have taken the risk of calling the girl in the middle of the day, and from police headquarters, but she was reasonably sure that she would not be disturbed or missed and she didn't feel that she could wait.

Lauren obviously thought it was strange as well because she answered hesitantly. After a moment she said, "I'm putting you on speakerphone."

Petra was momentarily nonplussed. And then she thought, *Well, Lauren must trust whoever she's with*, but she was still unnerved by the idea that someone else was sharing the phone conversation.

"Go on," Lauren said.

Her voice sounded hollow, as though she was speaking from the bottom of a well, the speaker on her phone evidently not brilliant. Quickly and concisely, Petra brought Lauren up to speed on what she suspected Lauren's father had done. She heard the gasp of shock and the murmur of another voice in the background, a woman's voice. Presumably whoever Lauren was staying with and the person she wanted to share the conversation with.

The voice that spoke next was not Lauren's. To Petra's ears it sounded old but firm and confident. This was someone who was used to being listened to. "And what exactly do you want Lauren to do about this?"

"Hello, who are you?"

"That, my dear, is something you don't need to know. What do you want her to do?"

Petra glanced at her watch, realizing that she must not stay away too long. "Lauren, I want you to think about anywhere locally your father might hide up, any properties that he might have owned that didn't show up on the formal records, anyone he might be staying with. We're pretty sure he's here, and it would make sense for him to have the kid with him. Make sense to him, anyway. He likes to be in control. So it stands to reason he's going to want to oversee all of the operation."

There was a moment of silence.

"I'm pretty sure I've told you all I know. But I'll have a think."

"Thank you. Look, got to go, I'll call you later tonight."

She thrust the phone back in her pocket and went inside.

* * *

Lauren stared at the mobile phone and then at Molly. "He's got to be stopped," she said. "Molly, we can't let him go on like this. One kid's dead. The other, well, I don't give much for her chances, do you?"

"No, my dear, I certainly don't. The question we need to ask is the one the police are no doubt asking: what made him target these two men? You get on your computer and see what background information you can turn up. You're far better at searching on that than I am and I have some phone calls to make."

Lauren nodded. She turned towards the stairs and then turned back. "Molly, I'm going to have to finish this, aren't I? He won't show himself, not the way the police want him to. He still has so many people shit scared that he can hide for ever."

"No, my dear, even frightened people will eventually decide that they cannot live scared. He will push them too far and they will either run or they will seek help, and either way they will betray his position."

"I ran, and it just got other people killed. Molly, I have to finish this. I have to finish him and you have to help me. If he knows I'm alive, then he will come after me, I could make him break cover."

"An option we keep very much in reserve," Molly told her. "You go and start your research and I'll start mine. The most important thing right now is not to let our own guilt and anger get in the way. To be frank, my dear, how you feel about this and your own part in it does not matter just now, you understand me? You must put that aside for the moment. Those feelings might well be of use later, but the child comes first and anything you can remember that might be of use to the police is your first priority."

Lauren nodded. "I know. I hate him so much, Molly."

"Of course you do, but revenge, as they say, is a dish best served cold. So keep your cool, my dear. Do what is necessary now. The rest will happen in due time."

* * *

It was Ginny Afton who gave them the information they wanted and made the direct connection to Kyle Sykes. She had been left largely alone for the first few hours, questioned briefly, brought refreshments, escorted to the toilet, but otherwise had not been the focus of attention. Deans's solicitor having expressed the need for a long conversation with his client, Denise and Petra switched their attention to Ginny, bringing with them tea and chocolate biscuits and sandwiches.

"I know you've had a meal break," Denise said to Ginny, "but we've not, so do you mind?"

She opened the first pack of sandwiches before she got a response. Ginny sat back with a sigh.

"I'll have a cheese and pickle," she said, "and then you can make sure that machine is on and we can make a start, because quite frankly I'm sick of all of this. I've been telling that stupid bugger for months, ever since Kyle Sykes reappeared and killed poor little Sammy, that it was only a matter of time before everything caught up with us. So let's just get it over with, shall we?"

Petra refrained from exchanging a glance with Denise. She could feel the other officer's tension and shock without needing to confirm it. Denise pushed the sandwich across the table, along with a cup of tea and a sachet of sugar. Petra glanced up to check the video was recording, having set the audio tape running when they entered the room.

"So, when did Sykes turn up?" Her tone was conversational, and she took a bite of her own sandwich.

"Three months ago." Ginny opened the sandwich and examined the contents. "They always put too much damn pickle in." She closed the sandwich and broke it in half. "Sammy was on duty. It was just coming up to ten o'clock. He'd let the evening shift out and was about to lock the gates when Kyle and his cronies drove in. They made Sammy call Ricky, and once Ricky turned up Sykes just shot Sammy to prove a point. To prove what a big man he thinks he is. Sammy never did anyone any harm, he was a sweet boy, just wanted to finish his studies and get a job. Sykes just stamped him out like it was nothing, and now Sykes has killed that baby, that poor little mite. Ricky, he reckoned that Sykes would just go along with the game, play it like it was always played, keep it purely business, but when has Sykes kept anything purely business?"

Petra felt Denise shift in her seat as she realized what Petra had understood, that Ricky Evans was involved in the previous kidnappings. She asked the question and Ginny nodded. "Nice little earner. No one got hurt. We modelled it on something that happened down south a few years ago, but that lot generally took teens or young adults. Ricky figured if we took younger kids they'd cause less trouble and get over the shock quicker. They were always looked after. We placed them with a registered foster carer. Ricky had the idea, but the organization, that was done by someone else. We helped with the logistics, Ricky was paid his cut, that was it."

"So, who else is involved?"

Ginny shook her head. Abruptly she took a bite of a sandwich, frowning presumably at the overabundance of pickle. She chewed and then swallowed before answering. "Way above my pay grade, love. I've told you what I know, that Sykes killed Sammy Marvin. I'll put our hands up to being peripherally involved in those kids being taken, but not these last two." She had clearly recovered some confidence now and felt that her obligation was completed.

Petra frowned. No one had told her about Deans's granddaughter. So how did she know?

"Last two," Denise asked. "And who might the second child be? We know that Joshua Banks is dead, and his body was found beside that of Sammy Marvin, which is why you were brought in. And we know that you had dealings with Paul Benson because he was seen at the warehouse. So who is this second child you're talking about?"

Ginny looked momentarily confused and then she shook her head. "Did I say two? No, I only meant one. I only know about the Banks kid because I was told about that one when I got here." She thrust the remains of the sandwich aside. "I want to see a solicitor now. I was told one would be provided for me."

"I'll make sure that's organized as soon as possible," Petra told her coolly. They gathered up the remains of the sandwiches and tea and left.

"Fuck." Denise drew the word out and leaned back against the corridor wall.

"Well, she certainly pulled some threads together," Petra agreed. "She'll clam up now, you just know it, but her statement gives us a bit more leverage with Ricky Evans. Do you believe her, that somebody else was involved? That Evans was just on the edge of things?"

Denise Allwood thought about it and shook her head. "I think he's in it up to his neck, but I don't think he could have done everything on his own. We'd already come to the conclusion that someone must've been on the inside, moving in the same circles as the families these kids were taken from, and that certainly isn't Ricky Evans."

Petra nodded. It was a good point. So who was it? "What if Ms Copeland isn't as innocent as she'd like to make out?"

"Definitely a possibility. But if that's the case we'll have a hell of a job finding her and maybe even extraditing her. A woman like that with money and resources could be anywhere. But if she was involved, why gather all this evidence?"

"I suppose some of it could have been useful in setting up the abductions. Some might have been so she could put extra pressure on the families later on. I don't know, but we could certainly do with finding her."

"There's still no indication that she's left the country. Not that that means anything. But this is progress. Now we've just got to see what Ricky Evans says about it. Let's see if Deans has finished taking advice from his lawyer."

"What's the betting that advice is 'no comment'?" Denise said gloomily.

CHAPTER 15

Back in the viewing room, Clarke noted that DC Sophie Hopkins was continuing her conversation with Brian Moore, father of young Gracie Moore and son-in-law of Superintendent Deans. A uniformed constable was taking notes, and all three of them looked up as the door opened and Deborah Moore came in. Her husband immediately rose to greet her, and for a moment she leaned with her head against his shoulder and her face buried in his jacket.

"God, what they must be going through."

Clarke glanced round to acknowledge Denise Allwood and to take the proffered coffee.

"We should all club together and get a decent coffee machine," she said and settled down beside him. "How's she doing? Sophie, I mean. Not an easy task for a DC, especially not a newbie like her."

"DC Hopkins is doing a fine job," he said.

Denise nodded.

"So, have you run out on DS Merrow?" he teased.

"I've been staring at stacks of paperwork and computer printouts until they're just a blur. So I volunteered for the coffee run. Petra has more stamina than I do when it comes to detail."

Clarke suspected the same could be said of him. Petra Merrow was dogged, her memory for minutiae phenomenal. He supposed she had needed that kind of focus just to keep her story straight when she had been embedded with the Perrins.

He and Denise watched as the mother of Gracie Moore sat down, clutching her husband's hand.

"I thought you'd be better with your sister," her husband said.

"I need to be with you. I need to help. I need to do something — I can't just sit there."

"Your husband's been telling me all about Gracie," Sophie Hopkins said gently. "About her friends, about the things she likes to do, about your daily routine."

Deborah Moore looked puzzled. "Why do you need to know that? She was snatched from our garden — what else do you need to know?"

Clarke knew that Sophie Hopkins had already explained all of this to the father, but she began again with the same calm tone she had maintained during the morning interview. "There are two reasons, Mrs Moore." She paused. "May I call you Deborah?"

"Debbie, please." The woman's tone hardened. "Only my father calls me Deborah."

"Debbie, I'm asking all of these things so we can build a picture of your day-to-day life and your daughter's day-to-day life, to see who you regularly come into contact with and try to establish why the men who took your daughter chose to snatch her from home instead of taking some other opportunity. It was a very risky thing for them to do, so we need to understand what was going through their minds and how they knew, for example, that the back gate was unlikely to be locked today."

"It was grocery delivery day," Debbie said flatly. "We order for the same time every week. It's easier for the driver to park on the back road and come in that way. The close is packed with cars at the weekend when everyone's home."

Sophie nodded. "Yes, so your husband told me. So the gate would have been opened this evening ready for the grocery delivery to arrive, and they usually arrive between five and six. Any other day and that gate would have been locked, isn't that right?"

"Yes. It's only left unlocked for a couple of hours. The rest of the time it's bolted and padlocked. We moved there so it would be safe, a safe place for Gracie to play. It's just a quiet road at the back, but dad suggested we put trellis on top. He said no one likes climbing a fence when there's trellis because it breaks."

She broke down again, collapsing into a tearful heap in her husband's arms.

"So who did the bastard tell?" Denise asked.

"There is nothing to suggest Deans told anyone," Clarke objected. "But everything to suggest that the family was being watched."

His gaze danced back across the bank of monitors. Tucker was in with Ricky Evans, and something about that interview attracted his attention. He turned up the volume. Ricky Evans and his solicitor sat across from DCI Tucker and a DS that Clarke didn't immediately recognize, new people from other teams across the region having been arriving all morning. There was, Clarke noted, suddenly an additional tension in Tucker's demeanour.

"So you're telling me that you were a confidential informant for the late DCI Frankland." Tucker's tone was cold and disbelieving.

"Indeed I was and had been for the last decade. DCI Frankland and I go back a long way. I was sorry about the way he died, nobody deserved that. And we both know our friend Sykes was responsible. He might not have wielded the knife, but he certainly wanted it done."

"I think you might find that it was Gus Perrin that wanted it done," Tucker reminded him. "Perrin was looking for the undercover officer he had discovered was operating within his organization. He had Frankland tortured to try and get that information."

"You're forgetting something," Ricky Evans said. "By the time it came to killing Frankland, Perrin and Sykes were working together — they had a common aim. Sykes's daughter had killed Perrin's son and then taken off. Sykes had to make amends. Besides, Kyle Sykes must have thought, if you lot can get somebody into the Perrin organization then perhaps you can do the same to his. Everybody was paranoid — for that matter, everybody still is."

"So, assuming just for one minute I believe you, what sort of information were you passing on to DCI Frankland?"

In the viewing room, Clarke was suddenly aware that Denise Allwood was swearing, her slim body very tense and very angry. Glancing at her, he could see her face was flushed red and she was glaring at the screen. If looks could kill, he thought.

"He'd never have anything to do with the likes of Ricky Evans," she declared angrily. "He wasn't like that."

"I doubt DCI Frankland knew anything about the kidnappings," Clarke observed quietly. "But you know as well as I do that we go where the information is. We don't always have much choice in who imparts it."

But she was shaking her head. This, he realized, was intolerable to her. Frankland had been her mentor and her friend and he had died horribly, refusing even under torture to give away the name of the young woman he had sent undercover.

"DCI Frankland was as straight as a die."

"Frankland was also a pragmatist," Clarke said. "Look, I didn't know the man very well. He was retiring just as I arrived." Not that he actually retired, not really. He'd continued to be Petra's point of contact long after that, and it looked as though he had also continued to run confidential informants. Clarke pondered the significance of that, and wondered who had known and who Frankland had reported to.

Ricky Evans was sitting back now, relaxed in his chair, or as relaxed as it was possible to be in the uncomfortable seat. The solicitor was looking at him speculatively, and Tucker's face was almost unnaturally blank. Finally the solicitor moved. "I think it's time for a break while I consult with my client."

The screen had blanked by the time Tucker came into the viewing room and dropped his folder on the desk. Clarke and Denise turned to him, Denise clearly ready to challenge what Ricky Evans said. Tucker held a restraining hand. "I know," he said. "I know. But we can't rule it out. It seems such an odd thing for Evans to be making up."

"He makes it sound as though it was a recent thing," Clarke commented. "Up to the point when Frankland was killed. Frankland had retired, though, so unless we think he was doing this off his own account, someone must've authorized it. Maybe someone who knew about the kidnap gang and suspected Ricky Evans might be involved."

"Maybe we should go and ask the chief constable. He seems to know everyone," Tucker said heavily.

Clarke filled him in on what was happening in the other interviews, and then Tucker announced that he was going to go and find something to eat while the solicitor was busy with Ricky Evans — who knew when he'd get the chance again? Clarke turned back to Denise. "So, how well did you know DCI Frankland?"

Denise Allwood looked despondent. "When I first came here I didn't know anyone. He was nice to me. He was really good at that kind of informal chat that a lot of senior officers aren't. He'd immediately notice if someone wasn't happy, or someone was insecure, or someone was just having a bad day, and he'd just quietly give them a coffee, call them in for a quick chat about something else and check that they were all right. I know he ran a lot of CIs. He was good at it. I saw him in action on a few occasions, and he had this way of making them feel as though he cared too. It's what he was good at, but that doesn't mean it wasn't genuine, you know?"

Clarke nodded. It was, he thought, well worth looking back through Frankland's records, and mentally added that to the list of cold-case data that needed to be on Petra's and Denise's lists. Perhaps this was something *he* should be looking into, given the involvement of the two women. Denise would cool down later and be able to look at things with a detached eye, but it seemed unfair to pile this additional task on them right now. First he would talk to Deans and to Craig, see what they knew about Frankland's operations. Were they officially sanctioned or was he freelancing? And if he was, then why and for whom? Clarke knew that officers that went undercover for a long period of time often ended up with a blurred view of where their duty began and ended, but he also knew their handlers likewise could end up with a skewed vision of what was justifiable and what should be kept outside of the usual boundaries. He had called Frankland pragmatic, and he had no doubt that was true. Had he gone beyond pragmatism, beyond reacting to circumstances to creating the circumstances?

Clarke told himself that he was getting ahead of things. Frankland was probably a side issue, and the important thing now was little Gracie Moore, finding her and bringing her home before it was too late. Somewhere deep inside himself he felt a clock ticking, and he knew everyone else on the team had that same sense that they were running out of time.

Denise mumbled something about going back to see how Petra was getting on. At the door she turned back. "I can't help thinking that Patricia Copeland is in this thing deeper than she liked to let on, that's she's either in danger or she is a danger."

Clarke bristled. "How do you mean? She struck me as a woman under threat and doing her best to escape from that threat."

"Maybe she knew so much because she was in a position to know so much. What if she was part of this and she decided she wanted out?"

Clarke nodded. It was of course something he had thought of. "If we find her we can ask her."

He watched as Denise turned and walked away. He knew she had a point and he was also certain that Patricia Copeland had been very much afraid when he had met with her. And where the hell was she now? He should have brought her in for interview, should have called for reinforcements — an image of him trying to wrestle her into his car and bring her back handcuffed somehow didn't gel. She was the kind of woman who would have decked him had he tried. Besides, at that point he had viewed her as an informant, not a suspect. But even as an informant he should have brought her in for formal questioning. At the time he had been so focused on keeping everything as quiet as possible, been afraid for the child, and that had impacted on his actions. He had not wanted to attract any more attention to the farce of an investigation he and Petra had been forced to undertake, but of course all of that had changed now. Joshua Banks was dead, and Clarke could not help but think that he was in part responsible for this. Logic had nothing to do with it.

CHAPTER 16

Monday morning dawned, bleary eyed. At the briefing Petra got the impression that no one had slept any better than she had. Not knowing how the day was going to progress, she had checked out of the hotel and bundled her possessions into the boot of her car. She needed to do her laundry at some point, she thought, as she regarded the meagre bundle that now made up most of her worldly goods, and she'd have to work out later where she was to spend the night.

Clarke was not in the briefing room. Denise told her that he'd gone to meet Mr Banks so he could make a formal identification of his son's body.

"Didn't that happen yesterday?" Petra was surprised. Formal identification was usually made as soon as possible.

"Didn't feel he could leave his wife. I think a relative has come to stay and the doctor has her sedated."

"God," Petra said. "I can't imagine what that poor woman must be going through."

The briefing began and tasks were assigned, the team brought up to date with all findings. Denise and Petra were to leave immediately to meet the family of a previous kidnap victim who had agreed to see them. The meeting had been set up at some posh country club Petra had heard of but never expected to visit. She didn't hold out a lot of hope that it would add to their fund of intelligence, but you never knew what might prove useful.

Standing in the car park, waiting for Denise, her thoughts drifted to Lauren Sykes and to the strange elderly woman who seemed to be her current guardian. There had been authority in that voice of a kind Petra had encountered before. This woman was used to being obeyed. She had called Lauren again late on the Sunday evening, but there had been little to say. The girl was clearly shocked and angry at what her father had done, but Petra had caught an undercurrent that went beyond anger.

"Don't do anything stupid, will you?"

"Like what?"

"Like thinking you can do anything about Sykes. Leave it to the police, Lauren. Don't put yourself in danger."

"I won't do anything stupid."

Petra had to be satisfied with that.

"Right, we ready for the off?" Denise asked. She looked as tired and anxious as Petra felt.

"I've programmed the satnav. This place is in the middle of nowhere."

"Of course it is. You don't want to be bothered by the hoi polloi when you're as rich as Croesus, do you?"

"Not unless they're washing your floors."

* * *

There were some things, Clarke thought, that burned themselves on to your memory, waking you in the night for years to come. The sight of little Joshua Banks lying on the mortuary table, his tiny head carefully swathed so that only the largely unmarked face could be seen, was one of them. Robert Banks, a barely contained bundle of rage and pain, his body contorted by the force of his emotions, stood beside him at the small window. His howl of grief was confirmation enough. The constable standing on his other side led him away, murmuring words of comfort that the man almost certainly could not hear, and Clarke followed.

In the waiting room Banks turned on him. "This is your fault. Your fucking fault. All those other kids, all of them, they came back alive!"

He was so close that Clarke could feel the spittle land on his face. He stood his ground and waved away the constable, who had hold of Banks's arm and was attempting to guide him away. If Banks decided to thump him, Clarke knew there wasn't a dammed thing either of them could do about it. The man was beyond caring about little things like assaulting a police officer.

"Those kids came back because the gang who took them . . . it's not the same people who took your son."

"Of course it is. They sent me that number to call, they—"

"The number they gave you was not for one of the families who had children taken. It has nothing to do with them."

"Call the number. I spoke to a woman. She said . . . she said . . ."

"The number was for a pay-as-you-go phone," Clarke told him gently. "A phone that's most probably at the bottom of the canal by now. It wasn't the same people, Mr Banks. There was never any intention of giving you back your child."

He knew he was hurting the man, that he was destroying what little bit of belief remained that he had done the right thing. "Mr Banks, there is nothing more you could have done or done differently. We believe the end result would have been the same."

The man's knees seemed to collapse beneath him. Clarke and the constable eased him into a chair. He curled in on himself, his heavy body slumping forward as he covered his face with his hands and wept uncontrollably, sobs sounding as though they were torn from the depths of his lungs and belly. Clarke sat beside him and waited for a break in the storm.

After a few minutes the man quieted. His hands shook as he took a proffered cup of water and the pack of tissues the constable produced. Clarke gave him a grateful nod, then took the pack and opened it for Robert Banks, that simple action now quite beyond him.

"So who?" Banks choked out.

Clarke hesitated.

"So who?" Louder this time, the rage not far below the surface.

"We think Kyle Sykes might be behind it."

"Sykes?" he sounded utterly bewildered. "Why the hell? Oh God. I don't understand."

"Mr Banks, I need you to do something for me." Clarke's tone had changed. He was all business now. This man needed a focus, something positive that could at least make him feel he was helping out. With luck that feeling might even turn into fact. He noted the constable's startled expression at his sudden change of tack, but he knew he had played it right when Banks sat up, wiped his eyes with an already sodden tissue and nodded.

"I want to kill the bastard."

"Of course you do. But, Mr Banks, I couldn't let you do that, even if we knew where he was. What I need from you is anything and everything you can remember about your dealings with Kyle Sykes. Any conversations you had with the man. Any business dealings he was involved in. Any tiny detail that might not be in the official records."

He paused. Banks nodded. "I'd like to go back to my wife now."

"Of course. The constable here will drive you back to the hotel." Their house was now an official crime scene, with CSI in every room, so they had moved out to a rather plush hotel — though, Clarke reflected, it would be no comfort now, no matter how many damn stars it had.

"I'll call my PA," Banks said, his voice just a little steadier now. "Tell her to help in any way she can."

Clarke didn't bother to explain that Jocelyn Mulligan was already collating anything she thought might be relevant.

"Thank you," he said, then nodded to the constable that it was time to go.

Once Banks had left, Clarke called DCI Tucker. "Not that it's any surprise, but the ID was positive. The poor bugger's falling apart, but I told him we believed Sykes was involved and set him the task of thinking about anything that might be useful to us."

"We had an interesting sighting picked up on CCTV," Tucker told him. "Paul Benson. It looks as though he may have paid a visit to Gus Perrin."

"Perrin? That is indeed interesting. Where did he go after that?"

"Out of town. We don't yet have a direction of travel, but if he takes the motorway or even one of the major A roads then ANPR should pick him up."

"Unless he changes cars. No, but that is an odd one, isn't it? We assumed he'd switched allegiance to Sykes, but what if he's still in Perrin's employ? Sykes told me, that day he tried to blow my brains out, that he'd been loaned by Perrin, but we've made the assumption that the arrangement has become a more permanent one." He thought for a moment. "So, does Sykes know he's still in contact with Perrin? And does Benson heading out of town suggest that Sykes is holed up elsewhere? So far we've no concrete reason to assume he's in Wandsborough. Only the use of the same body dump. We've had no firm sightings."

"Which doesn't mean he isn't here. No, Sykes likes to be close to the action. My bet is that he's somewhere close by."

"So, what's Benson up to, I wonder? If we could pick him up . . ."

"I'll raise a glass to that," Tucker told him.

CHAPTER 17

The country club was pretty much what Petra had expected. They were stopped at the gate, their identification scrutinized, a call made to alert the house manager of their arrival, instructions given as to where to park their car. A drive half a mile long brought them to a large Jacobean-style house, where a man was waiting to wave them into a parking space.

Holding out a hand, he introduced himself. "Jeffery Bean." His smile, Petra thought, seemed genuine enough, as did the barely concealed curiosity.

They followed him inside. The reception area rose to double height. The floor was tiled, and what looked like a genuine suit of armour stood beside the wide and heavily carpeted flight of stairs. The space was panelled to head height in dark wood, above which hung paintings that Petra eyed with interest. It crossed her mind that Carole Perrin would have liked the juxtaposition of what looked like eighteenth-century portraits and contemporary abstracts, as though whoever had curated the display had deliberately wanted to provoke a response. She missed Carole so much, and knowing she had betrayed a genuine friend hurt appallingly at times.

She glanced at Denise, who was looking around with undisguised interest and who, she guessed, would have loved to have quizzed this Jeffery Bean about the place.

Bean led them up the stairs. The carpet absorbed all sound, Petra noticed. They paused outside a massive dark-oak door, and the house manager knocked, opened the door and gestured for them to go in. He closed the door behind them, and Petra was struck by the fact that she could not hear his steps receding as he walked away. Three men and a woman sat in a rough semicircle. Two more chairs were set opposite. *Like we're about to be interviewed for some posh job*, Petra thought. One man, the oldest of the group, rose and came over, hand outstretched.

"Marley Cole. Of Marley, Cole and Binns. Please come and sit down."

Petra took a seat. She was suddenly aware that the usually confident Denise Allwood was ill at ease. Digging deep into her own diminished stash of confidence, she looked at the others gathered opposite, introduced herself and Denise and asked, "And you are?"

Marley Cole had taken his seat and retrieved his cup from a side table. The man at the other end of the row spoke first. "Bryn Daniels. My firm represents Mrs Deacon here and her family." He indicated the woman next to him.

Deacon, Petra thought. Another of the names on Patricia Copeland's list but not someone they had expected to meet today. She looked at the third man. "So I'm guessing you must represent the Reader family?"

The man nodded but looked uncomfortable.

"You understand that anything revealed here today is in confidence," Bryn Daniels said. "That we have agreed to speak with you on the understanding that we may be able to provide you with useful information. That recent events have emphasized that this state of affairs cannot continue and we, as a group, recognize the moral obligation not to withhold information that might help with the enquiry. But you must also understand that this is as far as it goes. Any attempt to drag these families through the mud, to reveal what happened to them to the public or to involve them in any subsequent court case will be resisted using every resource they have at their disposal."

Beside her Petra felt Denise shift in her seat and could almost feel the angry retort. She spoke before Denise had the chance. "You'll have to take all that up with our bosses," she said. "All we know is that yesterday morning the two of us and the rest of our team were standing on a patch of waste ground looking at the body of a little boy who'd been snatched from his home and then cruelly beaten to death. So you'll excuse us if we hand the technicalities on somewhere else. We just want to catch the bastard who did it." She knew she should probably have modified her language, but she saw a brief smile twitch across the mouth of Marley Cole.

Denise now seemed to have gathered herself. "As I understand it, your families were fortunate. They got their children back unharmed. But I'm sure you can imagine what it's like for the poor parents of little Joshua Banks. They're falling apart, and they can't understand why this is happening to them."

Bryn Daniels glanced at his client. "To be honest, DS Allwood, neither can we. The Banks family, as we understand it, are comfortably off, but they're hardly in the same bracket, financially, as the previous families that have been targeted."

He let the question hang for a moment. Petra said, "We have reason to think there are other motives this time. But that's not the issue here."

"No," Denise said quietly, "the issue is a dead child. So you can understand why we want all the information we can get."

"Especially as a second child has been taken," added Marley Cole.

Petra stared him. "And how did you know that? No public statement has been released."

"One hears things, DS Merrow. Anyway—" a briefcase sat beside his chair, and he reached into it and withdrew a folder — "we've collated everything we know. I hope it will be of assistance, but as my colleague has explained, our clients will not cooperate with any enquiry that exposes them directly."

Petra took the folder. "Are the names Ricky Evans or Ginny Afton familiar to any of you?"

She was met with blank looks. "I'm afraid not," Marley Cole told her, but she noticed him writing their names in a small notebook.

"What about Patricia Copeland?"

"Ms Copeland? Of course." Mrs Deacon was speaking for herself now. "We all know Pat. We all knew her before this dreadful business, of course, as a business associate. But . . ." She hesitated and glanced at the others. "To be frank, I don't know what we'd have done without her."

"Oh?" Denise's tone was a little accusatory, but Mrs Deacon did not seem to notice.

"She happened to be with me, at some lunch or other, a few days after . . . after this dreadful thing happened. I'd tried very hard not to let anything slip, to show that I was upset. I was afraid of what might happen if any of us gave the game away, so we were all trying to carry on as normal. But she seemed to sense that something was wrong. I'm afraid I confided in her. In the end she brokered the deal that got our children back."

The man from the Reader family who had not yet spoken looked discomforted. "Mr Reader?" Petra asked. "She also acted on behalf of your family?"

"She played a part, yes. We were told: no police, no solicitors. You have to understand, all of our usual fallbacks were taken from us. We have people in our companies whose only role is to close deals. Obviously, in a situation like this—"

"You were as helpless as anyone else would have been," Petra said quietly.

The man glowered at her. Again there was the hint of a smile from Marley Cole.

"If that's everything?" Bryn Daniels said and began to rise from his seat.

Petra and Denise stayed put.

"You said that Patricia Copeland brokered the deal that got the children back. I'm not sure I understand. What did she do?"

An exchange of glances between the group told Petra that this was considered a strange question. Did this DS not understand what was involved?

"Well," Mrs Deacon said, "she had already dealt with the kidnappers when her niece was taken. She spoke with their representative, arranged for the transfer of the financials and where the children were to be left for us to collect. As you can imagine, we were not in the best shape to deal rationally with any of this. Nothing can prepare you for that kind of thing. Nothing."

Petra nodded. "And you've stayed in touch with her since? I'm sure something like this, such a traumatic shared experience, it must create bonds that—"

Mrs Deacon was shaking her head. "To be frank, I think we all found it difficult afterwards. Every single time we saw Patricia after that it was like being reminded, you know? I suppose we all just drifted apart a little."

"It happens," Mr Reader agreed. "We were grateful, of course."

"And did you have the impression that Ms Copeland wanted more than simple gratitude?" Denise asked.

"I'm not sure I understand what you mean." Mrs Deacon's voice was suddenly sharp.

"And I think we've finished here." Bryn Daniels was clearly not going to be deflected this time.

Petra had not been aware of him summoning anyone, but the door opened and the house manager stood there. A smiling, friendly presence — ready, Petra thought, to politely dispose of guests that were no longer welcome.

"So," Denise said once they were back in the car. "Did we actually gain much from that? Apart from serious carpet envy. How thick was the underlay, do you reckon?"

Petra laughed. "Maybe that's where they bury the bodies. Depends what's in the folder, I suppose. But yes, we know a bit more about the role Patricia Copeland played and, reading between the lines, that she felt she deserved more of a reward than she got. Either that or they began to suspect she might have been involved."

"Either way it looks like they closed ranks, first against her and now against us. Makes it more important that we try and find the Copeland woman. If you ask me, she's up to her neck, one way or another. DI Clarke should have brought her in."

"On what charge? Maybe he should just have shut her in the boot and sorted out the details later."

"That wouldn't have worked. He drives a hatchback."

"True."

Petra waited until they had been waved through the gate and then got on the phone to Clarke to relay what they had learned. The folder she had been given was open on her lap, and she flipped the pages to see if she could glean anything else. "A lot of this seems to replicate what was in Patricia Copeland's files," she told him, "but we'll work through the details when we get back."

They had, he told her, finally got a warrant for Patricia Copeland's home and office. As neither was local they were working with another force. He was heading over there next.

"That's progress, I guess." She paused. "How was the identification?"

"As bad as you might imagine," he told her. "If I never have to do that ever again it will still be too soon."

CHAPTER 18

"So . . ." Clarke paused, watching Ricky Evans carefully. "Tell me about your dealings with Ms Patricia Copeland." It was a bit of a shot in the dark, but he was rewarded by a slight tick at the corner of Evans's eye and a discomforted shuffle on the hard chair.

"Who?"

"Well, if you're behind these other kidnappings then you'll have dealt with Patricia Copeland. We know that in at least three of the abductions she negotiated with the kidnappers. So I imagine that you'd be familiar with the name, if not with the lady herself."

"No comment."

"Okay then, let's look at this from a different angle. Maybe you're not the big fish you'd like us to think. Maybe you're just a bit player in this. Maybe someone else, someone much higher up the food chain, arranged for the kids to be taken and the ransom demands to be made. I mean, I don't see you as a multimillionaire, Ricky. You've not been flashing the cash like I'd expect for someone who's demanded more than a cool million a time for the safe return of these babies. And they are babies, Ricky. Defenceless, innocent little babies. And one of them is now very much dead."

Ricky Evans sat up as though stung and leaned forward across the table. "That has nothing to do with me."

"No? So are you pulling the 'Sykes made me do it' card? You can't have it both ways, Ricky. Either you're the brains behind this or you're not."

He pushed a photograph of Patricia Copeland across the table. "Maybe you'll recognize her face," he said, "even if you don't remember her negotiating techniques."

Evans slumped back and crossed his arms. He looked away from Clarke, from his solicitor, from the camera and the recorder. Separating himself from it all. "I have nothing more to say."

* * *

Ginny Afton was more forthcoming. She seemed intent on giving the impression that she was bored with all of this, but Clarke sensed that she was in fact quite shaken and more than a little scared. She looked at the picture and nodded. "Patricia Copeland. So what?"

"How do you know her?"

Ginny laughed. Clarke could feel her relief that she could laugh at something. That she could feel anything other than tension and dread. "She owns the warehouse, doesn't she? Technically, she's our landlady."

"She's your what?"

Ginny was laughing harder now. "Didn't you know that? Didn't you lot do a background check? Sladen Industries. They own the whole site. And Sladen Industries is Patricia Copeland, though she uses her married name on the paperwork. Cullen. Patricia Cullen. Though she divorced him long since."

Mentally, Clarke regrouped. "And Patricia Copeland negotiated with you over the ransom demands for two of the kids you took."

"I never took anybody."

"Oh, sorry, did that hurt your oh-so-sensitive feelings? For two of the kids that were taken. From the Reader and

Deacon families. Lily Reader, who was eleven months old at the time, and Timothy Deacon, who was just on a year old."

Ginny shrugged. "I don't recall the details. Anyway, I didn't have anything to do with it. Oh, I knew it was going on, but I never got involved. That was Ricky's game."

"Until it wasn't. Until it became Sykes's game. The rules changed then, didn't they, Ginny?"

"She's got a sister," Ginny said, seemingly apropos of nothing. "Celia. She deals with the day-to-day. Pat Copeland is always off doing something or other. Raising funding for investments or something. Me, I'd invest in bricks and mortar any time. You know where you are with property, don't you? They had a bit of a falling out about it a while ago. Pat Copeland wanted to sell off a big chunk of their portfolio and the sister disagreed. Or so I heard. She has a brother too."

"Yes, it was the brother's child that was taken. But of course, you know that."

"You don't know what I know."

"So tell me. Tell me about this sister."

"What, Celia?"

"Celia Copeland."

"No, she married, didn't she? Celia Myers she became. Like as two peas in a pod, they are."

She seemed to lose interest then, and after another ten minutes of Ginny refusing to answer anything more, Clarke left the interview and went down the hall to the incident room. "Celia Myers," he said. "Any record of her leaving the country in the last few days?"

"Anything useful, like a date of birth?"

Like two peas in a pod, Ginny had said. Twins? He suggested they try Patricia Copeland's date of birth and paced anxiously while the check was made.

"Saturday evening. Flew out from Heathrow."

"Fuck. I think we've been chasing the wrong woman. I think Patricia Copeland might have used her sister's passport."

* * *

Patricia Copeland's home and the cottage where Clarke had met her were out of the jurisdiction of the local force. Warrants were issued and DI Tucker went over as liaison. Warrants were also hastily arranged for the home and businesses of Celia Myers. Clarke headed over to her house and left instructions that Petra and Denise should follow him when they returned. They had a much better overview, Clarke figured, of the connections, both business and personal, and would therefore be in a better position to judge what might be immediately useful.

They arrived an hour after he did.

"Did you know Patricia Copeland had a sister?" he asked Petra as she and Denise got out of the car.

"Yes, and a brother. But you know about the brother. The sister, Celia Myers, she's CEO for a couple of big property management concerns. It's all a bit tangled. We handed a lot of stuff over to the forensic accountants and they've also got bank statements, company accounts and anything else we could lay hands on, but we suspect we've only just scratched the surface. Most of it was beyond us, so we handed it off to those who could make sense of it, but like we showed you yesterday, top-level business is an incestuous world. Everyone knows everyone and a hell of a lot of them seem to be related one way or another." She paused. "Maybe not incestuous. *Dynastic.* Inherited and passed on and then merged and married into and—"

"I get the picture. Reminds me of the Perrins and Sykes, trying to pair their kids off. Except Lauren was the only kid. Perrin junior was almost old enough to be her father."

"A bit of an exaggeration, boss," Denise objected. "He was, what? Thirty-one, thirty-two? She was seventeen. He'd have had to have started early."

"Doesn't make it any better."

"No," she agreed, "but the issue wasn't his age, it was that she had no choice. It's proper consent that matters. That's what I think, anyway."

He glanced curiously in her direction, wondering what brought that on, then decided he would let it go. They paused on the driveway to look at the house. It was modern, not more than a decade old, Clarke reckoned, and the sort of thing that was usually advertised as 'architect designed', as though other houses were designed by trained monkeys or accountants or something. Then, gloved and bunny-suited, they stepped into the property.

The door opened into a broad hallway with stairs rising in the middle and four doors leading off. The forensic teams had already moved in, and they followed the designated pathway into what seemed to be a small study. Filing cabinets stood along one wall, a desk close by the window and low, wide architect's plan chests were set along the opposite wall. Various business qualifications decorated the wall — it seemed Celia Myers was a trained architect and recipient of several awards. Clarke's eye was caught by a photograph of two women who, as Ginny Afton had said, looked like peas in a pod, though closer inspection suggested that they were not identical. One, the woman he now recognized as having introduced herself as Patricia Copeland, was a little taller, her face a little more lined, but they were alike enough for Patricia to have used her sister's passport.

Petra and Denise were already examining the filing cabinets.

"So what do we have?"

"A very neat filing system," Denise said. "This one seems to be building contracts and rental agreements. Celia Myers does a lot of work for local housing associations, and Sladen Industries has maintenance contracts for a lot of rental properties both here and, well, I'd say within something like a fifty-mile radius. We'll have to go through to see if there's anything useful, see if there are any links to anything or anyone else."

"Employee contracts, suppliers and so on are in this one," Petra told him. She moved over to the desk and he went to examine the bigger plan chests. On the face of it these contained architect's drawings, blueprints and sketchbooks. He flicked through these curiously and then froze. "Look at this."

They came over to him. "What are we looking at?" Denise asked. He had forgotten that neither of them had visited the Banks home. He pointed at the drawing of the rear elevation of a large house. "That's the room Joshua Banks was taken from."

The sound of car tyres on gravel distracted them. It was followed by the slam of a door, and a woman's voice demanding to know what the hell was going on. Clarke, his colleagues in tow, strode out into the hall and stood by the open front door.

"Celia Myers?" Petra said.

"Presumably so." Seeing her, Clarke could see that she didn't look exactly like her sister. She was shorter and more slightly built, and she was incandescent with fury.

"What the hell is going on here? What has that stupid cow done now?"

"What's the betting the cow is sister Pat?" Petra said quietly. But not so quietly that Celia didn't hear. She turned sharply to look at them.

"So, where is she, then? And what the hell are you doing in my house?"

CHAPTER 19

Celia Myers looked unimpressed, even though Clarke had taken her into the most comfortable of the interview rooms — the one with carpet and proper chairs — and sent out for decent coffee. He wanted this woman onside, at least for now.

Celia Myers's passport had gone. She usually kept it in her desk drawer, and although this drawer was locked, the key was kept in a box on her desk and her sister of course knew where it was. Celia Myers herself had a pretty solid alibi for the last ten days. She'd been in hospital having a minor operation on her wrist and then booked into a health spa. There she had taken advantage of every treatment on offer, slept a great deal and generally taken some time for herself, she explained to Clarke. A neighbour had called the health spa to tell her that the police were at her home. She was not happy to have had her break interrupted.

"It's been well over a year since I had more than a weekend off, so I felt I deserved it. Pat may own the businesses but she leaves the day-to-day running to me, so it all falls on my shoulders. And believe me, just lately she's been scatty as hell. I've not known whether she's coming or going. First she wants one thing, then she wants another, then she's talking about selling things. Then she's talking about reining back parts of the business or expanding into other areas. I told her months ago, she had to make some proper decisions. We couldn't go on like this. We were haemorrhaging money because she couldn't make up her mind what she wanted to do, and she's been like that for the last eighteen months. So I thought, why not, I'm going to take a break. I didn't even tell her where I was going. For that matter, she didn't ask."

"Did you know about the kidnapping?" Clarke asked her.

She blinked and looked at him as though he was making no sense. "What kidnapping? What the hell are you on about?"

"Eighteen months ago your niece was snatched from her home and a ransom demand was made."

Her incredulity was obvious. "What the hell are you on about?" she said again. "Just what are you talking about?"

"She never told you?"

"No one said anything. I don't know what you're talking about."

"How often do you see your brother and his family?"

"Next to never. We don't get on. We haven't done since we were kids. We exchange birthday cards, Christmas gifts, via Pat usually. Look, our parents made it very clear that they wanted boys. They got two girls, then they got a son. Pat was self-sufficient and confident even when she was a little thing. Brian was the youngest, and our parents thought the sun shone out of his bum. I left home to go to university and I rarely went back. Pat was working, and when I graduated she helped me financially till I got my doctorate and then gave me a job. I never asked the rest of the family for a damn thing and I can count the number of times my brother and I have seen one another in the last ten years on the fingers of one hand. Twice for funerals, once for a wedding and once for the reading of our mother's will. Dad left everything to her, then she left most of it to his son and heir. Pat and I got on with it together. She has a good business head when she's not . . ." She paused as though suddenly realizing that she was rambling on. As though the impact of what Clarke had said suddenly hit home.

"I don't understand about the kidnapping. What the fuck happened?"

He filled her in on the main detail as she listened, her expression appalled, and he was more and more convinced that her shock was genuine.

"Eighteen months ago," she said, "I was away in the US for about a month. I'd gone to a conference and then I had some business to do over there on Pat's behalf. All of this must have happened when I was away." She paused thoughtfully. "That was the longest I've been away in years. The conference lasted four days. It was in Atlantic City. Pat knew I really wanted to go and she knew I hadn't had a break in ages, so she told me to take some time. Most of what I do day to day is nothing to do with my degree or my doctorate, and she knew I was missing the creative side. I had a brilliant time," she said softly. "I had no idea anything bad was going on back here. Don't get me wrong, I couldn't care less what happens to that brother of mine, but that doesn't mean I want his kids to suffer."

"And she gave no sign that anything was wrong?"

Celia shook her head. "No, not really, she seemed a bit tired and distracted when I got back, but I assumed that was because she had been handling both sides of the business. I'm usually there to take the load off."

"And since then?"

"Like I said before, she seemed . . . off her game. Nothing major, not until this last month or so, and these past few weeks she's just been all over the place. We don't often argue, not really, but she's been making such stupid decisions lately. Liquidating assets in such a public way when she could sell things quietly. It makes the business look bad, makes it look as though we might be failing when we're really not. I asked what was worrying her, but she was so damn dismissive in the end we just had a row. I told her I was going to get my wrist sorted out then book into a spa for a few days, and she just said 'good', like she was pleased I was going to be out of the way. So where has she gone, and why has she taken my passport?"

"Have you ever had dealings with a man called Kyle Sykes?"

Celia laughed as though it was the most stupid thing she had ever heard. "Kyle Sykes? You've got to be kidding. You steer clear of a man like that or you don't last long. Okay, so I'm pretty sure he's had interests in some of the businesses we dealt with, same as Gus Perrin's lot. They've got fingers in so many pies it's impossible to know if the contractor you've hired is paying a kickback or the materials you bought come from a supplier he's got a so-called legitimate interest in, but we do our best to keep away from trouble. Anyway, hasn't Sykes disappeared into the wild blue yonder?"

"Apparently not. So you know nothing about the other children who had been abducted?"

That look of incredulity was back. "I don't understand."

Cautiously he outlined what had been going on over the past few years — children taken, ransomed, returned. The possibility that parents had been blackmailed into surrendering business interests. He was aware that this last was currently speculation, but from what Petra and Denise had found it seemed that the return of the children had not ended the agony for the parents.

"I knew nothing about any of this. And you can't think Pat was involved, surely?"

"Right now we don't know what to think about your sister."

Celia seemed to be processing all of this information. "You think Kyle Sykes is involved, don't you?"

"Lately, yes."

"And you think Pat knew about this? You think she was running away from him?"

"Sykes is a dangerous man. You know that. Now is there anything your sister might have said or done that might lead you to believe she's had contact with him?"

She shook her head. "Pat has more sense." She didn't sound convincing.

"Sykes doesn't always give people a choice," Clarke said.

Celia's face paled. "You think he was threatening her? That's why she ran away? If that's the case, then I'm glad she's got my passport. I hope she's far away by now."

He paused, then changed direction. "What do you know about Ricky Evans?"

"Rents a warehouse from us. Bit of a creep, but I've only met the man a couple of times. The rent is paid on time. Couple of years ago we had to threaten enforcement proceedings if he didn't clear up the land around the warehouse. It's his responsibility and some of his storage was causing a fire risk. I did go over on that occasion. There'd been an inspection and the threat of legal action, so I felt I should go in person. I spoke to him, but mainly I dealt with Ginny Afton, his PA. She dealt with everything and sorted it out. Why?"

"And do you know Mr and Mrs Robert Banks? He's the CEO of Tyburn Recruitment."

"Sure, why? We use them when we need IT support. They recruit good people. Pat knows them better."

"Why is there a drawing of their house in your sketchbook?"

"Because I drew their house. I'm not sure I understand the question. If you've gone through my sketchbooks you'll have found drawings of all sorts of houses. I draw houses, it's kind of what I do. When I'm not running the business day-to-day I keep my architectural practice on. Banks wanted an extension building. Okay, it's not the most exciting thing in the world, but it keeps my hand in and just occasionally I get to build a whole house."

"Isn't it enough just to take photographs?"

She smiled, probably for the first time since he began the interview, and it transformed her face, softened the lines around her eyes. She was prettier than her sister, Clarke thought absently. Less ruthless? Or maybe just less scared. Patricia Copeland had definitely been afraid.

"Photographs are fine, but when you draw something you have to look and look hard, so it helps with my thinking process," she told him. "I drew the back of the house because that helps me. Sometimes I give my working drawings to the client when the project is finished. They like that sort of thing."

He nodded. It made sense. Whether he believed her or not, he had yet to decide. "Did you ever meet Anthony Dronfield?"

"The man who fell off the multi-storey? Yes, once. He was in Pat's office. Why?"

"Did she tell you why she'd employed him?"

She shook her head.

"Though I suppose if you claim not to have known about the abduction of your niece, then she'd be unlikely to enlighten you."

"I'm not claiming anything. I didn't know."

"But you didn't find it surprising that she was employing a private investigator?"

"Well, no. She did it all the time. That was, I think, the first time she'd employed Mr Dronfield, though. She usually went through an agency."

"Which one and what for?"

"Um," she frowned. "Ridgeway and Pinks. Or is it the other way round. It'll be in the files. As to what, she was often responsible for paying out large sums of money to contractors and the like. We got stung once, years ago — paid a large sum up front to what looked like a reputable firm and the bastard fucked off. Oh, we weren't the only one's he'd stolen from. Turns out he was up to his ears in debt, so he decided to take what he could and run for the hills. So, after that she was all about due diligence. Ridgeways, they specialize in all things to do with credit and finance."

"But Dronfield was different."

She shrugged. "I asked, she told me it was a personal matter. I let it go."

"A personal matter?"

"Look, I just assumed she'd met someone and didn't want to find she was dating a loser. It's happened. She's suspicious of potential gold diggers. Compared to Pat I'm just the hired help. She's worked bloody hard and she's benefited from that. It's made her careful, I suppose."

"Suspicious, even. And has she been seeing anyone?"

"Not that I know about. Look, I've been really patient. I've answered all your questions the best I can. I've not even asked for a lawyer. But I really have had enough now. So, can I go?"

"I'll need a formal statement and I'll almost certainly need to do an interview under caution. If you want legal advice, you're free to ask for it."

"And if this goes on much longer, I will. Are you planning on charging me with anything?"

"For the moment, no."

"Then I'll be leaving."

"And where will you be going?"

"I'm going back to the health spa. I've three more days of rest and relaxation booked. And just think, you don't even have to tell me not to leave the country because, look, no passport. My darling sister has seen to that."

"She was scared," Clarke said.

"Yeah, I guess she must have been to take off like that." She grimaced. "Look, I'm not the cold-hearted bitch you've got me pegged as being, but Pat didn't tell me about what happened to Amelia. She didn't tell me anything about what happened to our brother's family and, like I told you, I don't give a damn about him, but if I knew anything I would tell you. His kid's an innocent party in all this."

"You didn't know your brother and his family have also gone abroad?"

An eyebrow raised at that. She shook her head. "Why should I know?"

"And it doesn't bother you that they've all left you to take whatever fallout there might be?"

He saw her wince, knew he'd hit an open wound. "What do you mean?"

"Pat and your brother are beyond reach. You're still here. Pat was undoubtedly very much afraid and so, it seems, was your brother. I find it significant that after their child was returned, your brother and his wife settled back very much into life as normal. They seemed to consider the matter closed and the threat gone, and yet a week or so ago they left home suddenly and told no one where they were going. They didn't even warn you that something might be wrong, that they were in some kind of trouble — danger, even — and that you might be at risk too." He paused to allow that to sink in. "Where would they have gone, do you think?"

He could see the cogs turning as she thought all of this through. He half expected her to demand police protection. Then she seemed to gather her resources and convince herself that he must be exaggerating. He hoped, for her sake, that he was.

"His wife is from Seattle," she said. "They might have gone to her family. I don't have the address, but it will be in Pat's address book. In her office, right-hand desk drawer."

The search team would have that by now, Clarke reckoned. "And your sister? Is there anywhere you think she might have gone? Any friend she might have trusted?"

"Trusted?" Celia laughed suddenly. "You might say that my sister had trust issues, Inspector. Her marriage broke down because she thought he was cheating. Anyone new she met she had checked out before she got too friendly and risked anything. Credit checks, financials, background, and I don't just mean business associates."

"Has she always been this way?"

"I don't know," she shrugged. "Maybe, but it got worse after that deal I told you about went wrong. That thieving bastard could have ruined us before we'd even got started. After that she wasn't much into taking chances. She's a bit of a control freak, if I'm honest."

Suddenly she looked tired as though this final admission had drained what was left of her resources. "Can I go now?"

He nodded. "But we need to know where you are. Stay at the health spa or whatever it is and let someone know if you see anything you think suspicious or unsettling. I wasn't joking about your siblings going off and leaving you to take the flack."

She looked shocked, then the professional mask was back in place. Both sisters were practised at that, he thought. He gave her his number, but emphasized that if she was scared, she should just dial 999 and ask for help.

"You really think I might be in danger?"

"I think it's best to be careful."

The constable who had been sitting in on the interview escorted Celia Myers out and a moment later DCI Tucker came into the interview room.

"Didn't know you were back?"

"Got in about an hour ago, so I've been drinking coffee and watching you lot work. You think she's telling the truth about being kept in the dark?"

Clarke considered. "I think she's telling the truth about not knowing about the abduction and about the problems with her family, but I suspect her sister saw her as a weak link, knew there were things about the business and everything else that she wouldn't choose to know about. She puts on a good front, but I think she's not nearly as tough as she likes to make out."

"And the sister? Patricia Copeland? How tough is she?"

"Hard as nails, I'd have said. But I've seen men who reckon they're rock hard crumble when the likes of Sykes is involved. I think she's pragmatic enough to know when to leave the game."

"And you reckon she left her sister in the shit."

"I don't think her sister figured in the calculations. I think maybe she's got so used to only partly including Celia in everything, of seeing her as an unequal partner, that it didn't occur to her someone might see it differently. She probably just assumed that with her gone Celia would be left alone."

He glanced at his boss's face and grinned. "I said she was tough, I never said she was particularly wise. I'm sure she's a really able businesswoman, but the Kyle Sykeses of this world throw everyone curveballs. They're hard to predict just because they don't behave in any logical way. Or at least not in a way that makes sense to anyone with half a brain."

A constable knocked on the door. "We found the book, sir. There was a Seattle address and a couple of phone numbers." He handed Tucker a slip of paper.

"When she mentioned the address book I sent word to look for it," he said. "We've brought a ton of stuff back from the raids on the house and the office. Petra and Denise are going to kill me when they see it all. Right, I'll see what we can turn up in the States." He paused, his expression suddenly more serious. "And I'll also give Superintendent Deans's daughter a call. Not that we can tell them much, but there were a dozen missed calls waiting for me when I got back. I'd sort of hoped the Myers woman would give us something to work with."

"Even if she had known about the previous abductions, that's no guarantee the information would have been helpful in this case. This time it isn't Ricky Evans making the running, or whoever was pulling his strings." Clarke was bitter now. "This is Kyle Sykes we're dealing with, so all the previous cases count for nothing."

CHAPTER 20

"We're the last here. It's time we all headed for home," Clarke said, surveying the mountain of boxes and folders that overspilled the little office and now probably violated fire regulations as it filled half the corridor.

Denise Allwood glanced up at the clock. It was almost nine at night and they'd been on the go since just after six that morning. "God, no wonder I'm shattered."

He saw Petra grimace and wondered where home would be for her tonight.

Denise reached for her coat and then her phone. As she made her way down the corridor, they could hear her talking to her partner and suggesting he order takeaway.

"Sounds like a good plan," Clarke said. "Look," he added on impulse, "come back to my place and we'll order in. My belly feels like my throat's been cut, as my old man used to say."

He saw her hesitate and then nod. "I'll need to book in somewhere first. I checked out this morning. I didn't know how the day would pan out and, well, you know. Some of the chain hotels out towards the motorway have late check-in. So it'll be okay."

He felt she was reassuring herself rather than him. She followed him to his flat in her own car. He stopped off to collect a meal he'd ordered from the office from his favourite Chinese takeaway and, walking back to his car, he noticed she was glancing anxiously up and down the street. He tapped on her window. "Everything okay?"

"Blue car. It's driven round twice, slowed up as it's gone past." She shrugged. "It happens."

"You've got the reg number? We should—" He caught her expression. "Of course you have. And of course it won't help."

He got into his own car and she followed him the rest of the way to the flat. Was she being paranoid? he wondered. But no. She had every right to worry.

His thoughts drifted to the parents of the missing child. Another night without their kid. Without knowing where she was or even if she was still alive.

He directed Petra to one of the guest parking spots and checked the outer gate was locked before taking her inside. A dark blue saloon paused in front of the gate and then sped off. He felt a shiver of fear run through his body, remembering his near-death experience the previous year. He had been shot — he had believed that he was going to die. But at least the threat had been immediate, something he could react to, ultimately something that had happened and then gone. What must it be like to live with that constant but unspecified level of threat, day after day, night after night? He wasn't sure he could cope with that.

* * *

Petra settled back in her chair, trying hard not to fall asleep. It was good just to sit for a while and forget there was a world outside. They hadn't talked much while they ate, both realizing just how ravenously hungry they were. Afterwards, Clarke had made coffee and the conversation had somehow drifted to her time undercover. It was odd, Petra thought; usually she avoided any intrusion into her memories of that time. It was past and gone and left nothing but a bad feeling

— one that pervaded her thoughts about the present and the future as well. But somehow she felt comfortable with Clarke, and the conversation had become oddly personal without feeling intrusive.

"So, did you care about him?"

She watched him pause, as though not sure how to phrase the next question.

"Did you love him?"

Petra stared into the depths of her coffee cup. The dregs were cloudy, and when she swirled them tiny fragments of sediment broke the surface. She wondered if it was possible to read coffee sediments like you could read tea leaves. Had she loved Billy Hunter? No, it hadn't been love, but she had known him for more than three years, lived with him more than two, shared some really good times. Yes, she knew what he was, and in the beginning that really bothered her. It had frightened her, but she had carved out her position within the Perrin organization, had developed her own skills, a talent for photography taking her into places she could never have expected. She had photographed parties and social events, weddings and even the odd funeral. Gus Perrin had approved her images before they had been printed, of course, but after that they had found their way into local papers, society magazines even. She had been well on the way to actually having a proper career, that's how crazy her life had been.

"I didn't love him, but I grew to like him, or at least I liked parts of him. He could be fun. He had a wonderful sense of humour and real style. And after a little while I stopped feeling that I had to be on my guard all the time and I relaxed. The truth is, I relaxed and I felt I belonged more fully than I've felt at any time in my life. And that's what makes it so hard, knowing that I was wrong to feel that way but knowing that it felt so good."

She could sense him looking at her, and when she glanced up he wore a puzzled expression on his face as though trying to work things out, trying to give her a fair hearing. She got up and crossed to the window, staring down into the street. It was raining, a slow, steady late-spring rain, washing the streets clean and heavy enough to obscure the view of the city. "Sometimes I think I should just go away," she said. "Leave the police and put it all behind me. But then I know I can't because I've got to face the coroner's court, and the accusations the Perrins are bringing and Billy Hunter's family, and I guess . . . I guess part of me can't blame them for what they're feeling."

"You are not responsible for Billy Hunter's death. He was shot in the head — he didn't do it to himself. Gus Perrin or someone close to him did away with him. You weren't to know."

"That's bollocks and you know it." Her voice sounded harsh and she realized suddenly that she was close to tears. She did not want to cry in front of this man. She had come to like Clarke but she wasn't ready to cry in front of him. "He died because he didn't see through me. He died because he believed I was exactly who I said I was. Gus Perrin killed him in retribution."

"Gus Perrin has killed a lot of people in retribution. It's what people like him do. Billy Hunter knew what he was into. He could have died a dozen times over given the life he led."

"But he didn't, did he?"

"Do you enjoy punishing yourself? Do you enjoy the guilt trip?"

She flinched. The counsellor she was seeing had asked her something similar, but not as baldly. She turned on him angrily, unable to keep the tears at bay now. "How dare you?" She clasped the coffee mug tightly, resisting, just, the urge to throw it at his head.

"I dare because somebody's got to ask the question. Look, I've seen what that kind of guilt, that kind of self-loathing and punishment can do to a person. I'd rather not see it happen to another friend."

For a moment or two all she could do was stare at him. She wanted to ask, what person? She wanted to ask if he was lying about this. She wanted to ask if he really saw her as a friend, but in the end she did none of those things. She crumpled to the floor as sobs torn from the very depths of her belly rose to her throat, choking her. She felt him take the mug from her hand and then help her gently to her feet and over to the sofa. Then he sat in silence beside her, not touching her, not speaking, but somehow just being there while she sobbed her heart out. And when she had exhausted herself, she must have fallen asleep because when she woke she found that she had a blanket covering her and that it was dark outside and there was no sign of Clarke. He had left a small lamp switched on and a pillow and another blanket on the sofa. Looking at her watch she saw it was 1 a.m. and that he must have gone to bed.

I should leave, Petra thought, and then, *Oh, what the hell.* She shed her boots and trousers then lay down on the sofa pulling the blankets tight around her body. Within minutes she had fallen back to sleep, and when she woke again it was daylight and there were sounds of breakfast-making coming from the kitchen. She saw that it was 6 a.m. and she had slept solidly for longer than she had in months.

Clarke came through from the kitchen carrying another mug of coffee and set it on the table beside the sofa. He smiled.

"Breakfast will be about another fifteen minutes."

"We should be at work."

"Morning briefing's at eight. We're fine. You know where the bathroom is. If you need a clean shirt take one out of the wardrobe."

She sat for a few minutes just drinking coffee, then went and showered and borrowed a shirt. It was too big for her. It would have been too big for her even before she lost weight, but now it hung loose and shapeless, even when she tucked it into her trousers, though with her jacket on it didn't look too bad. She could, she supposed, go down to the car and get her own clothes, but did she have anything clean? Getting her laundry done when there was nowhere she could settle had been a major chore.

Looking in the mirror she saw that her face was drawn and gaunt, and whatever had possessed her to cut her hair that short? She'd done it one night with a pair of nail scissors, wanting to eradicate . . . something. Herself, maybe? Definitely the woman who had lived with Billy Hunter and had expensive haircuts.

Petra took a deep breath and then went back through to the kitchen.

"Bacon, eggs, mushrooms and toast. And don't tell me you're not hungry. Yesterday was as busy for you as it was for me, and one Chinese takeaway won't make up for that."

"I'm not sure I had breakfast yesterday."

"Well, if you want more we can cook more. If we run out we'll go to the shops. There's not much room in here, just a breakfast bar, so take a tray and we'll go and sit in the other room. There's coffee, or if you want tea I'll make some."

"Coffee's fine," she told him. "Thanks," she added, realizing that she was in fact very hungry and that, oddly, she felt better. Not good — that would take more time — but better. She had slept in a safe space and she had cried for the first time in months, and somehow she was not ashamed of the fact.

For a while all they did was eat, demolishing bacon and eggs and mushrooms and then toast and marmalade and then making more toast and, having run out of marmalade, eaten that with jam.

"I've not eaten that much in months." She felt bloated now, knew that she'd overdone it, but she didn't care, didn't give a damn. The food tasted good. How long would this sense of euphoria last? she wondered. How long before she crashed again? And then she stopped wondering and decided she would just enjoy it while it lasted.

They took the trays back to the kitchen, washed up together and then she stood in the doorway wondering whether she should leave. Instead she asked, "If you hadn't become a policeman what would you have done?"

He smiled back, and a warm laugh followed. "I would probably have followed my dad into the family business and we'd be on opposite sides of the law now. As it is, I think knowing my dad and his cronies has given me an insight, shall we say. And can I also say, that's both of us with an unusual insight, so let's put it to good use shall we?"

She nodded and then found herself asking, "Can I crash on your sofa again tonight?"

She watched his face closely but he didn't seem surprised. "If you give me a hand to clear out the box room, you can sleep in there. There's a futon thing I got for when I occasionally have friends staying over, but the room's a mess. It gets used as a dumping ground." He shrugged. "All the stuff I don't want to deal with."

"Thank you," she said. "But the Perrins will know where I am."

"Probably, same as they know where we work, where we shop, which pub I like to go to — we can't stop the Perrins knowing things. Since Kyle Sykes got in here and shot me, the security has been beefed up. The CCTV and key codes on the front door are monitored, there's a key code to get on to this landing, my door is reinforced and you've seen the deadbolts. More than that I cannot do."

She nodded. Out on the street, in the office, going through her day she could only protect herself so far, but if she could sleep safe that would be a major help. "Thank you," she said, conscious that it wasn't enough. But what more could she say? He smiled at her and she figured that for him, that would do.

CHAPTER 21

"No doubt you'll all have heard the news item involving the bogus social worker who took a child from a foster home two days ago. We now have confirmation of a link to our case."

Petra exchanged a look with Clarke, their conversation coming to mind.

"The foster parents were shown a picture of Joshua Banks and confirm that this was the child who stayed with them from the early hours of Friday morning and was taken from their home on the Saturday. We all know the end of that story. So, DI Clarke, you'll be heading over to speak to the foster family and the local force involved in the abduction. The parents and their little girl are currently staying with family. The mother has worked with a police artist to create an image of this bogus social worker." He paused as copies were handed out to the team. Petra saw Clarke tense.

"This woman, she looks like the bogus DI Mace," he said.

"In which case I'll be having another talk to Superintendent Deans," Tucker said.

Twenty minutes later Clarke had left, and Petra slipped outside to call Lauren.

"He's got to be somewhere local," Petra told her. "Have you thought of anywhere, however unlikely, that he might have holed up? Lauren, I know I'm asking a lot but there's still—"

"A kid missing. You think I don't know that? Look, I've been thinking. There are places I remember from when I was little, but I couldn't tell you addresses or anything like that. Do you have an email I can send something to? Best I can do is describe what I remember and see if you can make any sense of it. Sorry, but that's all I've got. I've already told you everything I know for sure and everything I could guess about."

Petra sighed. She knew Lauren was right. The girl had provided so much intelligence already, but she couldn't help but hope that she might have remembered something more. Something truly significant. She gave Lauren her email address and thanked her. At least the girl was trying.

"I'll be sending from a one-time-use address" Lauren warned her. "You won't be able to reply. And Petra, this is the third time you've called me from the same number."

"I know, I'm sorry." It had just been hard to get to the shops for food, never mind spare SIM cards.

She returned to her little office, a nagging worry at the back of her mind that she was taking too many risks, and not just with her own welfare.

Denise was already there, as was Sophie Hopkins. "So, box number 523," she said. "Well, that's what it feels like, anyway."

Petra nodded. Even with DC Sophie Hopkins helping they were drowning in the sheer volume of probably irrelevant information. "We need some focus," she said.

"I'm all for that."

"Right, well the boss says that Patricia Copeland's brother and his family haven't shown up in Seattle. So, Sophie, you work your way through her address book and any other contact books that have been logged into evidence. Denise, you start by hassling the forensic accounting bods, see what they've turned up. We need to know if anything has changed in the past, say, three months, because that's when we're guessing Sykes might have come back on the scene."

"Why are we guessing that?" Sophie asked.

"Because that's when he shot Sammy Marvin dead. It's the best guess we've got. I'll go back to the previous abductions, see what we've missed."

"What makes you think we've missed anything?"

"Because when we first looked through the folders it was with the assumption that Patricia Copeland was trying to gather information that might help the families, or maybe even assist in any future investigation. But think about that in light of what we know about her now. She was closely involved in three separate negotiations. What if she was closely involved in more than that? What if she gathered all this intel for her own purposes?"

"Then why give it to DI Clarke?"

"Maybe as a smokescreen. Maybe to misdirect while she took herself far away? Maybe because with Sykes in play she was genuinely scared. But if we re-examine the evidence from a different angle, we might get a different viewpoint. Frankly, we've got to start somewhere. There's another thing we should be looking at now we've got a better handle on the different business interests of those involved. We know, for instance, that Kyle Sykes had a controlling share of the parent company for Tyburn Recruitment. Businesses equal property. I mean, they've got to have somewhere to operate from."

"And you think we might have missed somewhere that he could be hiding out." Denise nodded. "Can you generate a list and we'll divvy it up between us, see if we come up with any empty properties."

Petra breathed a sigh. It would take a bit of sleight of hand to slip the property details Lauren had promised her into the mix, but it was possible. Chances were they'd come to nothing anyway, she told herself.

She looked around at the landscape of boxes and evidence bags and then at the other two women.

"Good luck to us," Denise said.

* * *

Ninety minutes after he had left base, Clarke was sitting in an untidy but comfortable sitting room with a family liaison officer from the local force, a senior social worker called Mrs Jonas and a very distressed young couple, Clara and Pete Etheredge. This was Clara's sister's house, and the sister, plus her two children and her niece, Zara, were currently in the kitchen trying to stay quiet and out of the way.

"I saw the picture on the news," Clara said, "of the little boy who was found dead. It was Joshua. It was the little boy taken from my house."

"It wasn't your fault," Clarke said softly. "There was nothing more you could have done."

"But he was in my house! We were meant to be protecting him. I knew there was something wrong. That's why I went to get my phone to call Mrs Jonas. I knew something was off and I only left them for a moment while I went through to the kitchen to get my phone. But that was enough. I heard the door open and we both ran through into the hall, but it was too late. She just shoved him in the car and took off and I couldn't get to him in time."

Her husband put an arm around her shoulders. Clarke could see that he was as devastated as his wife. "We have fingerprints from the clipboard and the forms she was carrying and from the door handle. We have your description and the artist's impression you helped to create. That's so much more than we had before," Clarke told her, but he could see his words were barely getting through. "What would really help the investigation is if I could understand . . ." He paused. He had been going to ask, *how this could happen*, but that sounded so accusatory. ". . . the mechanics of it," he said. "How this woman got hold of the correct forms. How she knew enough to sound at least convincing."

Clara turned an anguished look in his direction. "I should have known." She broke down and fled the room in tears. With a murmur of apology, her husband followed.

"I'm sorry," Clarke told Mrs Jonas. "I've no wish to cause them more pain."

"Nothing you can do about that," Mrs Jonas told him bluntly. "Now, the mechanics, as you call them. I've already given that a good deal of thought. The forms themselves could be mocked up if someone could get hold of an original, and I don't imagine that's going to be impossible. Anyone working in fostering or adoption, a court official, a parent or foster parent, or anyone known to any of those groups or individuals could *theoretically* get access. Most of our confidential material is online and access is difficult, but if a child is removed because of an emergency then sometimes the paperwork is put together in something of a hurry."

"And the paperwork in this case, was it convincing?"

"It would not have stood up to close scrutiny. Clara is experienced enough to have noticed that something was not quite right, even if she couldn't be sure what it was, and she's dealt with enough emergency placements that she knows what the process should look like, both in terms of paperwork and the individuals she deals with. As she told you, her instinct was that something was off — unfortunately she wasn't able to prevent what happened. She'll have to live with that, and you or I or anyone else telling her there was nothing she could have done will bring no comfort, because there *is* none. Clara and Pete are brilliant foster carers, excellent parents." She shrugged helplessly. "I can help you to understand the process and I'll do all and anything I can to help with the investigation, but can I suggest—"

"That I leave now," Clarke nodded. He gathered his things together and made for the door. As he passed the kitchen he could hear weeping and a woman's voice trying to offer comfort. It reminded him, painfully, of the Banks family and the heartrending sobs of Joshua's mother.

Clarke sat in his car, not sure what he was waiting for but not quite ready to make the return journey. He felt drained, exhausted, helpless, and not sure what he could do to remedy that. Mrs Jonas left the house and came over to his car. Clarke wound the window down. "This is my personal number," she said, "and my office number and my deputy

June's number, in case you can't get hold of me. I'm going to ask her to send over a copy of our normal protocols so you can see how things are usually done, and I'll also try to collate my thoughts on the matter. You might get something useful. I don't know if it will help, but frankly I'm at a loss as to what else to do."

"The fallout from this—"

"Will be horrendous. As it should be, though the wrong people will pay the heaviest price, even if you manage to catch those responsible. A child has already paid the heaviest price of all."

Clarke nodded. He watched her walk away and get into her car and knew that what he was feeling was at least shared. Not that the knowledge made anything better.

"Fuck," Clarke said aloud. "Fuck." He banged both hands so hard on the steering wheel that his palms hurt. He drove away, hating himself for the relief he felt that he didn't have to comfort anyone in the house he had just left, knowing that even attempting that would be beyond him.

CHAPTER 22

The small sitting room was dark but there was still brightness in the sky, so Molly left the lights off and she and Lauren sat in companionable twilight. Molly poured them both a glass of sloe gin, homemade the previous winter. She had always thought of it as a winter drink, one for cosy evenings and firelight, but tonight, despite the day having been warm, she felt chilled to the bone. Looking at Lauren, the girl's face pinched and pale, she guessed Lauren felt the same. Molly always left soft blankets on the sofa, and Lauren reached out now and pulled what had become her favourite, the blue-and-white check, over her lap. She wrapped her cardigan tight across her chest, pulling the sleeves down to partly cover her hands, a habit Molly had noticed she had when she felt tired or stressed. It was a *tell*, Molly thought. An external signal that betrayed what the girl was feeling. It was something she should advise against. Then she caught the thought — this was just a teenager, an ordinary young woman who might have been through extraordinary circumstances but was at heart just a seventeen-year-old girl who, with luck, would go on her way and live a normal life. Molly wasn't used to preparing people to live normal lives.

"Did you send those other details to Petra?" she asked.

Lauren nodded. "There were three other places I remembered from when I was a kid and mum used to take me to visit friends. I've told her all I can remember, but it was a long time ago. After mum died . . . after she was killed, I never saw any of those people again and I never visited the houses." She shrugged. "I think that's it, now. I really don't know anything more."

"You've done all you can," Molly told her. "For now, at least."

"Do you think that little girl is dead?" Lauren asked.

Molly wondered if she should prevaricate. Is that what normal people did? She sighed. When were either she or this young woman normal people? Lauren might eventually manage to regain some semblance of the ordinary, but for now circumstances had militated against that. The girl needed and expected honesty. "I think it's likely," she said sadly. "But I also believe that you should never give up hope until hope is provably gone."

Lauren nodded, taking that in. "How many people have you helped, Molly? How many lives have you saved?"

Molly looked over at her young friend and then refreshed both of their glasses. This, she felt, was definitely not a night for staying sober. She reminded herself that Lauren was only seventeen and then decided she was far older than that in experience, so what the hell.

"Oh, I don't know. More than a few, I suppose."

"A lot more than a few."

Molly smiled at Lauren and laid her head back against the wing of her chair. "You don't count the lives saved. You just recall the lives lost. Especially as you grow older and your own mortality becomes more of a pressing concern."

"So, how did it start?"

Molly got up and took a photograph from the wall. It was one she had seen Lauren examining many times. It was faded and creased and it depicted a young Molly, newly married, all blond curls and hopeful expression, and her husband, his dark hair slicked back and a broad smile on his face.

Gently, Molly touched his smile. The third person in the picture was also young and also smiling. His black skin had faded to grey as the picture had washed out from too much exposure to the light, from time, from touch, from being carried and creased. From tears.

"I watched him die," Molly said. "He was a friend. He believed so strongly in the future of his country. Our first posting was to what had been the Belgian Congo, to Leopoldville. The colonial powers had just pulled out and the real fight for the future had just begun. The power grab. The conflict between rival interests within the country being fed by others from outside who could just see the opportunity for making money."

She pursed her lips. "The country stood on the verge of civil war, but you know, my dear, what I remember most was the sense of excitement. Of possibility. Of friendships and courage and . . . Oh, I'm getting old and maudlin, aren't I?" She took another sip of her drink. "And this isn't helping, I suppose."

It was Lauren who now reached forward to refresh her glass.

"He was a friend. I know what it's like to see a friend die. You know that, Molly."

"Yes, I suppose you do. And like your Harry, he died in part to protect me because he knew that in protecting me he might just manage to save his son's life. He lied, refused to tell them where I was hiding or that he even knew me. I could do nothing, Lauren. Had I come out of hiding I would have died too, but more than that, his little boy was with me and I'd promised to keep him safe. I learned that day that you do not make promises lightly."

She paused, sipped more of her drink, continued. "The fact that I was white and British might *just* have saved me. Knowing the consequences of killing someone like me might just have caused them to pause, but frankly, at the time I don't think that even crossed my mind. There was the boy to take care of. I had to protect the child. I was only a few years older than you are now and I was inexperienced and I was scared out of my wits. But I did know that nothing could have saved my friend — they had decided that he was a traitor because he'd been working with us as an interpreter. He was going to die, and so I had a choice. Stay in my hiding place and make sure his sacrifice was worth something or die with my friend and know that they would have no hesitation in killing his child as well. Once people become part of a mob they lose all sense of self, of decency, of reason. And believe me, my dear, it doesn't matter who they are or were or what background or ethnicity or religion. Once people surrender their own will to that of the mob, they lose themselves. Irrevocably."

She remembered so vividly, hiding in the empty shop, certain that she was only putting off the inevitable, that they would finish with him and come looking anyway. She could see young Lauren's thoughts running along the same lines. Molly knew how she had crouched in the dark and heard Harry's cries as her father and his men had torn him apart.

"I escaped, with his son. But I swore I'd never stand by and watch anything like that happen ever again, not while I still had breath in my body or resources I could use to make that change. My friend died for his little boy but also for me, both as protector of his child and as his friend. Just like Harry died for you and like all the men and women down the years who have made just the same decision. The same sacrifice. These are debts that can never be paid, my dear. I suppose I've just spent my lifetime trying."

"What was his name?"

"Adis. His son was named after him. He grew up to be a fine young man." *Before he too died needlessly*, she thought. But that was a story for another time.

Molly leaned forward once again and brimmed both their glasses, even though Lauren had barely taken more than a sip from hers. She raised her glass in a salute to the dead. To the living. To the people who had filled her life with so much joy and so much sorrow. But mostly, "To the lost ones," Molly said. "May they find their way back home."

CHAPTER 23

The same evening as Molly and Lauren spoke of their dead, Paul Benson was watching the sea.

When he had first taken the decision to leave, he had driven aimlessly. He had found himself heading north, for no better reason than that was the direction the motorway was heading. Later he had gone off on to A and then B roads, wandering the countryside, and as though magnetically drawn there found himself not far from the cottage where Harry and Lauren had hidden. Parking his car on the verge, he walked up the track, feeling the air freshen as he reached the beach and stood looking out at the cold greyness of the North Sea. There were some things that remained consistent, he thought. That the sea on this coast would be freezing even in summer was one of them.

He turned to face the cottage and then walked steadily towards it. There were a few people on the beach this evening, the sun not yet fully gone down. People walking dogs and a woman and two kids flying a kite. No one seemed to take any notice of him. Rags of crime scene tape clung to posts and hedges, a reminder of what had happened a little over six months before, and he was surprised to see that someone was in the cottage, standing in the kitchen washing the dishes as though this was just an ordinary place where people did ordinary things and nothing dreadful had ever taken place. He found himself wondering how long it had taken to wash the blood from the floor and walls and even the ceiling. He was not disturbed by what he had done or what Kyle Sykes had done that night or what he himself had done to the policeman, Frankland, a stubborn bastard if ever there was one. Paul Benson did not imagine *he* could have stood up against such pain, and he could not really comprehend why Frankland had suffered as he had. Or Harry Prentice, for that matter. And for what? For some stupid girl who couldn't do what she was told, or in Frankland's case a woman who had no right to be doing what she was doing. Who the hell sent a woman undercover? He'd not had much respect for the police, not even when he was a kid, but the idea that they could send a female UCO into the Perrin organization completely eradicated what little had been ingrained through social habit.

Though maybe he now did have an inkling. Maybe that was why he had walked. Paul knew he was a man who did not fit into society, and he had found his place with Gus Perrin, or so he thought. So when his boss had told him he was to spend time with Kyle Sykes he had accepted this as part of the job. But everybody, he figured, had lines they couldn't cross, and he realized and recognized that those lines had no logic to them. When Sykes had killed that kid he had crossed a line that Paul did not even know he respected — overstepped a boundary Paul did not even know he had set. Gus hadn't understood that.

The woman in the kitchen looked up and saw him. She frowned and Paul began to move away, realizing how threatening he must seem, a big man watching her from the twilight. It was a thought that usually pleased him, but this was not the time or the place for it. A man came out of the cottage and asked politely and, Paul realized, with an edge of anxiety, "Can I help you?"

"No, mate, I was just walking. I've driven a long way and I needed to stretch my legs." He turned and strolled away, aware that the man was scrutinizing him carefully. He should not have come here, he thought, and was not certain why he had. He had just followed the road and it had led him back. He ambled back to his car, and by the time he reached it he had almost made up his mind. An hour later he had found a small hotel on the edge of the motorway services and checked in. His phone had been switched off since he had left Gus Perrin's house — and his employ. Gus would be after his blood by now and Kyle Sykes prepared to tear him to pieces, no doubt, because that was what Sykes did. He switched the phone on now, listening and watching as the missed calls and missed texts pinged and flashed into life. He deleted them without reading, searched online for a number and then made one call. Then he dropped the phone to the floor and stamped on it hard, watching with satisfaction as the screen and the plastic and the battery all popped in different directions. Then he ground it under his heel until he was satisfied it was dead before scooping up the remnants and dropping them into the bin. Then he lay down and went to sleep. His last thought was that whatever was going to happen would happen, there was nothing else he could do about it and that he wasn't sure he cared anyway.

* * *

Petra felt as though she had only just fallen asleep when she was woken by Clarke knocking on the door. The urgency was unmistakable. She sprang out of bed, pulling on her dressing gown and flinging the door wide. "What's up?"

"We've got a lead on Sykes and also a possible sighting of Paul Benson. The couple who own the cottage where Lauren and Harry were holed up reported someone behaving oddly. They've got used to crime tourists over the past few months. They bought the place cheap this spring, apparently, and now they live there full-time. They reported a man matching Benson's description hanging around outside. The local police are taking a mugshot over this morning."

"Not somewhere I'd want to live. But what the hell was he doing there? If it was him. And what's this about Sykes?"

"Anonymous phone call came in through Crimestoppers a few hours ago. It took a while to be routed through to the right team. But a man called and gave them a location. An old farm out on the Lowndon road. A surveillance team confirm the place is occupied."

"Wow. You think?"

"Gotta hope. Get dressed. They're assembling the team. Firearms will go in first, but Tucker wants us both on scene."

"Good." She ducked back into the little box room and grabbed some clothes. The previous evening she had helped Clarke tidy it enough for the futon to be rolled out and for her to arrange her few possessions. Oddly it already felt like her space, despite the remnants of Clarke's stuff stacked against one wall. Glancing at her watch, she saw that it was 3 a.m. Her heart was thumping and she realized it was not just adrenalin but shock — the farm was one of the locations Lauren had mentioned in the email she had sent last evening. The note in the email said she used to stay there with some friends of her mother's, but the place had been abandoned for years, as far as she knew.

Minutes later they were in Clarke's car and heading towards police headquarters.

* * *

The briefing was already underway when they arrived, DCI Tucker sharing the honours with the chief firearms officer.

Petra studied the photographs of the farm that she'd been handed on entry. A main building, two barns and a collection of outbuildings that looked semi-derelict. Whoever had taken the pictures had used an infrared camera and the image was shades of grey and silver green. *Ghostlike*, she thought, *otherworldly*. More disturbing were the warm bodies showing in the picture. At least two men on guard and who knew how many more in the house.

"The team sent out to the house snatched the photographs and did what obs they could, but they were in no position to be able to hang around. They identified two men patrolling the perimeter and a third crossed from the farmhouse to this building here. It looks like a barn. He went inside and they didn't see him come out again in the few minutes they were there. A light came on briefly in an upper window, which indicates at least one other person in the house. Make no mistake, we are regarding everyone on scene as armed and dangerous. Let the firearms team do their stuff. Everyone else hangs back until they've secured the area."

A murmur of anticipation drifted through the room. She glanced around, noting the tension on the faces. Denise sidled up to her. "Let's hope this is it," she said.

"You coming out with us?"

Denise shook her head. "Sophie and I are holding the fort here, coordinating as the bodies are brought in. Live ones, that is," she grinned. "Tucker's going out with you, Clarke and a couple of others, but this has got to be their show." She nodded towards the head of firearms. "This is Kyle Sykes. No one's taking any chances."

"And what if the kid's there?" Petra fretted.

Denise gripped her arm sympathetically, then was called away. A moment later they were moving out and Petra was once more in Clarke's car and following the small convoy out on to the main road out of town. The heavy armoured vest she wore over her fleece jacket cut into her thighs. She tried to find the pressure reassuring, but she knew Sykes's men were trained to go for head shots, not centre of mass. She tried to remember how she knew that and decided that Gus Perrin must have mentioned it. Just one more bit of ragtag information she had inherited from her time undercover.

"What if he spotted the surveillance team?" Petra said.

"They've pulled back, but they're still in the area. I think they'd know if there was any movement at the house. The annoyance is it took so long for the initial intel to get through to us."

She glanced at her watch. It seemed as though hours had passed but it was actually just after four, though already there was a lightness in the sky. Absently she wondered when sunrise was at this time of year. A few minutes later Clarke pulled up behind Tucker's car. They were to go the rest of the way on foot. Only the armed response units would drive on to the site and they would go in fast and hard. She recalled the map they had been shown: a gated road led across the fields from the back of the farm, though the main entrance was off this road, and the house was set back perhaps a hundred yards. There was a ditch and hedge, what had been a proper gateway but now was just an opening between rotten posts. The surveillance team, crouching in a thankfully dry ditch, had found a small gap in the hedge through which they had been able to take their photographs and their video, such as it was. Though the hedges were high enough to prevent the house from being overlooked from the roadside and gave some protection to those approaching from the road, once the teams had gone through the gateway and into the yard there was no cover. The barn and the other outbuildings stretched out on either side of the house making the yard a potential killing zone. There had been discussion about sending a second team to the rear of the house via the gated road, but that would slow everything down. A vehicle stopping and starting to open the three gates between the house and the back road would be heard and probably observed. So no, she understood, it all had to be done from this one point, but it worried her immensely.

Moments later the time for worrying or speculating was over. The armoured vehicle roared in through the gateway. And then the shooting started from inside the house.

"Fuck!" Clarke said.

They knew we were coming, Petra thought.

They had accompanied Tucker as he moved forward and were now close to the farmyard entrance. Tucker dived down into the ditch behind the hedge and Petra and Clarke followed him, Clarke just behind him furthest away from the gateway. Petra was on the other side, a position that afforded her a slightly better view of what was happening in the yard, if she lifted her head and peered through the branches at the base of the hedge. The lights from the armoured car lit the scene, so bright it almost looked monochrome. The sky may have begun to lighten but dawn was still some way off, and the contrast caused by the fierce artificial lights made it feel even darker around them, as they crouched low. Tucker was calling in backup — a second team had been put on standby just in case. It should only be minutes away. Petra was listening to the gunshots and trying to figure out how many men might be holed up inside the house. Four, maybe five. She turned her head this way and that, and decided there were three men in the house and possibly two in the barn. She didn't think there were any shots coming from the other outbuildings. Lifting her head above the edge of the ditch she could see two other members of the team on the opposite side of the road, scrambling through a farm gate and into the ploughed field beyond. *Sensible*, she thought. There wasn't a lot they could do to help, so best get out of the way.

A stray bullet thudded into the bank just beside Tucker's head and he swore vehemently. Then, urging Clarke ahead of him, he began to crawl back along the ditch towards where they had left their cars. Petra lifted her head and peered once again through the thicket of twigs and leaves. The firefight seemed to have lasted for ever, but she guessed it could only have been minutes. There was automatic gunfire now, coming from the house. She could hear the commander urging his team to pull back. She guessed they were going to use the armoured car as a weapon to drive straight into the barn or the house. She thought she could see a body on the ground, but her view was obstructed and she wasn't certain. She turned, preparing to follow Clarke and Tucker, when an almighty explosion shook the ground and laid her flat on her back in the ditch, legs in the air and arms flailing. Her ears were ringing, but dimly she thought she could hear Clarke shouting something. Smoke and dirt filled the air around her. Suddenly she felt a hand on her ankle dragging her along the bottom of the ditch, and as she tried to struggle free, something hit her in the face. She identified it as a fist just before she passed out.

CHAPTER 24

Clarke and Tucker had been knocked off their feet by the explosion. Scrambling upright, they made it back to the cars, coughing and choking on the dust. "What the fuck was that?" Tucker demanded.

He was back on the radio again, demanding to know when the backup would arrive, trying to contact the firearms commander to find out what was going on.

"Safe to say they were expecting us," Clarke said bitterly. "Where the hell is Petra?"

"She was right behind me. Then the world exploded."

Clarke moved to go back the way they had come. Tucker grabbed his arm and then, just as abruptly, let go. "Just keep your head down."

State the bleeding obvious, Clarke thought. He dropped down into the ditch and crawled back the way they had come, reached the point where they had all been together, then went on towards the gateway. Uprooted hedge now half-filled the ditch, blocking his way and forcing him to climb back on to the verge, but there was no sign of Petra. The empty space where the hedge had been now gave him a clear view of the yard. People were struggling to their feet, or rushing for cover or, more disturbingly, lying prone and unmoving. The sound of vehicles and sirens alerted him to the fact that the second team had arrived, and he thought he heard the sound of a car engine receding into the distance, somewhere at the back of the house. Staying low but looking past where the hedge had once been, he peered into the yard and at the house beyond, the whole illuminated by the lights of the police vehicles. No sign of Petra. In the open yard at the front bodies lay — it looked like two armed police officers and two others. Not just prone figures, he thought, but almost certainly dead. The commander was now shouting "down on the ground, down on the ground", and Clarke realized they must have made an arrest.

The gunfire had ceased, and Clarke was suddenly aware that he could hear a child crying. She was here! She was alive! It had to be her, Deans's granddaughter. His first instinct was to rush across the yard to try and find her, but the place was full of armed police who probably wouldn't have much patience with that plan.

The second team sped past him and skidded in through the gateway. He followed them in, hands raised and shouting his name and rank. The scene was a war zone. There was a large pit in front of the house and an impressive-looking crack running the length of the front wall. Debris had been spread in all directions — substantial rocks, timber, bales of straw. Still no sign of Petra. One of the armed officers spotted him. "Out!" he shouted. "Just get the fuck out of the way."

"One of our team is missing," Clarke told him.

"You see them here? Out and stay down! There may still be snipers in the house."

Clarke retreated hastily. So where the hell was she? Staying low, he began to retrace his path alongside the ditch, wondering if she might have crossed the road in the confusion and scrambled into the ploughed field with the rest of the unarmed team. The air had cleared a little now and he was about to cross the lane when on the bank, half buried in mud and roots and leaves, beside what was left of the hedge, he saw something. He fought his way back into the branch-filled ditch. A single trainer, laces still tied. He was sure it was hers. He reached out to touch it and then drew back. Maybe she hadn't just lost the shoe, maybe someone had pulled it off her foot, and whoever that someone was might have left fingerprints or DNA. He hauled himself out of the ditch and stood just staring at the trainer for a moment, quite forgetting the instruction to keep his head down. This little area was now a crime scene of a different kind. There was a missing officer.

* * *

Petra woke in a confined space. Her hands were bound behind her back, a rag that smelt like shoe polish had been tied around her mouth and another across her eyes. The sound of a car engine, the rocking and bumping of the vehicle, told her that she had been crammed into the boot of a car.

Her first emotion was one of panic. She was trapped and she was tied up. She knew at once it must have been Sykes and his people who had her, and she knew what Sykes did to those who crossed him. She forced herself to calm down. Tried to get a hold on her breathing, was aware that she was now gasping for air and in danger of passing out again as she hyperventilated. She forced herself to slow her breathing, to try and concentrate on small, concrete things. Was she hurt? She didn't think so. Apart from where some bastard had thumped her. As though the memory brought it on, pain flared in her head and jaw. She moved her head, neck and jaw experimentally, as much as she could, given her bonds and her cramped position, and decided with relief that nothing was actually broken. Slowly and methodically she mentally examined the rest of herself. She seemed to be missing a shoe, and her entire body felt as though it had been beaten up. No, she thought, dragged along the ground, though the flak jacket she was still wearing, which was now digging uncomfortably into her neck and shoulders, had probably saved her from the worst of that. She was conscious that objects in her zipped fleece pockets now jabbed painfully into her hip. Her keys, her phone . . . and the other phone was in her other pocket. She had automatically grabbed it from her coat just before she left Clarke's flat. *Shit.*

The car jerked and bounced and her head made painful contact with the boot lid.

Momentarily dazed, she fought once more to think clearly. Just what had happened?

She could recall the explosion, the sudden clap of noise followed by a roar, followed by falling debris and choking dust, and then she remembered someone grabbing her ankle and pulling hard. She had kicked out hard with her other foot — or at least she thought she had. The sock on the jaw had put paid to everything, so maybe she'd just intended to.

Clarke would know by now that she was missing. Would guess what had happened. Wouldn't he? Someone might have seen her being dragged to the car. Her assailant must have got her across the farmyard somehow or other. She could recall no vehicles being parked in front. So did that mean that they had escaped across the fields and the gated lane? Reason told her they must have done. In the chaos after the explosion just about anything could have happened before her colleagues had time to regroup. They'd have been afraid of other explosive devices, of booby traps or incendiaries or God knows what.

No one would have been hurrying after her abductors, that was certain. They would, she realized with a sinking heart, have been far too busy dealing with whatever casualties they had sustained and with trying to figure out what the hell had happened.

Another bump, this one not so hard, the sound of gravel beneath tyres. The car stopped and there were voices. Then the boot was opened and Petra was pulled out, slung across a broad shoulder and carried inside a building. A door was opened and she was dropped to the floor, then the door closed and she was left alone.

CHAPTER 25

Everything seemed to move in slow motion for Clarke. He had returned to Tucker to report that Petra was now definitely missing. He emphasized that he'd heard a child crying, that the child was somewhere in the building. He suddenly realized how angry he sounded — he was shouting at his commanding officer — and how helpless he felt.

"We'll find her." Tucker laid a hand on his arm and forced him to turn around and take notice. "We will find her. Now let's see if there's anything useful we can do to sort this mess out." He had led the way along the road and back to the farm entrance, the other two of their team coming across to join them. An armed officer stopped them at the perimeter.

"This scene is not yet secure," she said. "We think the kid is in that building over there, but we're not allowing anybody in until we're sure there are no IEDs or booby traps."

"One of my officers is missing. We believe the OCG have taken her."

The woman looked concerned but would still not allow them through the perimeter. "Two vehicles were seen heading across the fields, down that track. They smashed through the gates and got away under cover of the explosion and the chaos afterwards. That's all we know. I'll get my commanding officer to come to you when he's got a minute. As you can see, we've got our hands full right now, so it might be best if you just keep out of the way."

Fuming, they retreated to where they had parked their cars and Tucker sent the rest of the team back to base, deciding just he and Clarke would remain. Though there was little they could usefully do, neither could bear to leave. Just after 6 a.m., a loud bang shook the ground beneath their feet. Tucker was on his radio instantly and was told that it was a controlled explosion but that they could now get into the outbuilding where the child was held.

"Poor little bugger must be terrified out of her mind," Tucker said. "Come on."

This time they were allowed through the perimeter, and Clarke noticed that most of the attention now seemed to be focused on the house and the barn. An officer came out of the other outbuilding carrying a small child, who was howling at the top of her lungs. Paramedics took her and sat her in the back of the remaining ambulance.

Clarke went over. "How's she doing?"

"She doesn't seem hurt, but she's cold and hungry, and I expect she really wants her mum."

Clarke closed his eyes and breathed a sigh of relief. At least one thing had gone right that day.

CHAPTER 26

Two men had come into the room. They had unbound her hands long enough to remove her stab vest, empty the pockets of her fleece and run the hands none too gently over the rest of her. Then her wrists were bound with a broad zip tie, which was pulled tight enough to bite into the skin. One of them gave her a shove and she fell heavily to the floor. The door closed once more and she heard the lock click.

Petra struggled to sit up and then to bend her face down towards her shoulder, trying to rub the gag or the blindfold or both free. Through sheer persistence she managed to move the blindfold enough so that she could see slightly underneath it, enough to figure out where the wall was. Grateful that she still had the use of her feet (obviously they didn't think she could run off anywhere), she hobbled awkwardly and stiffly over to the wall and rubbed her face against a surface that felt like woodchip, pulling the blindfold free. She looked around. She was in a small room with no furniture apart from one chair and a wooden stool set beside the window. She crossed to the window and managed to poke the curtains aside enough to see through. Outside the sun had risen and it was bright. She was looking on to an overgrown garden surrounded by a high hedge with trees beyond. So where the hell was she? There must be a road close by because they had driven here. She could see just a glimpse of gravel and remembered there'd been a crunch under the wheels and then under the feet of the man who had carried her in. So they had to be close to a road, there had to be traffic, so if she could just get out of the house there was a chance she could find someone who could summon help. A sound outside the door caused her to turn, but no one came in. She watched the door nervously for a few minutes, reminded all too abruptly of another angle to her current predicament. Kyle Sykes — and it had to be him, didn't it? — now had possession not just of her own mobile, and all the numbers it contained, but also her unregistered phone that contained only the number she used to reach Lauren. She was glad that she had no idea where Lauren was, so no matter what Sykes did to her she couldn't tell. She couldn't deliver that final betrayal.

She turned back to examine the window. Could she get it open? At first glance it looked as though it had been painted closed, layers and years of gloss badly applied to the old sash frame. A second look told her that the wood was rotten and the glass only loosely fitted in the frame. It could be broken if she had the time and the means, but it would make a hell of a noise.

Turning her back she leaned against the window, feeling for the catch and trying to raise the sash. To her surprise it budged, just a little. Not having anything else to do with her time, and needing something to occupy her mind before she gave into complete despair, she began to work the catch up and down the millimetre or so that it would go, rocking the frame backwards and forwards, trying all she could just to get the window moving.

She lifted herself up on to her toes, sat on the narrow windowsill and leaned back against the frame. It moved again, just a little. She pressed harder against the glass, feeling the frame give. Then a sound at the door had her moving again, and when the door opened she was standing in the middle of the room.

Two men entered, grabbed her arms and marched her out and into a second room on the other side of the hall. Sykes sat there, enthroned in an ageing armchair, a third man standing beside him. The man looked vaguely familiar and she guessed that he was one of Sykes's regular crew, but she didn't recognize the other two at all. Sykes had her mobile phones, one in each hand, and seemed to be weighing them thoughtfully.

"So what do we have here?" Sykes said. "A second phone. What would a nice law-abiding police officer be doing with a disposable phone?"

Petra held his gaze, refusing to seem intimidated, though her insides felt like jelly and her legs as though they could no longer support her weight. He set the second mobile aside and focused on her work phone.

"Unlock it," Sykes demanded.

She felt one of the men cut the binding around her wrists. Blood returned, fierce and painful, and she almost dropped the phone now thrust into her hands.

"I said, unlock it," Sykes repeated, and somehow she managed to input the code.

The phone was given back to him. Then her hands were pulled behind her and her wrists bound once more. Blood still throbbed in her hands, pain spreading up her arms.

She watched as Sykes skimmed through the contacts. "I see an old friend," Sykes said. "Someone with whom I have unfinished business."

She stood there, helpless, as he called Clarke, a feeling of hope surging inside her that Clarke would know at least what had happened to her, countered by a feeling of despair that it would make no difference whatsoever. Her colleague wouldn't even know where to start looking — this house could be anywhere. Sykes was out for revenge, so whatever he did now would put Clarke in even more danger. He held all the cards here.

Clarke must've answered quickly because Sykes smiled. "Ah, Inspector Clarke. I have a friend of yours here. This is just a courtesy call to let you know that at the moment she's alive and well. What might happen next of course . . . well, I leave that to your imagination."

He rang off then and switched off her phone, then picked up the other one.

"I'll speak to him again, when it suits me to do so," he told her. "Now, let's see what this is all about, shall we? Just the one number. Exclusive."

Petra closed her eyes. Things, she figured, were about as bad as they could get.

Sykes listened as the phone continued to ring and for one blissful moment she hoped that Lauren had decided that she didn't want to speak to Petra and would ignore the phone call. And then the call was answered.

"Hello," Lauren said. She sounded anxious, Petra thought. The look on Sykes's face was a picture of disbelief, shifting to realization and momentary anger and then, as he realized just what this meant, pure evil delight.

"Hello, Lauren," Sykes said. "I have a friend of yours here. I'm sure you can guess who it is."

* * *

Clarke stood by his car and stared at the phone. He tried to dial Petra's number but her phone was now switched off.

Tucker was watching him. "What?"

"That was Sykes, calling from Petra's phone. He's got her."

"How the hell?"

The firearms chief was calling to them and automatically they walked towards him, Clarke still stunned, not sure what to do next. Tucker was saying something, but Clarke could not take it in. They followed the armed officer upstairs in the farmhouse and into a room at the front. Dimly Clarke remembered the observers saying that a light had come on in the upper room when they had been watching.

"Fuck," Clarke said. The room was set up as a control centre, CCTV cameras fed into screens that showed the full 360 degrees of the house, as well as a couple of hundred yards either side of the entrance gates to the yard, out on to the road. Even as the observers were photographing them, Sykes's people must have been filming. They knew exactly what had been going on, and the only surprise was that they had not cleared out sooner. Or was that a surprise? Sykes would have enjoyed drawing them in. Losses had occurred on both sides: two of Sykes's men were dead, another three arrested, but two police officers had also been killed and another two severely injured. And the operational disruption was massive. The first armed response team, those caught up in the initial firefight, had been stood down and would not be able to resume duties until they had been debriefed and the investigation into their actions completed. All routine in the circumstances, but what was left of that team was now out of action and would be intent on analysing what had gone wrong, in licking their wounds and mourning their losses. The second team was still onsite but would have to be relieved and similarly debriefed. Additional bomb disposal experts had arrived, and the forensic team would move in as soon as the area was deemed safe enough. So much manpower tied up in one small place, and that was before you considered the consequences of the dead and injured. The damage Sykes had caused would take a while to recover from, Clarke thought, as he glanced down the road to the cordon, behind which the press corps, local TV and radio had already gathered. No doubt they would be joined by the nationals very soon. A police operation of this size was not going to go unnoticed, especially when there were gunshots and big bangs involved. This was not going to do anybody's reputation any good at all, and while Clarke wasn't particularly bothered about that on a personal level, he felt for those who had just been trying to do their job but whose judgement would now be called into question. The one saving grace was that the child was safe and well.

And how did the so-called DCI Mace fit into all this? Who was she? Dangerous, that's *what* she was, but identifying her was not going to be easy. Yes, Clarke was certain he would know her again, but was she actually a police officer, or was she simply acting the part? If so, then her knowledge of procedure indicated that she knew and understood enough to seem convincing at least in the short term. Though, he considered, he had not been in her company for very long and, already thrown by the strangeness of the circumstances, he had accepted who she was and what she was without too much question. If he had spent longer with her, would he have become suspicious? He honestly wasn't sure. Had she been at the farm?

"Any idea how many people were here?" he asked the officer who had shown them up to this room.

"No, but we're guessing that at least three escaped. Two are dead, and we have two in custody. A lot of personal possessions have been left behind, and there were eight bunks in all, one set aside in its own room and the others distributed around the place."

Clarke nodded. "Okay to open the window?"

He peered out, looking down towards the cordon at the end of the road. He caught a glimpse of someone he thought he recognized. Cameras were being raised, long lenses capturing him as he watched them. He withdrew his head. No real surprise that Jonathan Roan should be present. After all he worked for the local press, but something jangled in Clarke's head and he wondered how he could organize an informal chat with the man without compromising anything.

Tucker spoke his name and he realized from the tone that his boss must have been trying to get his attention. Tucker indicated one of the screens. The police technician was running one of the recordings. Clarke watched the explosion blossom from a few yards in front of the house, one camera blinking out and another feed cutting in. The blast came in low, spreading outwards rather than upwards and tore the hedge up by the roots. Whatever kind of blast it was, it was really pretty small, Clarke thought. It just felt much larger and more impressive. Yes, it had torn through the hedge, and yes, it had left a crack in the outer wall of the house, but it had merely rocked the armoured car and knocked people off their feet. It wasn't the blast that was deadly. That had been the gunshots. He caught sight of Petra, and a man diving down into the ditch and grabbing hold of her, though the veil of dust in the air obscured much of the action. And then an obviously unconscious Petra was slung across the man's shoulder as he raced towards the back of the house.

"Sykes must have spotted her," Tucker said, "and thought a chance of taking revenge was just too good to miss."

Clarke nodded grimly. It occurred to him that Sykes had just as much of a grudge against himself. If their positions had been different, if Petra had moved ahead of Tucker, he might have been the one that Sykes sent his man after. He liked to think that he would have had a better chance of fighting his way out of the situation, but the truth was, in the confusion of the blast and the dust and the speed of what happened, he would probably have been just as helpless.

"So where the hell has he taken her?" Clarke muttered.

"That we can't know, and we can't do any more here either, so we're going back to base."

Clarke felt that he should argue — Petra had been taken from here, the child had been kept here, Sykes had used this as his base of operations — but the sound of vehicles entering the yard alerted him to the fact that the forensic teams had just been allowed in — the explosives experts had decided the place was safe. And Tucker was right, there was nothing more they could do at the farmhouse, not immediately at any rate. They would just be in the way.

CHAPTER 27

With a bit of work Petra had managed to move the gag from her mouth, though her lip was now split and sore and the damp rag clung to her neck. She was back in the room where she had been dumped when they had first arrived at the house, Sykes evidently having no use for her at the present. She was surprised he had not questioned her about his daughter, about where she might be, about how he might get to her. She assumed that would be happening sooner or later and he would not be subtle. The fact she couldn't tell him anything wasn't going to be any measure of defence. She hoped to God that Lauren had now dumped the phone and broken all possible contact, and that whoever it was that was looking after her would have the wisdom and the knowledge to deal with the situation. It disturbed her greatly that the person Lauren seemed to be with was just an old woman. What the hell could someone like that do against the likes of Kyle Sykes?

There seemed to be more activity in the house now, and from time to time she heard Sykes shouting instructions, though she could not make out the words. Men marched up and down the corridor, ran up the stairs, slammed doors and generally made a noise, but no one came to look at her. They would get around to her sooner or later, she knew that, and in the meantime she knew they were just allowing her own fears and anxieties to do their work for them. After all, didn't the police do the same? Leaving a suspect to sweat it out for a while before interrogation? Though she had no doubt Sykes had a different kind of interrogation in mind.

Twice she had heard a telephone ring — two distinct ringtones, so she guessed two different mobiles. No one had offered her food or water, and she was thirsty but decided that was the least of her worries. She had gone back to work on the window, exploring it as best she could with her hands tied behind her back. She tried to break the zip tie but they had used thick, heavy-duty plastic that just cut into her wrists whenever she moved them. She wriggled her fingers to keep the circulation going, but the pins and needles were excruciating, and the bruised, aching feeling in her fingertips felt like she'd been out in the cold for too long and then come into a warm place.

She had realized quickly that working on the frame of the window was a nonstarter. Rotten it might be, but it was deeply recessed into the sash boxes, and though it might move and rattle it was too firmly ensconced to be of any use to her at all. The window itself was divided into small panes separated by flimsy-looking transoms and a lot of loose putty. She balanced on one leg, with a foot against the glass, and pushed experimentally, feeling the whole thing give. She'd have to be fast but it might be possible to get out that way.

Noise out in the hallway brought her away from the window and she stood uncertainly again in the centre of the room, wondering if this presaged her interrogation. To her surprise she heard voices and then what she assumed must be the front door open and then slam. A car drove away. She wasn't sure what time it was, but from the position of the sun — and the fact that her body was telling her it was close to lunchtime — she guessed it was something like late morning. So who had gone and who remained in the house?

Footsteps in the hall receded, and she crossed to the door and pressed her ear against the wood, listening, but could hear nothing useful. Whoever remained was not in the hall, and it sounded as though they might have gone upstairs. She knew there had been four men in the house: Sykes and three of his goons. Had someone simply gone to get food or other supplies? They had taken the car, but that in itself didn't mean anything. She'd never known Sykes's men to go anywhere on their own — like the Perrins they tended to work in pairs — so maybe two had gone and two stayed.

She retreated from the door and stood hesitantly in the centre of the room wondering what to do next. If she stayed, she would be killed, and her death was likely to be drawn out and painful. If she took the risk and tried to get out through the window, what were her chances of success?

She went back to the window and looked out. The drop wasn't bad. Undoubtedly she would get badly cut, but as long as she didn't slice through anything vital, that was survivable. She looked for cover, speculated about how to get out on to the road. The garden was fairly overgrown, but she wouldn't get far before they realized that she was gone. She could hardly break glass quietly and she couldn't free her hands.

Stay or go? Stay and be certain that she was going to be killed or take a chance and try to get out? There was no real option . . .

* * *

"Petra started collating a list of properties," Denise told Clark. "She'd been looking into business interests not just of Sykes but of anybody associated with him, both legitimate and otherwise. The farmhouse was on the list and there are a whole load of locations we were just working our way through. I just thought this morning, I'd see if the farmhouse was on the list, and there it was, so it's just possible that Sykes might have taken her somewhere else we already know about."

Clarke glanced down the list. The farmhouse was midway down the first page and there were two other pages after that.

Addresses. Petra had also been noted the name of the owners wherever possible, alongside any other information she could glean. He crossed to the OS map they had pinned to the wall, the location of the farmhouse circled. He traced the road they had taken to get there and then the gated road across the field, which was the way that Sykes and his men had got out.

"So we know they left this way and this track comes out on to the small road. What's it called? Coopers Lane. If they turned left, it leads to this village, Coopers Croft. It's worth canvassing the village, though we have no idea what cars they should be looking out for." He paused. "Actually, though, we might have. Sophie, see if you can find out if the cameras at the farmhouse recorded vehicles at the back."

"If they went right," Denise said, "then this eventually loops around and back into town, but there are three, no four, turn-offs before that. Thing is, will he have holed up locally or will he have just fucked off out of here?"

"We have to hope that he has gone to ground locally," Clarke said. He knew that there would be search teams going out, but if they could suggest a possible start point, narrow down the search parameters, that would help enormously. "So do we have any properties on the list that fall within this area?"

Eagerly they began their search, but it soon became obvious that there was nothing within a five-mile radius that Petra had recorded on the list.

Sophie returned and said that the tech teams would get back to them about the cars, but it might take a little while.

Clarke got a bigger map. A ten-mile radius. Nothing. They searched for an hour but came up dry.

"What about property owned by Patricia Copeland?" Sophie suggested. "I mean, she's up to her neck in this one way or another. She and her sister own the warehouse where Ricky Evans runs his business. Maybe . . ."

Clarke looked eagerly at Denise. "What do you have?"

She grimaced. "The challenge in all of this has been digging down through the shell companies and figuring out who owns what. Celia Myers sent over a list of business interests and we'd started working through that." She extracted two folders from the stack that to Clarke's eye seemed random. "Start with these," she said. "I'm going to give Celia Myers a call, see if we can short-circuit the search parameters."

Tucker came back into the incident room and Clarke could see him casting an eye over his assembled troops. The room was packed with desks and computers and bodies, all generating yet more intelligence. Five officers were manning telephones, taking calls from the public. Clarke had yet to see any of them come up for air.

Tucker had been interviewing Ricky Evans again.

"Anything?" Clarke asked.

"A whole load of nothing. He's 'no commenting' everything except his bloody name. Ginny reckons he's just too scared of Sykes to give us anything."

"And did *she* have anything to say?"

"Just that she's glad we got the kid back. She knew about the farmhouse, though. It belonged to Joseph and Bly Matheson. Both now deceased. Joseph Matheson was rumoured to be a fixer for Sykes back when he was still a small fry. Bly was a distant relative of Sykes's wife."

"What happened to them?"

"Ginny Afton reckons they got caught up in the fallout when Sykes's wife was murdered. He set about cleaning house of anyone he suspected of disloyalty, and they were on his list. I looked through the records. Disappeared, bodies never found. The place was just left to rot. You have anything?"

Clarke explained what they had been doing and that so far they'd made no progress.

"We've people out canvassing the whole area. Something will turn up," Tucker told him, but Clarke knew the lie of that. Even a one-mile radius around the farm was a massive undertaking. Five miles would need additional manpower called in from other forces. They needed to narrow things down.

Was she even still alive? And why take her? Sure, Sykes wanted revenge but he could have had that at any time. No one could protect Petra, not if either Sykes or Perrin decided to make that final move. Gus Perrin was a pragmatist — if he could extract his pound of flesh in ways other than actual murder then he would most likely do so. Especially if, as in this case, the law was helping him out. Sykes was more impulsive. Clarke decided that he must have seen Petra and decided it might be fun to take her from under their noses. It would tie up more resources, cause as much mischief as possible and allow him to take his time doing whatever he wanted with her.

This last thought chilled Clarke. He realized he had come to count her as a friend and not just a colleague. But worse than that, he had been there when she had been taken. Most likely, just a few yards away, and he hadn't even realized she was gone until it was too late.

He thought about the foster mother who had turned her attention from her charge just for a moment, and that had been enough. Of the daughter of Superintendent Deans, who had assumed her child would be safe in her own garden. For the first time he really felt he understood how vulnerable Petra must have felt these past months. Knowing that any moment could be her last — any lapse in attention could spell disaster.

Clarke had seen what Sykes had done to previous victims. He was not someone who would delegate — he enjoyed inflicting pain far too much. Sykes would cut and slash and even disembowel, just because he could. Because nothing mattered to him and the lives of others were, in his eyes, less than nothing.

Clarke swallowed hard, turned back to his lists and his map and began his task again.

CHAPTER 28

She had balanced herself as best she could, drawn back the foot clad in her one remaining shoe and was about to strike. The sound of the car returning stopped Petra. She froze then regained her balance and skittered back into the centre of the room. The front door slammed open and a moment or two later the door to the room she was in swung wide. Once more she was grabbed and half carried, half dragged through to where Sykes was waiting.

"So," he said. "Where is she?"

This was it, Petra thought, the end. She hoped it would be quick — knew it wouldn't.

"I don't know."

"Like fuck you don't." He held a knife in his hand. Nothing fancy, she noted abstractedly, just a cheap craft knife, the kind with snap-off blades. Was he afraid she might blunt them? The ridiculous thought came from nowhere.

And then there was only pain. He had slashed her arm, laying the bicep open, hitting bone. Petra screamed and dropped to her knees. He slashed again, catching her temple, the blade skidding into her hairline and catching the tip of her ear.

Dimly, through a haze of pain, the blood dripping down into her right eye, she saw him raise a mobile phone to his ear. Heard him say, "I don't have to tell you what else I could do to her, do I?" She could hear Lauren's voice now. Frantic and afraid.

"I'll come to you," she heard Lauren say. "Just don't hurt her again. Please, dad, don't hurt her again. I'll meet. Just me and you. We can talk. We can—"

Sykes ended the call. Petra was hauled to her feet again and taken back to the room on the other side of the hall. She was dropped to the floor and the door closed and locked. She curled into a tight ball in the middle of the floor. Blood poured from the head wound and from the slashed bicep. With her hands bound behind her back she could not even apply pressure to the wound and in fact could barely move her wounded arm.

He'll kill her, Petra thought. If she meets him then she's dead and so am I. He'll kill me just for the hell of it and everything she had done to protect Lauren Sykes, everything Harry Prentice had done, would be for nothing.

She felt sick, woozy from the shock and pain, and when she was suddenly jerked back to full consciousness by the sound of the front door slamming again, she realized she must briefly have passed out.

Or maybe not so briefly. Outside the sun had moved around to the other side of the house and long shadows told her it must now be late afternoon. Her arm hurt abominably, blood soaked her sleeve and her side and had run down her arm to coat her fingers. The head wound still dripped blood. To add to her misery, she badly needed to pee.

Awkwardly, she manoeuvred into sitting position and then stood unsteadily. She listened. Not a sound in the house. Had they all left? Not likely, she decided, but someone had gone out, though there was no telling how long for.

She closed her eyes. Stay here and she was going to die. She took a deep breath, struggled once again to get her balance and then kicked out at the rotten wood and ancient glass.

* * *

Lauren stared at the now-dead mobile phone. "He'll kill her. Molly, he'll kill her!"

"No, my dear, he won't. Men like him like to enjoy their victories. He'll want her alive until after he deals with you. That way he'll be able to gloat about what he did to you while he deals with her."

Lauren stared at Molly in horror. The older woman sounded so calm, so matter of fact. "We have to do something."

"And so we shall. But we must do it right."

Lauren forced herself to draw a deep, controlling breath. She nodded. A slip of paper caught her attention. While she'd been on the phone to her father, Molly had scribbled instructions. *Tell him to meet us here.* "This place where you told him to meet us. Where is it?"

"It's a little over an hour from where we think Sykes must still be and a little closer for us. If we leave now we'll get there ahead of him. And I know my ground, Lauren. He doesn't. We can turn this to our advantage, my dear. Between us we can finish this."

"He won't come alone."

"I don't expect he will. Now, you go and get Harry's gun."

Lauren felt a jolt of shock run though her body. Then she nodded. As she turned for the stairs she saw Molly go to the stick stand and take out one of her more unusual sticks.

"Molly?" Lauren paused on the second step.

The older woman twisted the collar that released the trigger mechanism, checked it carefully. Then she turned the ferrule that allowed her to load the shotgun shell into the hollow in the shaft. Satisfied, she looked up at Lauren and smiled. "Time it had an outing," she said. "Now go, get ready. We don't have much time."

Lauren took another deep breath. She could do this. Molly was right — it was time to finish things once and for all.

CHAPTER 29

Celia Myers stared at the map. "I don't understand why you think I can help," she said. "I've told you all I know. It's Pat you should be looking for."

"Dealing with your sister can wait," Tucker told her bluntly. "We have a missing officer. She was taken by Kyle Sykes. The likelihood that your sister had dealings with Sykes is—"

"God, Pat would deal with anyone if there was a profit in it. But she'd draw the line at someone like Sykes. He's in a different league."

"And he covered his tracks. Hiding behind legitimate interests. For the time being I'm willing to believe that she didn't know. Now, please, look at the map and tell me if anything strikes you."

She cast him an almost contemptuous look and then sighed and studied the map again. "He's over the hills and far away by now. You're kidding yourselves. What's he got to hang around for?"

"Who knows? But he has been for the past three or four months, as far as we can tell. Best guess is he's hoping to move in on Gus Perrin, same as Perrin did when Sykes was forced to vacate. It's possible he's gone. It's also possible he's not gone far. We have to explore every avenue in the meantime."

"And what makes you think she's still alive, this officer of yours?"

"We have to hope she is."

Tucker tapped the map. "The farm is here, the track leading across the fields is here, the nearest village is—"

"I know. You said all this already. Look, I know nothing about this fucking farm. The wood over there is where my brother used to go camping with the scouts. The big house over there is now a very expensive organic restaurant. Pat was going to buy shares at one time then she changed her mind. And before you ask it was because she had a meal there one night and said the service was crap. There's an outdoor pursuits place over there near the lake. We do have an interest in that one, I think." She paused, something striking her.

"What?" Tucker demanded.

"The families you mentioned. Where Pat was supposed to have brokered a deal. Did you mention the Reader family?"

"Yes," Tucker told her. "What about them?"

"Well, if I remember right, they're a major shareholder. There's some land adjoining that they want to build on, but that's still going through the planning process. The idea was to build a holiday park in the woods, sharing facilities with the adventure park."

"And?"

"And there's an old house there and a couple of outbuildings, from what I remember. Set well away from the road." She pointed to the edge of the map. Much further out than the search teams would have canvassed yet. "Is that the kind of thing you're looking for?"

Tucker considered this. "It's worth a look." He glanced at his watch: 4.15 p.m. Where had the day gone? He reminded himself that actually their day had begun around 3 a.m., and on one hand it seemed to stretch back for ever into the distance. On the other, the day seemed to have gone nowhere and achieved nothing. No, he argued with himself. The kid was safe. That was something.

He took one last look at the map and began to organize his team. It might amount to another heap of nothing, but anything was better than hanging around waiting for news.

CHAPTER 30

She was covered in blood. It ran slickly down her arms where she'd cut herself going through the window. The head wound had begun to bleed in earnest — she must have opened it up again, and her arm felt like someone was sawing through it with a blunt, serrated knife. The pain travelled through muscle and bone, down into her hand, up into her shoulder.

She had kicked hard at the window, scrambled out and fallen hard on to the gravel. Then, stumbling to her feet, she had run, expecting every second to hear a shout, a shot, to be dropped by a bullet in the back. Now she ran, blindly, dimly remembering that she had glimpsed a car on a road beyond the perimeter of trees and overgrown shrubbery. Her arms still bound, she found it hard to move quickly and she was horribly aware of the giddy, muzzy feeling in her head. How much blood had she lost? She tried to recall the position of the brachial artery — wasn't that close to where Sykes had slashed her arm?

Get a grip, she told herself angrily. If the blade had even nicked that, she'd have been dead by now, bled out on the floor of that sad little room in the long-abandoned house.

It felt like for ever but was probably less than a minute before she heard shouting and then the front door slam open and knew they had heard her and were in pursuit.

She stumbled, fell. Looked down at the ground and the trail of her own blood. Fuck. Heard footsteps, running steps on gravel. Heard a man's voice. It sounded like he was speaking into a phone. Her head was spinning, her whole body in pain, but she knew she couldn't stay put. She'd put too little distance between herself and the house and the blood trail was clear enough that a child could follow it.

Petra lifted her head and peered through the vegetation. She could see a man on the front drive, speaking into a mobile phone. Could hear another, but couldn't fix his position. If she moved now the man with the mobile would see her. If she stayed put he would find her anyway.

The other man had come outside and both now stood beside the front door, deep in conversation. She had expected them to come running out and for there to be more urgency to the pursuit. They had halted as though something had interrupted them and they were now as uncertain as she was.

Whatever had slowed them down, she had to take advantage of it. Cautiously, painfully, Petra began to inch into deeper cover. Instinctively she moved towards the road, praying that she could make it that far, that there was not a thick hedge or some other barrier blocking her way, that there would be someone coming along the road if . . . when . . . if she could make it that far.

Her foot struck something hard. She turned cautiously to see what it might be. A section of fence had fallen against a tree, the post at an angle, the panel collapsed and now almost overgrown with bramble and ivy. Running feet on gravel shifted her attention back to the house. One man disappeared inside while the other crunched his way back to where she had made her dramatic exit through the window.

This was it, Petra thought. Whatever had given them pause, it had ended now. She tried to get to her feet, but a red mist swam behind her eyes and her legs seemed unable to support her weight. She could hear his feet on gravel, hear him now with what sounded like a stick beating against the bushes and tall grass. Petra retreated further, some vague idea forming in her mind that she could hide beneath the broken fence panel, beneath the brambles and the ivy and the nettles. She pushed herself into the narrow gap beneath the panel and the rough, uneven ground. Felt the thorns pulling at her clothes and skin, the nettles attacking her bare hands and face, the ivy seemed to twine around her limbs, locking them tight, as though the vegetation was pulling her under and into the ground. She heard a shout.

This is it, she thought. Petra closed her eyes.

CHAPTER 31

Five thirty, Clarke glanced at his watch.

Nothing. The manager of the Outward Bound centre stood close by, nervously jingling keys and change in his tracksuit pocket. "I told you there was nothing much here," he said eventually. "We fenced it off to keep the kids out. It's due to be demolished in a week or two."

Clarke looked around again as though a second examination might reveal something he had not seen before. What was left of an old house, roof off, walls collapsed, stood against the line of trees, birches and ash already reclaiming bricks and mortar. A few outbuildings in a similar state of disrepair stood at right angles to what was left of the house. Even if he'd been completely desperate, Clarke thought, Sykes would demand more comfort than this location could offer.

"No," he agreed. "There's nothing to find." He felt the energy draining out through his feet and realized just how much he had been counting on this lead paying off.

"Look," the manager said, slowly catching on to what they were looking for, "there's the old Retford place just up the road. That's been empty three, four years since the old guy died, and I think the council is having trouble tracing family."

"Take us there," Clarke demanded.

* * *

It had taken about ten minutes to get back to their vehicles, Clarke chafing at every step of the way, but the going was rough and they could not push the teams faster through undergrowth and brambles. Clarke got into the manager's car, leaving Denise to drive his. The man seemed to have responded to the urgency, and Clarke didn't comment that he was obviously driving above the limit along narrow and winding country roads.

"How far?"

"About another mile."

Clarke spoke into his radio, enquiring as to the ETA of the armed officers he had requested. He knew that he should have called them in to the first location, but the truth was he'd been in too much of a hurry. Instinct told him that he would not get away with that a second time, and good sense reminded him that he could not risk his people if Sykes was there. He told himself that he had already taken too many risks.

The driver slowed and pulled on to a grass verge. Clarke had told him to stop before they got close enough to the house to be spotted. He got out of the car. "Stay here," he instructed the manager.

Denise had pulled up behind him and the other car behind that, tucking into the hedge. The armed unit was only minutes away.

"So what now?" Denise asked.

"We should wait here."

The manager got out of the car and came over to where they stood.

"I told you to stay put."

"I know, but I thought you might be interested in the public footpath that runs at the back of the house." He pointed back the way they had come, and a few yards further up the road a green fingerpost pointed to a rather overgrown but still passable trackway.

"The local rambling clubs use it, but it doesn't get that much regular footfall. It leads round the back of the house, so you might be able to see what's going on."

Denise looked at him. "Boss," she said, a warning note in her voice.

Clarke set off at a jog and a moment later was over the stile and into the field. The path ran straight for about a hundred yards and then turned abruptly left, over another stile, into another field and, he guessed, ran along the boundary line between properties. Another hundred yards took him to a place where he could see the house beyond the hedge. He managed to find a gap through which he could peer into the adjoining garden. He stood very still. There was no sign of movement in the house, but all he could see was the back wall and a row of windows and a garden grown wild.

He sighed and turned back, and by the time he reached the road the armed officers had arrived and had parked up behind their own little convoy. Clarke went over to speak to the officer in charge and explained that it might be possible to get through from the back of the house. Two officers were dispatched there and the others began to move forward towards the main entrance. Once more, Clarke had no option but to stand and wait. He glanced at his watch and noted that it was a little after 6 p.m. He seemed to have been awake for ever.

Denise came over to him and they leaned against the car, staring towards where the armed officers had now disappeared around a bend. "What did it look like?" Denise asked.

"It's quite a substantial house, certainly not derelict even if it has been empty for a while. I can only see what I'm assuming is the back wall, windows on the top floor and on the ground floor, possibly a door, but I couldn't see the ground floor well enough. The hedge is lower further down, so I'm hoping there's a way through. Put it this way, it's more promising than the last place we looked at."

Denise nodded and then tensed. In the distance they could hear shouts of "armed police" and then the sound of something breaking, but Clarke was relieved that there was no gunfire this time. Though was that really a good or a bad sign? Was this simply another empty building, another dead end?

A few long minutes later one of the officers came back round the bend and called them forward. "No one in the building. But they were here, and *she* was here."

Clarke and Denise hurried towards the house. The officer in charge stood by the front door and would not let them go in but instead took them around to the side of the house. "We found a flak jacket in one of the rooms, most likely DS Merrow's. There's a lot of blood in two rooms and there's this."

"Fucking hell," Denise said as they studied the broken window, the blood on the glass and on the sill and splashed across the gravel.

"Petra," Clarke said. Cautiously, aware that he was going to be contaminating the scene, but far more concerned that she might still be somewhere in the grounds, he followed the blood trail, Denise just a step behind him. The trail seemed to peter out once they had crossed the grass and were walking on loose mud and a tangle of overgrowth, nettle, bramble and other plants that he could not name.

"There," Denise pointed. "There's blood on the ground over there."

Cautiously he stepped over to where she had indicated and realized she was right. It had soaked into the ground, but enough of it had stained the bark and leaves for him to pick up the trail again. Then he saw the broken fence panel and for a moment he could not see how she could have crawled underneath, but something told him that she might have taken shelter there. He lifted it carefully, then shouted, "Paramedics! Now!"

Petra was unconscious, covered in blood and mud and vegetation, but when he reached out to touch her hand it was warm, and when he felt her wrist there was a pulse, faint but definitely there. He took her hand. It was slippery with blood and grimed with earth, but she was alive. He squeezed her fingers gently and then surrendered his place to the paramedics.

"She's alive?" Denise demanded.

"Yeah, she's alive." He looked down at his hand, the palm bloodied, and once more he felt as though energy was seeping out through his feet, but this time it was relief.

"So why didn't Sykes kill her?" Denise wondered. "How did she manage to get away?"

He shook his head. "I don't know. She obviously went out through the window, but . . ."

Where was he now? Clarke wondered. What would his next move be?

* * *

Cliff Turnbull could see that Kyle Sykes was not a happy man. They had been forced to park on a grass verge, climb over a five-bar gate and then scramble up the side of a steep hill. Evening was closing in on them, the last of the sunlight disappearing rapidly behind the castle, and all the way on the journey, which had seemed to take for ever, he had been cursing his daughter. Now, it seemed to Cliff, he was almost foaming at the mouth.

Cliff had gone ahead of his boss, puffing and panting a bit on the steep slope, but glad to be out of the car. Sykes was not good company when he was in a mood and, boy, was he in a mood now. Not, Cliff reflected, that he was ever exactly *good* company. He liked to keep everyone on edge. He said it was about keeping them at the top of their game, but actually, Cliff knew, he just liked seeing everybody scared.

Cliff didn't know what to expect from this little excursion but was certainly not prepared for the old woman. Leaning heavily on a stout walking stick, she came out of the twilight to ask politely if they had seen a little dog. "He's just a little chap, a Jack Russell cross, but he does like to burrow and he won't come back. I've been calling and calling him."

Fuck, Cliff thought. This was all they needed. Some old biddy out with her dog just guaranteed to get in Sykes's way. And people who got in Sykes's way ended up dead.

"No, I've not seen any dog. Maybe he's gone down the hill."

Sykes had reached the summit now, and the climb had not improved his temper. He glared at the old woman, and then at Cliff. And then came the inevitable instruction. "Deal with her," Sykes said.

"Oh, I don't think so."

Cliff stared at the apparition. She straightened, seemed to grow taller. She raised her stick, pointed it at him and for an absurd moment he thought that she was going to poke at him with it. He had moved to take his gun from the shoulder holster but he got no further than a vague gesture towards it before he felt a sudden pain in his gut and realized that he'd been shot.

Cliff fell backwards and the old woman lowered her cane. Sykes began to shout something, Cliff was vaguely aware of that, but then there was another voice, one he recognized, though he had never heard her sound so calm or so self-assured.

"Hello, Kyle," Lauren said. "It's been a while."

* * *

"Don't hesitate, and don't be tempted to monologue," Molly had told her. "You have nothing to say to him and he has nothing of any worth to say to you."

Lauren looked down at her father from her position higher up the slope. She felt strangely calm and oddly at peace with everything. The anger would come later, she knew that, along with the grief and, she hoped, the sense of relief. Those mixed emotions were really not going to go anywhere in a hurry. The present calm was simply a result of Molly drilling her in the use of this weapon, week by week, month by month, ensuring that she could handle it well, easily and automatically. No thought required — just point and shoot.

Sykes was laughing now. "Well, look at you," he said. "All grown up and with a great big gun of your own. I take it that belonged to Harry. Though it seems you've got another teacher now."

He cast a glance towards Molly, who had joined Lauren further up the slope. She was calmly reloading her strange weapon. Slipping a shotgun cartridge into the reinforced barrel, a couple of inches below the elegantly curved, horn handle. From her position she could watch Lauren and Sykes, and the man she had just shot. She appeared, Lauren thought, to be doing so with a degree of detached interest.

Lauren held her position, body square to her target, feet set shoulder width apart, knees relaxed. She had found a little bit of level ground and she had absolutely no intention of moving from it. She could feel Molly silently urging her just to take the shot, to get it over and done with. Molly liked things tidy. But the truth was, Lauren wanted to take a little moment or two. Although she had no intention of monologuing, as Molly called it, she did have a few things she wanted to say.

Her father was looking amused. "We both know you won't use that," he said. His hands were moving slowly to his pockets. Sykes, she knew, was always armed.

"Put your hands up, please," Lauren said calmly.

"Please? Oh my God." He was laughing at her now. "You're pathetic, you know that?"

"Maybe, but put your hands up anyway."

He did so this time — raised his hands, palms facing her, a look of pure contempt on his face. Lauren noted almost absently that Cliff had crawled a foot or so closer to the cover of bracken and bushes, but he now lay very still and she guessed that he was probably dead.

"You've killed a lot of people," she said, her tone conversational.

"What about it?"

"But I can't do anything about that. I doubt I know who most of them were, and I don't really imagine you bother to remember either."

"Why should I remember? Pathetic, the lot of them. Just like you."

"Yeah? Maybe, but listen, I'm only really interested in two. You killed Harry Prentice and you killed my mother."

"And you're not exactly pure as the driven, are you?"

"No," Lauren agreed. "No, I'm not. But I can live with that."

The laughter began again, harsh and contemptuous, and suddenly Lauren was fed up with talking. She'd had enough. She'd visualized this many times, this last confrontation with her father, run the film in her head until it was totally familiar — though she'd never really believed that it would happen. Every time she'd thought about it, she'd assumed it would feel dramatic, cleansing, victorious, but the truth was she was bored now and just wanted it done. Molly shifted position, catching Lauren's eye. She looked perfectly at ease, Lauren thought, waiting her out.

"You know what," Lauren said. "I think I just want to go home now."

She saw the look of faint surprise on Kyle Sykes's face and the look of shock the instant she fired, and then he fell and lay still. Still operating on automatic, following Molly's drill, she made her weapon safe, took a handkerchief from her pocket and retrieved the cartridge. Leave things clean, Molly always said.

"I'm ready to go now," Lauren told her. Suddenly she felt terribly weary.

Molly came over and took her arm and then the gun, which she slipped into the capacious pocket of her waxed coat.

She bent down as they passed Sykes's body, searched his pockets and removed his mobile phone. Then they made their slow way back to their car.

"I think I should drive back, while you take a nap," Molly said. "Things like this always take their toll."

Lauren nodded, aware of the tension and the energy draining out of her. That was probably, she thought, a very good idea.

CHAPTER 32

It was 7 a.m. the following morning when someone shook Clarke awake. Startled, he found himself staring up into Tucker's face. His boss looked rough, unshaven and exhausted. He looked pretty much the way Clarke felt.

He looked over at the hospital bed on which Petra lay. Sleeping now, sedated but safe. A heavy bandage covered her wounded arm and she was covered in cuts from the glass and one on her temple from Sykes's blade — but she would heal.

"Go home, get a shower and some food inside of you. I'll sit here for a bit."

Clarke got up and stretched. "What's happening?"

"CSIs are still at the scene. They've recovered a number of mobile phones and two handguns. Evidence that there were two cars at the scene from the two sets of tyre tracks and, as you know, a fair amount of blood in two rooms. It looks like Sykes attacked her in the room across the hall from the one where she was held. There's a large patch on that floor from where she must have lain for some time and then more on the window from where she kicked her way through. When she's awake enough to talk we'll get a proper statement, but it looks like they left in a hurry. There's no clear indication as to why."

"She said there was a phone call," Clarke said. "She was certain they'd come and find her, but there was a phone call and they seemed to change their minds."

"So presumably the two goons that Sykes left behind got some news that made them clear out. Anyway, we'll work all of that out later. Go home. Get yourself sorted out and grab a couple of hours' sleep. Nothing more you can do here."

Outside the morning was cool and clear and promised a bright day. Clarke was bone weary, arriving back at his flat with no real memory of his journey there. He showered and drank coffee, felt a little more alive. Made toast and added marmalade, remembering the first morning Petra had shared breakfast in his flat. That she was alive was such a profound relief that it caught him off guard. Of course he wanted her to be safe — he'd have the same level of anxiety for any colleague. But he had to acknowledge that this was a little more than that. She was fast becoming a valued friend and, he reflected, he hadn't collected so many of those in his life that he could afford to lose any.

It was now 8.15 a.m. Despite the coffee he was contemplating bed, for a couple of hours' inadequate but much-needed sleep, when his mobile rang. Minutes later he was back in his car, his head reeling.

He collected DCI Tucker from the hospital car park. "Are they certain?"

"A jogger found the first body just after six this morning. The local police found the second. One of the PCs thought the second body looked familiar, and the identification was made soon after. Sykes is dead, Toby. Single shot to the chest. The other chap may be one Cliff Turnbull, but we're still awaiting confirmation on that. He'd been with Sykes's operation man and boy."

Clarke nodded. He'd run across Turnbull. "And how was he killed?"

"Again a single shot, but he doesn't seem to have been killed outright. There's evidence he tried to crawl from the scene but didn't get far. Indications are he bled out."

"And this place where they were found?"

"About an hour's drive from here, about five miles outside Lichfield. Some kind of ruined castle next to a public footpath that's popular with joggers and dog walkers. Not exactly Sykes's territory."

"And no CCTV, of course."

"If he drove through Lichfield we might get lucky with the traffic cameras but . . ."

Clarke nodded. "You think Gus Perrin's behind this?"

"I think if Gus Perrin had been involved he'd have been a tad more subtle. There'd be no bodies."

Clarke nodded. Tucker was most likely right.

An hour later they were pulling in behind a marked police car. A long, low hill rose from the road and in the field beyond stood a ruined castle. A proper Norman-type affair, Clarke thought. They followed the path laid out by the CSI up on to the hill. Sykes lay at the foot of the curtain wall. He looked shocked, Clarke thought, as though death had come from an unexpected source, and he was seriously aggrieved by that.

The second body lay in undergrowth a little distance away, the short blood trail marking the distance the man had dragged himself before he had finally succumbed.

"Cliff Turnbull," Clarke confirmed. "So what happened here?"

"Time of death was sometime yesterday evening, as far as we can judge. It rained after ten and the ground was dry under Sykes's body, so most likely before then. It would still be light enough to take the shot but getting towards twilight. Whoever the shooter was took their brass with them," they were told. "CSI tell me that so far there's not so much as a footprint, not so much as a blade of grass out of place." He grinned. "Maybe whoever did this was a bloody ghost."

Then I'll have to get my Ouija board out and send a thank-you note, Clarke thought.

"It couldn't have happened to a more deserving bloke," Tucker said.

CHAPTER 33

Two weeks later, Petra had returned to light duties at work — glad of the distraction, if truth be told. Paul Benson had been picked up a couple of days after Kyle Sykes's death and now seemed intent on unburdening his soul. Most relevant to Petra was his confession to killing Frankland and also to taking the life of Billy Hunter, on the direct instructions of Gus Perrin, something his erstwhile boss strenuously denied. Gus Perrin was currently still at home on police bail but was keeping a very low profile and leaving the fight to his very highly paid lawyers. Petra doubted the allegation had legs — there would be someone else taking the fall, despite Paul Benson's forceful statement.

She wondered if Benson would actually make it to trial or if he would have an unfortunate accident while on remand. She found she didn't much care.

One thing very much to her benefit had come out of all this. If Billy Hunter's death was not due to suicide but to murder, then his family could hardly continue to accuse her of causing his death. It seemed that Perrin himself had considered it politic to make this point, and so the funding for the civil case that Billy Hunter's family had been preparing had dried up. He had made the very public statement that while he considered the police to have acted in an underhand and disreputable manner, Petra herself was undoubtedly coerced into playing this particular role. It was a statement that had taken her utterly by surprise, and caused her to wonder what game he was playing, but she was grateful to be off that particular hook and to feel the diminution of threat that came with it. Gus Perrin had signalled that she should be left alone. And Sykes, of course, was dead. There would still be an enquiry, but the threats were now manageable, legal, things she could discuss with the Police Federation rep. They no longer constituted a very real fear of a bullet in the back or worse.

Unlike Paul Benson, who, once he had started to tell his story seemed unable to stop, Superintendent Deans had maintained an absolute silence that neither his daughter nor his solicitor had been able to crack. What was he hiding? What did Perrin have against him? Petra was convinced that, with Sykes now dead and gone, fear of Perrin had to be the cause of the silence. But fear of Perrin doing what? Investigators were taking Deans's life apart looking for a triggering event — a moment when his actions had given someone else power over him. They would find it eventually, she was sure.

She still wondered about Lauren. Where was she? How was she faring? That she had killed Sykes was something Petra felt certain of but not something she could talk about, even to Clarke. Then, a few days after she had returned to work, a call was put through to her from the central switchboard and a voice Petra recognized said, "Good morning, my dear. I trust you are recovered."

"You." It was the older woman who had become Lauren's protector. "I didn't expect to hear . . ."

"No, and this will be the last time. Lauren wanted to let you know that all is well, that she's happy and safe and everything has turned out for the best."

"Was it her—?"

"No questions, now, my dear. No doubt the conclusions you've drawn are more or less correct. It's time to move on. For both of you to go your separate ways."

"I understand," Petra said, but it still hurt, far more than Sykes's blade had ever done.

"I know you said no questions," Petra added, "but can I just ask one?"

"You can ask."

"Okay, well, we've arrested the two men Sykes left behind, and one of them keeps talking about a phone call. Some old woman, he says, who called them on his boss's phone and told them that Sykes was dead. Was that—"

"I think people should know the score, don't you, my dear? Life was about to change for them and besides . . ." She paused as though considering how much to reveal. "Lauren had a fair idea of who might have remained loyal to her erstwhile father. She picked a name from his speed dial list as being a likely candidate. Petra, we had no idea at that stage if you were dead or alive or if the phone call would precipitate your death. We gambled on them buggering off, I suppose. If you were still alive, we felt it might give you an edge if they knew Sykes was dead. It could easily have gone the other way. I might not have been believed. They might have taken it out on you, but we couldn't think of anything else that might help. Though from what I hear, you'd taken matters into your own hands by then."

She sounded impressed, Petra thought, and was surprised at how much that thought pleased her.

The call ended then and for a few moments Petra stared at the handset, expecting, wishing, hoping for more. But no, it *was* time to move on. She had stopped falling, for now.

* * *

A few miles away Gus Perrin was sitting in his conservatory gazing out on to an immaculate lawn. Jonathan Roan sat close by, uneasily nursing a heavy, cut-glass tumbler containing what he assumed was a very fine whiskey. He had never been a whiskey drinker.

"And so," Gus Perrin was telling him, "you will continue to dig. I want to know who the Merrow woman sees, what she knows, when she sneezes, who she fucks."

"I don't know if—" Jonathan broke off as Gus Perrin's head swivelled in his direction and his close-set and intense blue-grey gaze settled upon him.

"You've taken my thirty pieces of silver," Perrin reminded him. "What makes you think you're in any position to argue?"

Light footsteps, heels clicking on the conservatory floor, caused both men to look towards the door. A woman entered and Jonathan noted her tailored suit and bright-red nails.

He cast Perrin a puzzled look.

"You two will not have met," Gus Perrin said. "Sheila, this is our young journalist friend. Jonathan, this young lady will be keeping tabs on DS Merrow from the inside. The two of you will liaise."

Jonathan swallowed nervously. "You're a police officer?" he asked, trying to make it sound accusatory — trying to express just a little outrage.

Gus Perrin laughed. "Oh no," he said. "Nothing like that. Just let's say that this lady has privileged access. Give him your mobile number, Sheila."

A few minutes later Jonathan Roan was on his way, walking carefully across the immaculate lawn on unsteady legs.

* * *

"You're sure you want to do this?" Molly asked.

"I'm sure. I did what I needed to do, but it's time to let go. Harry would want that."

Harry's gun had been disassembled and was now packed into various pockets — jeans, jacket, Molly's oversized cardigan. They began their slow walk along the canal path, just two women, generations apart, perhaps a great-grandmother and great granddaughter out for an evening stroll.

One by one, many steps between, Lauren took each last little vestige of her past, held it out over the still water and let it fall.

THE END

ALSO BY JANE ADAMS

MERROW & CLARKE
Book 1: SAFE
Book 2: KIDNAP

RINA MARTIN MYSTERY SERIES
Book 1: MURDER ON SEA
Book 2: MURDER ON THE CLIFF
Book 3: MURDER ON THE BOAT
Book 4: MURDER ON THE BEACH
Book 5: MURDER AT THE COUNTRY HOUSE
Book 6: MURDER AT THE PUB

DETECTIVE MIKE CROFT SERIES
Book 1: THE GREENWAY
Book 2: THE SECRETS
Book 3: THEIR FINAL MOMENTS
Book 4: THE LIAR

DETECTIVE RAY FLOWERS SERIES
Book 1: THE APOTHECARY'S DAUGHTER
Book 2: THE UNWILLING SON
Book 3: THE DROWNING MEN
Book 4: THE SISTER'S TWIN

DETECTIVE ROZLYN PRIEST
Book 1: BURY ME DEEP

STANDALONES
THE OTHER WOMAN
THE WOMAN IN THE PAINTING
THEN SHE WAS DEAD

Thank you for reading this book.

If you enjoyed it please leave feedback on Amazon or Goodreads, and if there is anything we missed or you have a question about, then please get in touch. We appreciate you choosing our book.

Founded in 2014 in Shoreditch, London, we at Joffe Books pride ourselves on our history of innovative publishing. We were thrilled to be shortlisted for Independent Publisher of the Year at the British Book Awards.

www.joffebooks.com

We're very grateful to eagle-eyed readers who take the time to contact us. Please send any errors you find to corrections@joffebooks.com. We'll get them fixed ASAP.

Made in the USA
Columbia, SC
06 February 2022

55576970R00150